"Hamilton spins this coming-of-age tale with the same sort of poignancy that earned her previous six novels high praise."
—*ENTERTAINMENT WEEKLY*

"A timeless classic, in its first appearance."
—KAREN JOY FOWLER,
New York Times bestselling author of
We Are All Completely Beside Ourselves

"Tender, eccentric, wickedly funny and sage."
—NANCY HORAN,
New York Times bestselling author of
Loving Frank and *Under the Wide and Starry Sky*

"Funny and heartbreaking, colored with a palpable wistfulness."
—*MIAMI HERALD*

"Everything you could ask for in a coming-of-age novel—
funny, insightful, observant, saturated with hope and melancholy."
—TOM PERROTTA,
New York Times bestselling author of *Little Children* and *The Leftovers*

"Peopled with vivid characters . . .
Hamilton gets it, all of it, about life and love
and growing up when you just don't want to."
—*THE GLOBE AND THE MAIL*

Praise for
The Excellent Lombards

"A lovely coming-of-age tale."   —*People*

"A book that thrilled me to read. THE EXCELLENT
LOMBARDS is, in fact, magnificent."   —Ann Patchett,
New York Times bestselling author of *State of Wonder*

"THE EXCELLENT LOMBARDS gives full voice to Jane
Hamilton's storytelling gifts. Frankie's tale of growing up on
the family apple farm is a love letter to a threatened way of
life and proof, once again, of Hamilton's extraordinary talent
for dramatizing ordinary lives with nuance and compassion. I
loved spending time in Frankie's world."   —Nancy Horan,
New York Times bestselling author of *Loving Frank*
and *Under the Wide and Starry Sky*

"Deeply affecting, a moving elegy for an idyllic way of life
that's slipping away as development and technology encroach
and children grow up and away from rural pleasures."
—*Miami Herald*

"Jane Hamilton's novel about a young girl's life on an apple orchard is full of oddball characters and tender scenes that will
linger in your memory."
—Tom Perrotta, *New York Times* bestselling author of *Little
Children* and *The Leftovers*

"There is a well-crafted tenderness in Jane Hamilton's THE EXCELLENT LOMBARDS that teases out the drama in ordinary life and quietly lulls the reader...Frankie's love of the farm is beautifully drawn in Jane Hamilton's perfect details, creating a sense of place so strong, at times the orchard seems to transcend setting to become another character in the novel...a poignant and sometimes witty coming of age story."
—*New York Journal of Books*

"A book with so much grace, wit, and resonance—this is one you'll read and reread. I surely did. I laughed, I cried, I pondered, I mourned. I took these characters deeply into my heart. Hamilton at her amazing best."
—Karen Joy Fowler, *New York Times* bestselling author of *We Are All Completely Beside Ourselves* and winner of the 2014 PEN / Faulkner Award

"A powerful coming-of-age story...Her penetration into the hearts of her characters is as profound, perhaps more so, than ever before...This is a very fine novel: Its people, their individual predicaments and their relationships with one another and with the land stay with the reader long after that last page has been turned."
—*Minneapolis Star Tribune*

"Hamilton's lushly pleasurable novel of radiant comedy, deep emotions, and resonant realizations considers the wonders of nature, the boon and burden of inheritance, and the blossoming of the self."
—*Booklist* (starred review)

"[Hamilton] writes with compassion and warmth about how

we see our family compared with how they really are, and who we can become when we finally cut the cord and fly free—like it or damn well not." —*The Globe and the Mail*

"This coming-of-age story is captivating and passionate, taking us back to being a child and believing in one thing whole-heartedly. Simply put, this is a book you won't be able to put down." —*BookPage*

"Tender and rueful...Richly characterized, beautifully written, and heartbreakingly poignant-another winner from this talented and popular author." —*Kirkus Reviews* (starred review)

"What a beautiful book. Its style is a wonder of accuracy—one enters its world in the fullest possible way. At the center is a girl whose fate is linked to the fate of her family's struggling farm, a place whose rhythms and details are miraculously evoked. Jane Hamilton, whose work I have long admired, has brought us again to the juncture of innocence and chance."

—Joan Silber, author of *Fools*, *Ideas of Heaven*, and
The Size of the World

"In THE EXCELLENT LOMBARDS, Jane Hamilton returns to her deep love of farm and land that is quickly becoming a thing of the past. As seen through the eyes of young Mary Frances 'Frankie' Lombard, whose idyllic life on the family apple farm begins to fray, it is at once a poignant coming of age story, and a profound look at the complexities of family, love, and loss in the ever changing cycle of life. It is Hamilton's masterful touch that brings it all together, that immerses us into a world as if it were our own. I loved being back in her warm embrace." —Gail Tsukiyama, author of *The Samurai's Garden* and *A Hundred Flowers*

"In THE EXCELLENT LOMBARDS the wonderfully gifted Jane Hamilton explores the lives of a family bound together and driven apart by land, money and inheritance. How intimately Hamilton understands her heroine's devotion to the apple orchard and how brilliantly she evokes the wages of time." —Margot Livesey, *New York Times* bestselling author of *The Flight of Gemma Hardy*

"Each character in this family has a story and a history to reveal. The parts play together like those of a great symphonic revolution, with the same sonic and emotional bombast you would find on a good night at Carnegie Hall...a beautiful book filled with flowing prose that will make Frankie and her family one of your favorite literary go-tos all summer long— and well after that, too." —*BookReporter*

"Exudes humor and compassion." —*The Toronto Star*

"Both a lively coming-of-age story and a deeply felt portrait of an endangered species, the American farm family." —*Milwaukee Journal Sentinel*

"Jane Hamilton can do anything, really...this timeworn plot still has vibrant life...It's all fresh and all strong because it's all Hamilton." —Literary Hub, "18 Books You Should Read This April"

"Jane Hamilton writes movingly of a young girl's changing views of her life and ambitions." —*Manhattan Book Review*

"Hamilton has always been a master storyteller, and THE EXCELLENT LOMBARDS is a story masterfully told. She doesn't give too much away at once, developing characters and places through well-chosen details, linking the past with the present smoothly, and keeping the story moving in such a way that readers may not realize how much they've learned—and how much they care about these people—until several dozen pages have gone by." —*The Wichita Eagle*

"A poignant coming-of-age tale that resonates with readers... beautiful." —*Romantic Times*

The Excellent Lombards

Jane Hamilton

GRAND CENTRAL
PUBLISHING

New York Boston

Thank you to Libby Ester, Mrs. V, Elizabeth Weinstein, and the Wonder Women. My gratitude, also, to the Hedgebrook Foundation. Not least, thank you to Deb Futter and Amanda Urban.

Grand Central Publishing
Hachette Book Group
1290 Avenue of the Americas, New York, NY 10104
grandcentralpublishing.com
twitter.com/grandcentralpub

Originally published in hardcover and ebook by Grand Central Publishing in April 2016
First Trade Paperback Edition: April 2017

Grand Central Publishing is a division of Hachette Book Group, Inc. The Grand Central Publishing name and logo is a trademark of Hachette Book Group, Inc.

The publisher is not responsible for websites (or their content) that are not owned by the publisher.

The Hachette Speakers Bureau provides a wide range of authors for speaking events. To find out more, go to www.hachettespeakersbureau.com or call (866) 376-6591.

Excerpt from "Bear" from *Headwaters* (W.W. Norton, 2013) used with permission of Ellen Bryant Voigt.

Library of Congress Cataloging-in-Publication Data
Names: Hamilton, Jane, 1957 July 13- author.
Title: The excellent Lombards / Jane Hamilton.
Description: First Edition. | New York ; Boston : Grand Central Publishing, 2016.
Identifiers: LCCN 2015044431 | ISBN 9781455564224 (hardback) | ISBN 9781455564217 (ebook) | ISBN 9781478939283 (audio cd)
Subjects: | BISAC: FICTION / Family Life. | FICTION / Coming of Age. | FICTION / Literary. | GSAFD: Bildungsromans.
Classification: LCC PS3558.A4428 E93 2016 | DDC 813/.54—dc23
LC record available at http://lccn.loc.gov/2015044431

ISBNs: 978-1-4555-6420-0 (trade paperback), 978-1-4555-6421-7 (ebook)

Printed in the United States of America

LSC-C

10 9 8 7 6 5 4 3 2 1

For WOM and his associates

The Excellent Lombards

. . . . *as we grill the salmon*
we spiked with juniper berries the other one thinks
the plural pronoun is a dangerous fiction the source
of so much unexpected loneliness

—from "Bear" by Ellen Bryant Voigt

EARLY

1.

This Story Always Starts Here

We were making hay. Everyone who was there still remembers it, how the sky was its usual high immense self, and as we went along a wash of clouds moved in, the ceiling suddenly quite low. There was the usual sweet smell of hay drying, the swallows swooping and scolding, and the oil and dust of the baler, a bitter black fragrance. It had been windy and hot when we started but the heat stilled, dirty and wet; or that was us at least, chaff stuck in our mouths, chaff in our bloodshot eyes, chaff like sequins on our clothes, our flesh. My father wore what were originally his dark-blue coveralls, the material over his back bleached by the sun to a pinkish white, the fabric drenched and glued to his skin. He didn't wear an undershirt on hot days, so you could see his thick chest hair—which always surprised me—that wet black fur. He had a wild foamy look, a person not to interrupt, no saying a word or crossing his path. My brother, William, was there, and our very distant cousin Philip, and the Bershek twins from down the road, and our hired hand Gloria, and me, and Aunt May Hill, we called her, across the wide field on the Allis-Chalmers, the baler spitting out the old-fashioned square bales.

Aunt May Hill was not a typical lady, May Hill our prize because she could fix any broken thing. She was sixty or seventy—we weren't sure. In the olden days they'd apparently called her a misfit but that wasn't quite right. My mother sometimes laughed a May Hill story away, saying she was certifiable, *mildly* certifiable, she'd say, aiming for accuracy. Eccentric, is all, my father corrected. We naturally assumed Witch. Whatever she was she'd been working on the baler for three days, trying to get the twines to make their knots, trying to remind the mechanism of its own intelligence. It seemed to work most consistently when, at my father's suggestion, one of us walked alongside it, just being there, not touching it, the baler in need of assurance or companionship or maybe it loved an audience. As much as we were generally afraid of May Hill we were grateful for her tenderness with that rattletrap.

"You guys can't upgrade or anything?" one of the Bershek twins asked, pulling down on his lid to get a bug out of his eye. "For the millennium, how about. Your great-uncle, or whatever, got the baler used in, like, 1955? That what your dad said?"

The twins were in high school and they'd bound around the field, leaping, skipping, doing barbell stunts with the bales—such goofs—as if they'd never get tired, as if the heat couldn't ever drop them flat. We, William and I, eleven and twelve years old, we knew better, knew enough to walk between the bales, no jetés, no handsprings for the Lombard children. We knew to conserve our strength. When we were small we'd had matching striped coveralls, sunglasses and leather gloves and boxy orange work boots, no one more serious or poised to make hay. We would have been enraged if anyone had called us cute. Even now we were still not quite ourselves in our tattered chambray shirts, the heavy jeans, the worn gloves, our caps tight on our heads, our clothes a costume plucked from our future, when we'd run the farm.

William didn't answer the twins and I didn't, either. We were not going to get a pop-up bailer, no, never have enormous round bales that only a machine could pick up. There was no point talking about the nobility of the labor, the ancient gathering up of the field, no use explaining it if you didn't get it at this late date.

Earlier in the day there'd been talk on the weather discussion board about the building of the system, the possibility of thunderstorms, 40 percent chance. My father had meant the baling to start earlier but there'd been the usual conversation, the long silences with Aunt May Hill, Aunt May Hill always reluctant to commit, worried that there was too much moisture in the mix, she the one who knew about danger. Nothing to do then but wait, kicking around until she agreed to start the work, until in her estimation the hay was near enough to dry perfection. But we had knowledge, too, we did, bending the stems, sniffing, the goods leafy and sweet, a vintage the sheep would be pleased to eat.

Finally, she took her place on the Allis, and soon after we fanned out, throwing the bales on the wagon, a rickety thing with no sides. My father always constructed the load, ninety bales that he stacked long ways and crossways, five tiers, the structure holding through the woods on the jolting trips to the barn, all of us riding on top, admiring the view. And ducking, to keep from getting clocked by the limbs hanging over the rutted path. There would be three to four loads, my father thought, maybe more. If Sherwood showed up, my father's partner, if he came we'd be done sooner.

It got hazy in the middle of the fourth load, the low sky a dull white and then suddenly—it was like that—all at once, out of the west, a wind, a black bank coming at us, the seams of lightning doing their zigzag, a quick count, one and two and three, the boom, the crack so close.

"Papa!" William cried. "We're not going to make it." William, who never called my father Papa anymore, was trotting alongside the wagon, gripping the edge, as if he meant to stop the whole contraption. There were thirty or so bales left in the field, another fifteen minutes to pick them up. My father was knocking one hard into place on the fourth tier with his knee, standing high, standing steady.

He didn't even turn to look at the roiling sky, pure wrath above, my father, who was a cautious person under most circumstances. We heard him say, "We'll be all right."

"We won't! It's almost here, it's— Pa! Look!"

A bale tumbled up at my father, and another, the Bershek twins on a roll, forever on a roll, my father grabbing the first by the twines, jamming it into a slot in the stack, Gloria on the wagon, too, thrusting the second up to him. Our cousin Philip had been driving, our cousin a native of Seattle, a city dweller. He jumped off the tractor and tore ahead of the wagon, hauling the bales that were far flung into stacks, consolidating them near our path. We wouldn't take notice of his usefulness, we would not, because in our opinion he couldn't have any real knowledge about weather.

"Doesn't Papa see it's going to hit?" William shouted at me. "Frankie! Doesn't he see?"

"I know it!" I, too, kept moving.

One of the twins called in my direction, "Good times, Mary Frances, good times."

Our father, the living skeleton, Exhibit A, underneath the coveralls nothing but hanging bones, and on display all the teeth, the hard grin signifying great effort, our father going at it as if he were still a teenager himself and not in his fifties; and yet of course he wasn't crazed and of course he would not ever put a single person—except himself—in any kind of jeopardy. But my brother yelled again, a frayed, tearful sound—"Come down, Papa! Let's get out of here."

The Bershek boys weren't stopping, my father wasn't telling them to, my father taking the bales ever higher as if another crack hadn't gone right over our heads, as if there really was sin, each worker supposed to wait in the open air for his punishment. Aunt May Hill in her floppy straw hat and sunglasses, Aunt May Hill almost glamorous if you didn't know how plain she was, had already driven the baler back to the barn and was safe. William moved faster, keeping on without meaning to, almost without knowing he was still working. In his head, I think, he'd made for home.

At dinner it was a story of triumph for my mother, the first drop, a drop so ripe, so heavy, that drop falling in the instant the wagon was unloaded, William in that second handing off the last bale into the barn. It was then that Sherwood, my father's cousin, turned up, arriving to help just when we were finished, a talent of his. We had to tell my mother that funny part of the story, Sherwood and his legendary timing. All together we had stood in the wide open door of the barn laughing at the force of the downpour, the rain soon hard as bullets, ricocheting off the metal feeders. In the field the bales had flown up into my father's hands, all of us moving as if in black light; time sped up for us even as the storm was outside of time. At the table my brother said very little. He couldn't be glad for the miracle, not entirely, a bitterness in his own self, for his doubt.

You know you believe it, I beamed to him across the platter of corn. *You know you believe the one pure thing!* William couldn't say the words out loud, didn't want to sound insincere or childish. But that night of the hay baling he was reminded of the truth. He knew what we'd always known, that our father could outwit a storm. It was so. It had happened. He knew there was no point, not in anything, if our father wasn't on hand, quieting the wind; and no point, either, if we weren't there to see it.

2.

Two Terrible Discussions

Our greatest fear must have been with us always because even before we went to school we did play at holding to our own fortress. We imagined war with the other family on the orchard. We considered it a siege more than a war, the standoff with our relatives, with our cousins who in ordinary life were our friends. It wasn't until we were seven and eight, though, that we were first frightened in real terms about the farm, both of us just beginning to suspect that the future, that empty wide forever, might contract, it might narrow and start to spin, it might touch down, sweeping us into itself.

We were on our way to Minnesota to visit our forgetful, wandering grandmother when we got the inkling. It was rare that we took a vacation all together, and more than anything we were excited about the seven-hour drive. The backseat of the van had been made up like a pasha's tent, beautifully draped and soft with our blankets and pillows, a box of tapes in alphabetical order, books on a makeshift shelf, magnetic games, a full tub of markers and new pads of paper, enough supplies to entertain us to the West Coast if for some reason that became our destination. Even though it was winter we got in the car an hour before departure to anticipate the pleasure of the trip, wrapped up and sitting mindfully in the tidy splendor. William had his red toolbox, something he couldn't travel without, construction always in progress of a mixed-race quadruped, part Lego, part Capsela, a few mutant Erector Set parts for the personality who might someday speak to us, gestures and all. We were only slightly ahead of the age of handheld electronics for every boy and girl, and yet how impossibly old-fashioned we sound already. The thermos of hot chocolate, that timeless delight, and the basket of apples and cookies and nuts were by our side.

We liked the setup so much William said, "Let's pretend this is our house, Frankie. This is where we really live."

I loved that idea.

For most of our lives we'd been mistaken for twins. I was as tall as William, and we both had light-brown hair, his softly sprouted and growing in a swirl as if from a single originating point at his crown. Mine was cut in a pageboy, thin and blunt. Looking at William, I always knew I was not ugly. We seemed for a time to have the same plain standard-issue child noses, his turning up slightly. Whereas I dreamed we were twins, Siamese even, conjoined in utero, attached at an easy juncture, the little finger shared, or just a sliver of the hip—whereas I often believed this had to be so—it would never have occurred to my brother to consider altering the details of our birth.

At first as we drove west to the Twin Cities we were happy.

My mother up front did her imitations of her patrons at the library, where she worked, and my father opened his mouth as if he were having a dental exam and howled. No one made him laugh as hard as my mother. She'd say the amusing line and then sit back to watch him at the enterprise of enjoying her little story. She had a black heart, she once said to him, the result of smoking, had she ever smoked? Could she have been so stupid and so terrible? And yet that shriveled charred heart somehow beating was a feature my father found funny, and therefore we must try not to worry.

For a while we sang along to one of the folksingers on our tape, songs about baby whales and delightful banana pickers and abandoned ducklings, songs we were getting too old for but nonetheless they were our favorites. We weren't self-conscious about singing, not quite yet, unable to help ourselves, belting out the *quack quack*s and the *Day-o*s. *Daylight come and me wan' go home.* Somehow William was able to sing and at the same time even in travel draw on paper tacked to a board across his lap, the artist making boy-type inky castles, tight lines, extreme architectural detail, the dungeons equipped with outlets and computer stations.

Halfway across the state my mother took the wheel and soon after we both must have fallen asleep.

"What are you saying?" She was speaking quietly to my father but urgently, the blast of her *t*, the incredulity in the word *what* the sound that woke us. We didn't move, both of us lodged against our windows, a little damp, a little drooly.

"I want him to be able to carry on the business, Nellie," my father said. "To make it as easy as possible for him to keep going. You'd want him to do the same for me."

"Carry on the business," my mother said, leaning forward, her face practically to the dashboard. "As easy as possible for him," she repeated.

"You'd better pull over."

"I'm not going to crash the car."

My father said, with deep apology in his voice, "I shouldn't have brought it up. We need a will, that goes without saying. I'm thinking out loud—"

"I just want to get it straight, your plan."

"It isn't a plan—"

"Your *thought* is to will the property and the business—every one of your assets—to Sherwood. To make it easy for him. The property that includes the house we live in."

My father looked out the window, which we understood to mean he did not wish to continue talking, something my mother didn't seem to know.

"It would be nice, Jim, it would be considerate, in the event of your death, to be able to remain in the house." She said that sentence so distinctly, and sweetly, too, it seemed.

"Nellie—"

"Just so I have it straight, is all. So I can prepare. You're giving the whole of everything to Sherwood—and Dolly, let's not leave Dolly out of the discussion. Imagine leaving Dolly out." She had to pause, stunned at such an omission. "If you're going to give the place up to them, I should probably start putting my spare change in a jar. So I have enough to care for our children, food, shelter, clothing, that kind of thing. A dime or two for college. In the event of your death," she added, her tone even more agreeable.

Our father dying? William's eyes were narrowed in concentration. Our parents were having a joke, I thought, or maybe playing a car game. My father dying and his business partner and cousin, Sherwood, owning every acre, this funny, hard game something like My Grandmother's Suitcase or I Spy. As for college, that also was ridiculous. William and I were never going away.

"Aunt Florence and Uncle Jim passed down the farm to you and Sherwood and May Hill." My mother reviewing ancient history.

"Yes, Nellie, all right, let's not go into a tailspin. Let's let the funnel cloud settle elsewhere."

"And so maybe you feel obligated to honor that history. Maybe," my mother mused, "Sherwood will build me a house out of the scrap metal in the sheep yard. Imagine the house that Sherwood could make! No, no, this will be fun."

We could tell she didn't mean real fun in this game of theirs. Sherwood famously invented all kinds of never-before-heard-of contraptions, and he tried to build regular tools and machines, too. It was unlikely—we knew this—that he could successfully erect a whole house.

"Our palace," she was saying, "oh, Jim! It will have a laundry chute, like a marble run, underwear, socks, washcloths skating down tubes through all the lopsided, slanting rooms, kicking off bells and whistles before they land in the washing machine. How great is that?" She turned to my father, looking at him for longer than seemed a safe driving practice. "The floors," she went on, "will be made of arable soil, you mow it instead of mopping. Plus, we can grow radishes under the table." Another hard look at him. "And play golf."

"Nellie," he said wearily. "Get off at the next exit, will you please?"

"I do understand that for you the farm is the most important feature of the world," she said quietly, and almost sadly. "I do know that. I'm not going to dwell on the money I put into the operation—gladly, I put the nest egg in gladly."

What money? We were always puzzled about money, whose was what, and why my father's jaw went taut when the subject came up. He turned around to see if we were still sleeping, our eyes snapping shut. "You do dwell on it." His voice was in the back of his throat, my father rumbling, a rare occasion. "You are dwelling. You dwellth."

"I dwellth not! I'm only thinking of the will, and how maybe you could, in that document, jog Sherwood's memory, for the final tally, this teacup, that teacup."

"He remembers," my father said. "Of course he does. He's grateful."

"*Of course he does!* My God, Jim."

They were blissfully quiet for a while but then my mother had to start it up again. "Anyway, the normal course of action, if you weren't going to make a sanctimonious gesture to your cousin—wouldn't it be to give your share into my custodial care until William and Francie could have a crack at it? Assuming they want to inherit the bounty of the ages. And carry on the . . . cult."

We recalled what she'd said about the farm. It was true that our orchard was the most important feature of the world.

"Assuming," she went on, "that the Queen and her right-of-way, and her other well-placed acres, doesn't ruin everyone." My mother called Aunt May Hill the Queen, a name that did not suit her.

"Would you stop talking? Please, Nellie."

Yes, yes, we were absolutely on his side—he should give her an apple to fill her mouth, a gentle stuffing.

"I think what you're saying, Jim, is that if I had ownership I'd screw Sherwood over. Which, okay, I admit, is sometimes an appealing thought."

My father was again gazing out the window, as if fields under snow was a landscape that had variation of untold interest.

"You actually," she said, "you actually don't trust me." She said this as if she'd been stricken by awe.

"That is absurd," he cried. "And you know it." Jim Lombard went ahead and at that very particular moment made a remark that was out of place in the timetable of the fight. He said, "There's a rest stop in two—"

When she lurched back against the seat, preparing to be shrill, I finally yelled, "What are you talking about?"

William took up the call, sticking his head between their high-backed seats, as tall as thrones. "You shouldn't argue."

"We're not," my mother spit, "arguing."

"It sounds like it," William pointed out.

My father, who was always truthful, said, "We are arguing."

"Here's what I want, Jim." My mother, for her part, did not like to leave a task unfinished. "I want Sherwood, when you're gone, to implement every single one of his lunatic ideas. May Hill will have to wrastle him to the ground, think of that! When the whole operation is in complete disarray William and Francie will step in and save them. That," she snapped, "is my dream."

We were not only further bewildered by their discussion but, more critically, unsure now about whose side we were

on. My father's for agreeing with us about their arguing or
my mother's for foretelling our marvelous future? I wanted to
cry because of their game and also because the conversation
reminded me of a secret I had, a sliver of talk I'd once over-
heard, something awful my mother had said to Gloria, the
hired hand. It was a snippet I couldn't even repeat to William.
They'd been in the kitchen maybe a year or two before when
Gloria asked my mother if she thought William and I would
stay on the farm when we were grown, if we'd want to take
it over. My mother said, "Oh, who knows! Don't you think
William's too dreamy and too interested in other things to be a
farmer? And Francie"—she burst out laughing—"is too full of
spleen."

Spleen? What was that? Why was it funny? For the life of me
I could not find out what *spleen* meant; I couldn't understand
the largest component of my character. I couldn't ask William
because what if it was a hideous stain or germ, amusing to an
observer, that was soon going to overtake my hands, my legs,
my face? The spleen was going to keep me from being a farmer
and when I remembered that fact I was very sorry for myself,
a sad glum girl.

In the car my father said, "We're going to get out and
stretch." In order to ensure that his wife take the exit ramp he
added that he himself had to use the bathroom.

"Take the ramp or not take the ramp?" my mother considered. "Make you hold it all the way to Minneapolis? Oh, Jim,
let me think about this."

They both then did something we couldn't stand. They
both unaccountably started to laugh. "You'll be the death of
me," he said to her.

"And then I'll be stuck with that asinine will. Jesus Christ."
They laughed again.

"If you croak," she said, "if you leave me with Sherwood and Dolly and May Hill, I'll hunt you down."

We could hardly move, William and I, in the parking area. My father giving the farm to Sherwood? My mother hunting him down—what did that mean? My father dying—no! He wasn't really going to do that, but the rest of us without a house? Sherwood building a metal home with a marble run? "I don't have to go," I said. Their sudden laughter, the way their argument seemed to end, was possibly the most confounding thing of all.

"Yes, you do," my mother said.

"I don't."

William squeezed his eyes shut for her, he bore down, as if he were trying to summon urine for her pleasure. "I'm fine," he concluded.

When my parents gave up on us and went off to the visitor center on their own I started to cry. We were left, we were left, we were left now and we were going to be left later, left without the orchard. William looked out the window to the cold travelers walking their dogs in the dirty snow. He was crying, too, the Lombard children as good as orphans, might as well start now, brother and sister, hand in hand, abandoned on the highway, an apple each, a favorite book, a few Jolly Ranchers, green only, a song to sing for company, nothing, nothing else, no place to roam but everywhere.

3.

The Situation

The orchard, the family affair, was a compound with three houses, three barns, four hundred acres of forest and arable fields and marsh, the sheep pastures, and the apple trees. The woods were wild and dense, no hiker's path of shavings, no sign at the start announcing points of interest, the lady's slippers hidden in the broad ginger leaves, the morels—we weren't going to tell anyone where they were. There was no warning about future dangers, such as the cougar maybe making a comeback in our state. By the far west fence there was an Indian burial mound that we took for the shape of an owl, and in a thicket nearby the remains of a settler's cabin. Once, digging around, we found a tin cup, dented and packed with dirt. William picked it up, he sniffed it, sniffed the rim, where lips would have touched. I asked should we take it with us? He held it in both hands, looking off into the distance, seeing, I guessed, the fairy-tale children of long ago. An ogre of course and a father with an ax. Without deciding exactly we buried the cup as if it were a little pet we'd cared for.

Home we went over the wooded hills. The last glacier coming down into Wisconsin had stopped just south of us, dumping its remaining load of gravel, ideal country for an apple orchard, the soil rich enough, the drainage superb. In truth, though, we were more interested in what was to come than in what had already happened in the time of weather and pioneers. William and I were the fourth generation born unto the operation, heirs to a historical property and a noble business, far more than our friends could say about their fathers' jobs and their houses on quarter-acre lots.

What worried us was a possible hitch, a potentially tricky web. Because we were not the only heirs. The major candidates in our minds were our good playmates and cousins, Adam, the oldest of us four, the boy for William, and Amanda, the youngest, the girl for me. They lived across the road in the manor house, a house far enough away and shrouded by trees so that it was not visible from our side. Amanda and Adam lived in Volta. William and Mary Frances lived in Velta. Our divided kingdom, William inventing the names, Velta and Volta, for what was true. Our cousins in Volta on the whole hated to work, disliked the out-of-doors, and never went into the woods unless their father coaxed them. Adam had cause to protest because he had the bee sting allergy, a cruel joke for a boy living in the middle of an orchard. But aside from their natural disinclination, their mother, Dolly, was always describing to them their college lives, way off, already excited about their adulthood in the city. So Amanda and Adam usually didn't trouble us too much, but what about the cousins who lived elsewhere, in Alaska or California, children whose parents had grown up on the farm, those strangers who might arrive and seize the road? Children we had never met. For the most part after our trip to Minnesota we forgot that our father might someday give the farm to his partner, to Sherwood, or maybe we heard our parents not long after discussing their will in reasonable and generous terms. With that fear out of the way we had to make ourselves afraid on our own steam, pretending we were royal orphans, our right to rule threatened by the thugs at the palace door. Then we put on our capes and crowns and we climbed on top of the old chicken shed for our rapture: Bring me my bow of burning gold! Bring me my arrows of desire! Bring me my spear!

There were many dwellings that we would someday own part of if the strict lineage wasn't interrupted. The manor house, the size of a ship, of a destroyer, was made of granite and cedar shakes, and had been built for our great-grandfather, the lawyer, the state senator, the gentleman farmer. Sherwood, Dolly, Amanda, and Adam lived in the downstairs, although my parents owned three-eighths of the entire house. We always wondered, Which part?—hoping one of the four bathrooms was in our share. Also, we would need a slice of either the up-stairs or downstairs kitchen. Aunt May Hill, one-fourth owner, was someone we didn't want to think about for any number of reasons.

For instance, when May Hill was a young person her father, a relative of ours, had accidentally suffocated in a silo on his farm in Indiana, and shortly after that her mother found a rope and hanged herself from a barn rafter. May Hill's brother was in college but she, a high school girl, had to be adopted by Sherwood's parents. One day she was a teenager at home and soon after she arrived at the Lombard farm in Wisconsin to take her place among a two-, three-, five-, and six-year-old— that was Sherwood—and a baby on the way. If she had been in a book we probably would have loved that downtrodden orphan. She was brilliant, everyone said. A solid girl, a girl with a large frame. When she grew older, instead of going to college or finding a job she stayed upstairs in her room reading, she tinkered in the tool house, she chopped wood, she studied auto mechanics on her own, and she invested in the stock market. It was common knowledge that she'd become rich. No woman we'd ever seen had such thick rectangular eyebrows. Not that we saw her very often. We understood that she did not like anyone, that she did not wish to see you on the path. The fact we knew most certainly was that, no matter her solitary habits, May Hill was the farm's pure gold. Because breakdown was daily and went according to the seasons: the Ford tractor and market truck sputtering in fall, the sprayer clogged in spring, the baler and mower fizzing in summer, the snowplow intractable in winter. Each piece of equipment poised to quit in the time of its urgent need.

Aside from May Hill's holdings everything else was split fifty–fifty between Sherwood and my father. Down the drive past the manor house was the apple barn where the customers came, where the cider was made, the apples sorted and stored, and behind that was the sheep yard for the flock of thirty ewes. Also, there in the yard, the museum of cars and other implements from as far back as 1917, plus rusted stanchions mostly buried, stacks of bicycles, wagon wheels, refrigerators, lawn mowers, barrels of used twine, chipped crocks—nothing of particular use but each item in a casual pose, caught as if in the middle of a task, as if trapped in time by lava or ice. You might think, studying the jumble, that the ancestors had done very little but ride bikes and churn butter. We sometimes worried that if Sherwood and my father had a real war we wouldn't be able to get to the apple barn to do business, to feed the sheep, to rattle around in the junk, to play with Amanda and Adam. We'd be prisoners cut off from the supply.

The war would start because of the ancient argument, and one irrevocable thing would be said, something bitter and true. Sherwood and my father would then fall silent not for a few minutes but for years. It would be a war with no punches and certainly no shooting, no physical injury of any kind because that's not how the Lombards behaved. The problem for Sherwood was my father, Jim Lombard, his cousin who hadn't grown up on the farm. Jim had only spent his summers on the orchard, working alongside his maiden aunt, Aunt Florence. Whereas Sherwood was raised full-time in the manor house, the boy who had always known he was the rightful and only heir. After college my father came to help out, to rescue the operation while Sherwood was in the army. To Jim Lombard's own surprise and joy, he never left. Sherwood came back from his posting, he and my father were made partners, one by one the older generation died, my parents got married around the same time Dolly and Sherwood tied the knot, Adam and Amanda were born, we were born, everything beginning all over again. But the tickler, the fundamental question lurked: Was my father, the city person, the interloper—did he belong? Did his pedigree and his summer roots constitute a claim?

When William and I learned a new detail of my father's story, or when we heard more about the argument as the years passed, each piece was usually an understandable part of the predicament. Very rarely did additional information surprise us. Because the feeling between Sherwood and my father, that hum, was outside of us and also within us; surely it was so because otherwise we would not have entertained the war as we did, considering our stores of food, planning to hold fast to our little house across the road, the falling-down clapboard heap my parents had done their best to rescue, built circa 1860. We plotted how we'd get to the stone cottage near the village where Gloria the employee lived, Gloria, in the role of the hired man, living in the original Lombard house in the state of Wisconsin. Would I have to hate Amanda, who was a year younger than me, or would we be like lovers who were separated, sending each other messages in code, the upholders of the best, the pure Lombard spirit? William and Adam would sneak notes, too, the children reminding the elders who we were.

By the time we were in high school we understood enough to consider the hardships each bore. For certain Sherwood and Jim had the same funny pride in their independence and parsimony, but even though their goals were identical and their love equally deep, still, the fact remained that there perhaps have never been two men more unsuited to be in business together, the pair a marvel of incapacity. Sherwood the visionary—how we sometimes loved him for his leaps, his forays into the future! And Jim the commander of all details, the prophet of routine. The force of each diminishing the other's power. But what the men respected in their situation, once they were business partners, was their rage, each for the most part keeping a lid on it, their semi-annual blowouts usually occurring in November and May. In-between times the majesty of the woods around the manor house and the size of the house itself, and the elegance of the apple barn, which originally had been meant for horses, and along the rise the dignity of the long straight rows of apple trees: All those beauties were a reminder of the grace and the good breeding of the Lombard clan itself.

There was a time when everyone came together in a purpose beyond farming. We were lost, William and I. After dinner we'd wandered down the lane that went out to the hay field, sure of ourselves because already at five and six we had helped with the hay in our complete costume: coveralls, gloves, boots, sunglasses, straw hats. It was the end of June and we'd started finding wild raspberries, straying farther and farther from the path, as sheep do, with no regard to the way back. After a while William looked up, his lips stained black, his eyes at once bright with fear. "It's getting dark," he noted. We started running, the thorns scratching our arms, our legs, our cheeks. Although we'd been told there were no bears or wolves in our part of the state, we knew that when night fell the savage beasts from out of time would emerge from their dens. We were already bloodied by the thicket, by mere plants. When we came to a hillside William led me up the brambly slope into a hole, a great gouge that had been made by a tree falling down. We climbed over the dead limbs and got ourselves into the torn earth, arranging ourselves among the roots. "Don't cry, Frankie," he said, but he himself was shivering. He held me in his arms and so although I was afraid, I was strangely happy, too. I started to try to sing a little song but he said we should probably listen for—for what? Our father, of course our father would come. Even though we knew he would find us, all the same we began to see—without speaking of it—the whole story of our being the dead children.

There was so much to miss in the life we wouldn't lead, the Lombard girl and boy who despite his dreaminess and her spleen were supposed to carry on the orchard, those two snuffed out before they could be the farmers. William and I continued to tremble as if it were winter. Ghosts, that's what we'd be, standing at our places at the apple sorter wearing our XXX Small brown cotton gloves, child laborers who were glad to undertake any task even in death. We'd been going to marry each other, my brother and I having solved that problem of adulthood early. It was William who'd firmly told me about the arrangement, who had the good idea, the two of us continuing on in our bunk beds, William above with his raspy breathing, that lullaby, the parents staying put in their room.

For a little while in the woods he told me a story that began this way: "Once there was a girl who lived near the end of the world. Her name was Miss Imp." Miss Imp! That was me, a girl who was always annoying everyone but in a way they secretly enjoyed. When Miss Imp got lost her house right on the edge of the world picked up its skirts and came to find her, it loved her so much. With that conclusion we listened to the darkness again, remembering that in fact we were still lost and were probably going to die.

Gloria was the person we first heard calling. "WILL-YUM! FRAAAAN-SEA!" Our own names out in the night.

William called back, "Here we are." His thin song like an insect's steady announcement in the grass, *hereweare, hereweare.* We heard in the farther distance my father calling and my mother's cries. It dawned on us that although they were looking they might not find us, and then what?

So William again took me by the hand, and out we crawled, back into the night, trying to find the voices, again stumbling, again getting scratched, our legs and shorts soaked with dew. We again wrapped our arms around each other, and went slowly. At the moment when we came out of a tangle into the back field the moon burst from under a cloud, a half-moon but there was enough light to see where we were. Instead of running, for the first time in our lives we cried tears of joy. That made us laugh, how funny that tears could be for something other than a wound or fear. We went skipping along the real path with the heavy ruts, the path that would take us to the manor house and the barn.

On our way we were surprised by Gloria, her headlamp shining along the rise. In our giddiness we'd forgotten that we were still the objects of the search party. She had to start whimpering, clutching us to her, and at the same time trying to shout for our parents, saying we were found. We kept holding hands, William and I stiff in her embrace. We had rescued ourselves and did not appreciate her claim. We hadn't been frightened, we insisted. Our cuts didn't hurt. No, we weren't cold. We'd known where we were the whole time. We knew the woods, our woods. We had only been out for a walk, hungry for some raspberries.

When we came from the path to the manor house, Sherwood and Dolly were walking up the drive from the east orchard, and Aunt May Hill was standing on the porch. Amanda and Adam were in the living room window looking out, pale and still on our account. Everyone had been concerned and everyone was now relieved, even, oddly enough, Aunt May Hill. There was chatter that we didn't pay attention to, my parents thanking the search party, Gloria recounting her part, Sherwood expressing gratitude to the moon herself for shining. He was the tallest Lombard, the man with the magnificent forehead and wild red curls, the man who right then made us laugh by baying like a coyote at the heavens.

In William's bed that night we continued holding hands, thrilled by our near-death and our own powers, certain just then that we would always find our way home.

4.

Our Gloria

Just as the farm could not have been the farm without Sherwood and Dolly and Aunt May Hill, we understood without ever thinking about it that Gloria, too, was ours. But that did not mean that we were hers. We didn't want to have to thank her for saving us, though we were told we must. But even if she had rescued us, say she'd found us in the jaws of a beast, that simple offering, *thank you*, those two worthless words were hardly compensation for our full long lives.

Well before that night, thanking Gloria for her many kindnesses, how best to thank her, was often a subject at the breakfast table. "She does so much for you," my mother reminded us, as if we could forget that Gloria had taught us to skate backward and leap, to knit dishcloths, to make cinnamon rolls in knots, to shrink great clumps of fleece into tennis-size balls for the cats, the short list of our skills.

"We do thank her," William said. "Thank you, thank you, thank you, thank you, thank you, Gloria."

He was the funniest boy in the world!

But the business about thanking her always reminded us of *that time*. We'd suddenly remember, we'd look at each other, quickly we'd have to look away. *May Hill*, we'd whisper in our minds. One long-ago afternoon we'd been in the tool house, a small building near the apple barn with the usual junk, boards with rusty nails in unruly stacks, coffee cans of bolts, drill bits in a mess on the workbench, the floor covered with tires and watering cans, broom handles and the guts of lawn mowers. A power saw, a pile of chain saws, gasoline cans. There was also a nest of kittens in a bag of rags; somebody had said so. We were clambering over a heap trying to find them when the door burst open. Aunt May Hill, the lady giant in her dungarees, her mouth ripped down to her neck. She waved her arms, more than two arms, four or five arms sprouted in order to scatter us.

We couldn't move. We were too terrified to cry out.

So then she had to say a word. We'd never heard that voice or the spell. It was a thin, high screech and long, the word. "Scram," it started—"bambow!" She wailed it again. "Scram-bambow!"

We each were exactly like a cornered cat when she said it, chasing any which way to get out, knocking over boards and cans, a box of old nails clattering to the floor. We ran without knowing where we were going, run, run, run and who did we smack into on the orchard path but Gloria.

"Whatever is the matter?" she said. "William? Mary Frances! What happened to you?"

We both fell into her arms. We couldn't help it. We started to sob, pressing ourselves into the available softness of her skinny chest. *Scram-bambow!* We'd never heard such a word, but worse, the voice, the screech—

"Oh, my darlings," Gloria cried, she herself crying with us. "Now, now." She urgently petted our hair, rocking us. We covered our ears as if we could keep that voice out of our heads. "It's all right, it's all right," Gloria crooned. "You're safe. You're safe with me."

We could never tell anyone about the real May Hill. Never tell about *Scram-bambow*. And even though we should have thanked Gloria for trying to soothe us we couldn't ever mention what had taken place in the tool house.

As time passed there were other things we learned from Gloria in addition to skating and crafts. For instance, we first learned about romance, William and Francie with a bird's-eye view of the swoon, Gloria falling in love with Stephen Lombard. Although that was a cautionary tale more than a how-to in-struction. And it was not a lesson we could thank her for, not least because she had to go away for several months to recover.

"Remember how much she loves you," my mother said reg-ularly, well before the Stephen crisis, as if we could know the exact amount, the stuff of love made in sizes or judged by weight.

She was a tall, pink-faced woman with heavy blond braids and thick glasses who had come to live in the cottage and work on the farm when we were babies, Gloria Peternell, who had always been with the apple business and the prop-erty. It never occurred to us to ask where she'd come from and why. When she was in our house she was almost like a mother for us and nearly like a wife for my father. But after dinner she'd go back to her cottage where she wasn't either of those things.

In the years and years before the Stephen Lombard episode, most every evening during the harvest long after my mother was in bed, Gloria and my father continued talking at the kitchen table, discussing what apples, out of scores of possibilities, they should pick in the morning, what varieties should be sorted in the sorting shed, what apples should be used in the cider that week, which workers should do what tasks. Gloria, strictly speaking, was the employee of both Jim and Sherwood Lombard but we all knew her devotion lay with my father. So that at some point in their nighttime discussion one of them would make a comment or two about Sherwood. That was the favorite part of their ritual, Sherwood always doing something beyond their comprehension.

"The Macouns are dropping," my father would say. "You can hear them. And he decides to patch the sheep shed roof?"

Gloria had one response when it came to Sherwood: She shook her head slowly, eyes cast down, as if she were a disappointed teacher.

"He's had all year to do the project, and he decides to do it now?" My father's disbelief was always fresh.

"I know, Jim. I know."

What, they asked, was Sherwood thinking? Even if the project couldn't wait, even if the whole shed was going to fall to pieces because of the leak, no matter what, the apple crop must always have priority. My father and Gloria seemed confused and upset, but if you looked closely you'd now and again notice on each the slight upward curl of the lip. It was almost indiscernible, that hint of what looked like *I told you so*. A righteous happiness.

"He won't speak to me," Gloria would report. "He walks in the barn, he sees me, he walks out again."

"That's appalling!" There it was, my father's little smile. "I can't stand it. I'll talk to him—"

"No! No, Jim—really. That won't make the situation any better. It's hard for him because—"

"Because, Gloria, in many ways you know more about the business than he does at this point. It's true. You understand the realities of the picking and selling, how each aspect goes hand in hand. If only he could see that we're all working together. Why can't he understand that? You and I, we aren't on some kind of team. We aren't on the opposing side."

"Of course not. Of course we aren't."

It was as if, we sometimes thought, a spell had been put upon both Gloria and my father, so that they had to keep reviewing who had said what and insisting there were no sides. We'd come downstairs in the middle of the night to get a drink of milk, the plastic bottoms of our pajama feet slapping on the steps, and there they were, not even hearing us, Gloria often with a naked face, Gloria without her glasses, rubbing her eyes. In her canvas pants, her faded T-shirt, and, you could tell, no bra for her little titties—even in the same old work clothes—Gloria without her glasses went from looking like welder woman to Nordic princess. If her braids were pulling apart after a long day, and if she'd undone them all the way, her yellow hair fell in its unlashed crinkles to her waist. She was so uncommon-looking with that hair down we were afraid of her, unsure of who she was. She suddenly seemed as if she didn't belong to the farm anymore.

My father and Gloria weren't in love, nothing like that. For love, for romance, we knew you had to be beautiful all the time and also you had to have little else to do. Gloria, we thought, should not wear her glasses if she wanted true love, for one, and for another she had a boyfriend in North Dakota, an older man with a messy gray beard and smudgy eyes who visited every few months. When he wasn't in the state we forgot he existed. This was a proper arrangement, Gloria enjoying my father's company best, and mostly being too busy for other friends.

My mother used to joke to her library patrons that she liked my father having an alternate wife, a spare, Wife Number Two, that the setup allowed her to go to bed at a reasonable hour, to hog the mattress, to read as long as she wanted to, and *Thank you, Gloria*, it freed her from having to hear every detail of the apple business, year in and year out. Sometimes she'd make a peculiar pronouncement, as if her short sentence was a truth from out of antiquity. She'd say, "When you are married to Jesus Christ you become mean."

Her patrons, the women, laughed.

She'd say next, "Gloria is Jesus's nice wife."

This, too, must have been funny because Mrs. Lombard's fan club always snorted at her quips. They laughed even though it was not a humorous fact that Gloria was nice. She was quiet and steady in her jobs as the hired man and Wife Number Two and the lady-in-waiting, and additionally she was the nanny and the scullery maid. All those helpers in one woman. Nellie Lombard was always singing her praises and thanking her and from the kitchen window if Gloria was outside pushing a wheelbarrow full of manure or digging a deep hole or dragging a sheep by its hind leg back to the shed my mother cried, "Don't strain your back! Gloria! Wait until Jim can help you." My mother, always considering Gloria's happiness and comfort.

But sometimes she also came downstairs in the night to get a drink and there Gloria and my father were at the table staring at the candle. My mother had to transform herself then, had to turn into the monstrous shape of a shrill housewife, a cupboard opening, we thought, and this ugly warty woman stepping out. "What is wrong with you people!" she'd cry. "You don't have the sense to go to sleep?"

"Oh!" Gloria pawed around the table for her glasses. "How did it get so late?" And she scuttled away home for a few hours of sleep, Gloria always up at daybreak for the great work of the harvest.

The tangle in our minds, the Gloria problem, if laid out end-to-end, went something like this: As much as she put her time and strength and creativity into the picking and the cider making, the selling at the markets and at our barn, and sorting fruit, and trying to keep order in the storage barn, and doing her best to preserve the peace with Sherwood; as kind as she was to Dolly and even to May Hill; and as much as she slavishly went marching side by side with my father during the day and throughout the seasons; could it be that more than all that activity she wanted to find an actual husband—someone different from the bearded old North Dakotan—and have her own children? Years were passing while maybe she secretly held on to that wish, and then an entire decade had gone by. Through her thick glasses, with her steady gaze boring down into our wobbly selves, she watched us grow up. She put her arms around us, clasping us to her, kissing our hair. My mother did that to us all the time, which was right, which was something we didn't have to hold still on purpose for. Gloria every year gave us handmade Valentines that said BE MINE, a message we knew she'd send us every day if the holiday calendar allowed her to. And sometimes she looked at us as if—if we weren't careful—we'd get beamed up through her magnified eyeballs into some magical Gloria realm that might be an uncomfortable place. She bloodied her fingers sewing me a doll with braids and a wardrobe to go with her and for William she made a knight with knitted chain mail. All those gifts were items my mother was incapable of producing, Gloria, in technical terms, a superior mother.

Our concerns therefore: If she couldn't have enough of us would she quit her post, abandon my father and the farm? Was it our responsibility to hold her? And if so, what did we have to do to keep her? That is, how much did we have to love her?

Always, when we were leaving her cottage, after doing an extensive cooking or sewing project, she'd solemnly give us one last instruction. "William. Mary Frances. Thank your mother for sharing you with me."

She was the only person outside of school who called me Mary Frances, as if she alone had license to call me by my real name.

William and I didn't say anything. Because: No matter our duty, we were not something to be shared. We didn't really know what she meant by saying such a thing, and also we were certain that if we conveyed that wrongheaded, awful gratitude to Nellie she would be furious with Gloria. So we didn't agree

outright to say thank you, and we never, not once, told our
mother.

It was late summer when Stephen Lombard appeared in the
orchard. That was his habit, showing up with no warning.
We were nine and ten. He was Sherwood's youngest brother,
another of my father's cousins, and here was a curious and unsettling fact: He had been my mother's boyfriend in college.
After their graduation she came to visit Stephen on the orchard
but somehow or other instead of going off into the world with
her classmate she married my father. The natural, right choice
but ticklish. Jim Lombard had been living for many years with
his aged aunt Florence, so my mother had to barge in on that
situation. She said that's what you had to do to catch a farmer.
Jim was a far older person than my mother, a previously un-
caught man who worked such long hours and so hard any
future wife had to run alongside him on the orchard path, grab
his collar, and say, "We are getting married right now, hold
still." It mostly seemed to us a funny idea, that Stephen could
have been our father.

After my parents fell in love, after my mother wed the Lombard family, Stephen went away. He eventually found a job
with a nameless American contractor instructing secret agents.
That's the story he told, anyway. He wrote manuals for the
CIA, he said, educating operatives about the country they'd
be living in, about the culture and religion, and also he figured out guidelines in the event of emergency, if the airport
blew up, say, if the embassy was attacked, if you were held
hostage by so-and-so or such-and-such. He had to go to the
region in question, do the research in person to best preach

safety to the recruits. We'd watch *Where in the World Is Carmen Sandiego?*, and my mother, passing through the room, might mutter, "Where in the hell is Stephen Lombard?" Sudan, for instance, was where, and Iran and maybe Egypt. Suspicious, unnerving places, no place that could ever be your home. This was what we all very much wanted to know for certain: Was he himself a spy?

Every few years he came back in the late summer to revisit his childhood by picking apples and to purchase his big shoes and the fleecy warm clothes he couldn't get in the desert. At least that's what he said he wanted to do at home, shop and help out on the farm. Maybe, though, he was in hiding. Maybe in his line of work it was important to disappear periodically. He didn't have an office in the United States, one of the clues he was a rootless agent, and also he wouldn't talk directly about his projects, and furthermore, he insisted that his job was really just entry-level grunt work. While he was in the trees, perilously reaching with his tremendously long arms for the highest apple, he'd gossip about foreigners as if they were people we knew. For instance, after the first World Trade Center bombing he was making idle conversation, saying, "Ramzi Yousef ordered the chemicals for the bomb from his hospital room. He'd been in a car accident, he lands in the hospital in New Jersey, he orders urea nitrate over the phone while a nurse's aide is in the bathroom, emptying the bedpan." The aluminum ladder made a warping sound as he reached for another apple. "The deal with these characters? They believe only jihad can bring peace to the world." No one in our neighborhood in 1993 was using the word *jihad* then, and we thought he was maybe talking about a beautiful, princely person named Jihad. Stephen Lombard absolutely was a spy, my mother always said.

"If he was truly a spy he'd have some completely unrelated job as his cover," was my father's position. "He'd lead safaris or be a mapmaker or a computer technician. A plumber."

"Not necessarily, Jim. Maybe the thinking is, he's doing something so obviously related to the CIA, it's staring you in the face so you don't suspect it."

"I think," William said. We all waited, wanting to know. "I think he is a..."

A what?

"A genie of the Orient."

My parents laughed.

I said, "He is! He is!" He was tall enough and he had a full lower lip and could cross his muscly arms over his chest in an imposing way. When he frowned, as genies must, his brows would surely make two slanting lines toward the bridge of his nose, a telltale sign.

The probable spy/genie stayed in our guest room even though Sherwood was his brother, even though the manor house had eleven bedrooms. Even though he was uncle to Adam and Amanda. He wouldn't stay in the upstairs with May Hill—no one did that—and he couldn't be in the downstairs house because there the Lombard hoarding trait was on full display, no place in Sherwood and Dolly's quarters for a person to fully stretch out. So Stephen stayed on our side of the road, in Velta; Stephen was ours, like it or not.

With or without his glasses the genie of the Orient was handsome, the planes of his large face broad and smooth, his lashy brown eyes tapering delicately, his supple mouth often nicely moistened with ChapStick. One of the things I liked about him was his dark-brown hair that curled prettily at the neck. I liked also how he dipped his head in a shy way when he came into a room, not letting anyone see his beauty, and when he spoke he held his hand to his chin and cheek, as if he were in hiding, as his true job must have demanded. He was a genius, my mother said, and complicated, which William told me a spy/genie had to be, pretending to be one thing when you were another.

Back to Stephen's appearing in the orchard in that summer of Gloria. She had just broken it off with the North Dakotan. Even though she'd spent a lot of effort on the boyfriend she hadn't been able to get him to do what she wanted. Why she hadn't fallen in love with Stephen in previous years we didn't know, or maybe she'd been pledged to the old man in their long-distance fashion.

A week or two after Stephen arrived we saw her walking out of the orchard with him at day's end, both of them with their picking bags slung carelessly over their shoulders. But wait, was it Gloria? Her head was tipped back, her face shining and open in a way that was not usual. He was different, too, his hand wasn't covering his cheek, Stephen unguarded, gazing down at her. Both of them heedless of any stone or stick that might be on the path. And one standard feature of Stephen, usually, when he got himself talking? He couldn't stop the story, the story driving hard and sure until the end, and beyond, the very end. Even so, you had to wait for a good while to be sure it was truly over before you tried to make a comment or ask a question or change the subject, no point in two people trying to squeeze through the needle's eye at once.

And yet, with Gloria on their walk that day, he was waiting, waiting for her to say her part. He was listening. He said a sentence or two, and then she spoke. Neither one was confused or struggling. Along they came, in and out of the lavish long rays of the late afternoon, the two of them sometimes bumping a little against each other and also, most alarming, looking at one another for an impolite length of time. We were on the roof of the old chicken coop and we felt funny watching them, somewhat dizzy even, as if we were the pair in the staring contest.

They came in for dinner and as usual Gloria and my father discussed who had picked what, how many bushels, how the trade was at the apple barn, what was tasting good and should be picked next, and what they should include in the market load. What was strange, bizarre, even, was Gloria's being almost bubbly. "Thirty-one customers," she sang out, as if there had never been such a number on a sunny afternoon. William gave me a *Huh?* sort of look. My mother moved around the table and finally she sat, pouring herself another glass of wine, Nellie Lombard on her own path to happiness. Gloria, who was usually hungry at dinner and eager, pushed her plate up to her glass of milk. She stared at the lamb chop, the ear of corn, the pink applesauce, the mashed potatoes fluffed with butter, everything we ourselves had grown, as if she had no idea what food was for. That's when Stephen started his story, when with good reason she could turn her full attention to the storyteller. We all knew his tales were always funny in parts, but also they were sad. They almost always involved him as the hero who does exactly the wrong or clumsy thing, so that even if we didn't want to we found ourselves listening.

He told the one where he was little, when he and his father

were picking in the Cortland line. His father, straining for a huge, deep-red apple growing from a leader that was impossibly high, fell eighteen feet to the ground. Thwump. There he lay in a heap. Five-year-old Stephen froze to the rungs of his own ladder.

"Oh, Stephen!" Gloria cried.

"One of my first existential crises," Stephen said modestly. "Where was God? Was there a God? What was God going to do for me?"

Everyone except Gloria laughed.

"Couldn't find God, but probably more important, couldn't locate my feet. Or my vocal cords. Not only my first existential crisis but my first stunning public display of ineptitude. If only I'd known how many more were to come."

Gloria smacked her hand to her mouth. It seemed as if she might cry. We all knew how the story came out, how eventually the father was loaded onto an old door for a stretcher and put in the apple truck and taken to the emergency room, that he'd miraculously sustained only a few broken ribs. There was no reason to cry.

William and I also knew we were supposed to love the fumbling, sweet boy, young Stephen, just as everyone else did. But how could we? When Stephen talked about his childhood we got the feeling he didn't actually believe that any child had come after him on the farm. For that reason we couldn't laugh or feel very sorry for him. He hardly seemed to notice that we were at the table, that we, Mary Frances and William, were the actual, real true children.

When he'd finished the story, the father alive and hardly wounded, Stephen abruptly pushed back in his chair and stood up. "Thanks," he said to my mother. "You cook lamb better than the Saudis."

My mother, so pleased by the compliment, tittered girlishly. Gloria watched him hastily tie his shoes and land a short pat pat on Butterhead, the old yellow cat. She stared at the aged tom, both of them glazy-eyed, while Stephen crossed the yard and started out to the hay field. After a minute Gloria blinked away her dream, she looked at her full plate, and then—what did she do but go to the sink and scrape all of that bounty into the bucket for the chickens.

"Gloria?" my mother said. "You all right?"

"Fine!" Gloria said so brightly we knew she had to be ill. Nonetheless she was putting on the smock she wore at our house so she could wash the dishes.

What's going on? It was my mother who first asked the question of my father with the look, eyebrows raised, the wide glare of alarm.

Next we knew Gloria was ripping off the smock, throwing it on the counter, and she was gone, out the door.

"Oooooh...sweeeet..." My mother's oath was coming from her mouth, a slow leak. "...Geeeesus."

"What's the matter?" William said.

"Do not, Gloria, go after Stephen." My mother spoke as if Gloria were still in the room.

"Is that what's happening?" my father wondered.

She shook her head mournfully, which seemed to mean yes.

"Why are you doing that, Mrs. Lombard?" William had started using her formal title when strictness was required.

"It's just that—it's just that if, if Gloria likes Stephen—if she likes him very much—he just won't—he just can't attend to—"

"Is that what's going on?" My father's same basic question.

"Yes, Jim, yes it is."

"Gloria likes Stephen?" I said.

"All the signs indicate yes," my mother explained. Not only was she the person in the family who knew about the world in general, but she had also once followed Stephen all the way from her college in Ohio to the orchard. So she should know.

William looked at me, I looked at him. We were thinking about how Gloria had recently scooped up a batch of late-summer kittens from our barn, the mother, Piggy, having eaten the first two, the glutton Piggy feasting on her own young. In rushed Gloria to rescue the remaining babies from both Piggy and my murderous father, who, if given a chance, would slit their throats, a quicker, kinder death, he always said, than drowning them in a bucket. What remained were three blind little mewlers who required feeding with a syringe. So, right away, if Stephen and Gloria got married, they'd have something like an instant family.

"It's not going to work out," my mother pronounced, pushing back to clear the plates.

My father, always hopeful where love was concerned, said, "Maybe it will, Nellie. Maybe he's ready."

"Oh God, Jim."

"He's got this sabbatical situation. Maybe he's ready for a new life."

"You know Stephen is not domesticatable," my mother said, going to her husband's chair, standing behind him, draping her arms down his front. "You know you are utterly out of your mind."

He smiled as if she'd given him a compliment, as if she'd said something factual.

"You're not crazy, Papa!" I cried.

My parents laughed, the way they did when, without warning, they were in their own realm where everything was funny. If anyone was crazy it was Gloria. She had flung down her smock. She'd torn away. So that's how it happened, not eating any of your dinner, abandoning the dishes, having to run to try to catch, maybe not even the man, but the love itself? None of it seemed like a good idea, but we weren't going to worry about Gloria's disappointment in the event it didn't work out. We wandered off upstairs to our room. We got to wondering whether, if it did work out, if she and Stephen would then have real children instead of cats. If they did, those children would be our cousins. Because Gloria was a knowledgeable gardener, unlike my mother, whose plot was a tangle, and because Gloria was interested in farming, those children might want to live on the orchard. They might want to take it over. Those future relatives would be our rivals, our enemies, and furthermore they would have extensive knowledge, something we had neglected to get. We would then be sorry we hadn't loved Gloria more, so that she would have been satisfied with just us.

That night, though, we forgot as usual everything that was going on around us, forgot to worry. My father always lay on the floor in our room in order to tell us a continuing story that came out of his own head. He could only do it lying down. The story featured a hero named Kind Old Badger. Kind Old Badger seemed doddery and was sometimes baffled but, surprising to some, he was remarkably strong and wise. Not to mention shrewd. The story highlighted William and Mary Frances, too, we who performed feats of astonishing bravery with the dearest of Badgers. We were always having to run swiftly over hill and also over dale, the two of us *run, run, running like the hobbie-a*, my father said. We knew what that meant and also couldn't have explained it. Neither Gloria nor my mother ever made an appearance in Kind Old's kingdom. They never had to *run like the hobbie-a*; they would have been unable to. My father also read us the stories about queens being in prison for years, and wife after wife getting her head chopped off. All King Henry wanted was for the right boy to be born, that child standing at the ready to take over when the time came. If my father temporarily ran out of steam with Kind Old we loved second best hearing about the princes and princesses wearing sables and golden gowns, studying the countries on the globe, realms that would be theirs once they assumed the throne.

5.

The Four–Five Split

In addition to the romance situation out in the orchard, Stephen and Gloria almost literally sitting in a tree, k-i-s-s-i-n-g, there was another crisis that summer that, although I didn't know it right away, also involved true love. At the end of July the thing William and I had feared for at least a year came to fruition. Time, we could see, was beginning to run as if it were leading somewhere, as it had not exactly done when we were very small, time occurring back then only in bursts. At any rate, the dread event took place, a radiologist and his wife moving not only to our town but into a house on our side of the road, next to Velta. Dr. and Mrs. Michael Kraselnik. They had two teenagers, David and Brianna, hard to think how students with KRASELNIK on the backs of their gym shorts would manage at high school, although we were hardly concerned with their problems. The prospect of their coming was at first so alarming William and I couldn't stand to imagine it.

For a full year the building of their sprawling four-story house had been in progress on land that should have been ours. My father and Sherwood had tried to buy the ten acres, as a buffer, they said, between the farm and the village, but they'd waited too long to make the offer and lost the chance. When the hole for the doctor's foundation was dug we looked on from our fence line. William's mouth, which under usual circumstances was like a little bunched bud, had the further tightness of a person gathering spit. To have neighbors on our side of the road? Even if we were separated by eight acres of orchard and a row of scrubby pines we would see, in winter, the lights of their château. This outrage could not, must not happen—the river, the river would know to flood, the water climbing the hillside, or a meteor might fall into the hole, a tornado smash the building to pieces. Or a sweep of flame would run through the timbers and the stacks of sod waiting to be laid—the doctor paying for earth as if regular old ground wasn't good enough for him.

But it wasn't just that a family was moving in, that we were going to have something like next-door neighbors on good farmland. It was stranger than that. Our town, as it happened, was not famous for its races and creeds or lifestyles. There were no blacks, no Filipinos, no Native Americans, the arrival of the Hispanics and the Hmong migration a few years in the future. We did have the men who operated the bed-and-breakfast, two or three adopted Koreans, an occasional Japanese or Brazilian AFS student, and the gym teacher, Miss Manning, so aptly named. For well over a hundred years, then, the job of drawing the line in the sand had been left to the English and the Germans. However, now into our field of Caucasian Christians and Catholics were going to come Dr. and Mrs. Kraselnik, from Chicago. The husband's people were originally from Poland, my father thought. "Ashkenazi Jews," he said to my mother because he knew those kinds of things, the history and dispersal of populations. They were moving because the radiologist had a job in Milwaukee and because his wife wanted to own a horse and raise vegetables. Most of all, for her children's sake, she needed to escape the tony Illinois North Shore where the high school students were crippled with sports injuries and also were under so much academic pressure they became drug addicts. That's what my mother said.

I first learned about our new neighbor when I was in Volta, at the manor house kitchen table, doing an art project with Amanda. Sherwood and Dolly's daughter was a round little ball of a girl with long black hair, a year younger than me, a girl who in a babyish way couldn't say her r's, saying *vewwy* instead of *very*, which the adults thought adorable especially in a person who was so intelligent. She was obsessed by topics such as the Suez Canal and Pompeii and predictably she went through a big hieroglyphics phase. Because she was my cousin I must automatically love her.

I was taking great care with my glitter art when Amanda told me, with a proprietary air, that the *KWaselniks* were moving in. Sometimes she irritated me more than anyone else I knew even though she was my playmate, and also loving her was mandatory. I didn't look up. A delicate puff, a little blow to the paper, to scatter the excess glitter, the cat coming into focus. I then pointed out that the information about the foreigners was not news, first, and second the family was going to be living on *our* side of the road. While I didn't want neighbors anywhere near the Lombard Orchard it seemed necessary in our conversation to make my rightful claim. "And it's the *KR*aselniks," I said in not at all a nice tone.

"They came ovuh to talk to Dad," Amanda bragged, ignoring my correction. "We alweady know them."

"They'll be in Velta," I said, letting loose the secret name, something I'd never done before, Mary Frances full of mystery, full of knowledge. "In Velta," I repeated, tossing my head.

Adam came through the hall and went to the refrigerator, opening it and removing a package of ham. He was going into seventh grade, possibly smarter than Amanda, preoccupied with NASA, Stephen Hawking, and especially the particle accelerator in Batavia, Illinois.

"What's Velta?" he said, rolling three thin pieces of ham into a cigar and sticking it between his fingers.

"We're talking about the Kwaselniks," Amanda said, as haughty as I'd been.

Dolly came up the back stairs just then carrying a basket of tomatoes. She had to be mindful to not activate a burglar alarm that Sherwood had made, one of my favorite things about the kitchen, the marble-type run that involved an egg beater, a cow bell, a wind chime, and a bicycle horn. It was a golf ball that got the whirring and tinkling and honking going.

"Don't eat that ham," she cried, Adam retreating with the booty down the hall.

Amanda's mother was nothing like a real Lombard, having before her marriage been a Muellenbach, a local girl, Dolly with a puff of black hair, everything about her soft, a little blurry, her round face with what kind of nose, what color eyes, how shapely the mouth? You couldn't recall the details in someone who was merely Dolly, tall enough, not thin but not fat, the mother who happened to be in the background.

Before she'd set the basket down she was talking to us. "If I was a doctor's wife I wouldn't work." Her slow easy speech filled the kitchen. "What would I do with myself?" She was fetching an enormous tray from the pantry. "What would I do with myself?" she repeated. She started to arrange the tomatoes on the tray. "She's not Jewish, she's not the religious one. Nobody would have argued with her if she'd kept her own name. But then she wouldn't be *Doctor* and Mrs. Kraselnik. You girls will be the doctors, the men lining up to sponge off you. If I didn't have a job in the apple business I'd ride my horse—me with a horse! Spend a lot of time grooming old Chief. And shopping for supplies, you have a horse you need supplies. Saddle soap, maintain the leather, nothing worse than brittle leather." Dolly was a champ at merrily keeping herself entertained, the interviewer and the subject in one person. "What else? A curry comb. And oats, got to have oats and a feedbag. And those Klan-type hoods, keep the gnats out of Chief's eyes. Mrs. Kraselnik is teaching the four–five split so you girls will both have her—that'll be nice for you. I'll bet she'll have pictures of Chief on her desk. I'd do steeplechase, get a black velvet helmet, that's what I'd do, taking the fences, a little noodge with the boot to the flanks, over you go, a little noodge."

Wait. Four–five split? What did that mean? I stared at Dolly, hoping for the same loop to repeat, as it often did, before she went on to a different loop. Amanda and I were going to be in the same class? Is that what Dolly had said? I was starting the fifth grade, Amanda in fourth, the two classes joined? My cousin looked up from her paper, she, too, registering the essential sentence. And yet she didn't seem alarmed. She said, "Mom says Mrs. Kwaselnik is intwested in geogwaphy, that we'uh going to pawticipate in the National Geogwaphy Bee."

"I know," I lied.

"Mrs. Kwaselnik will want me to bwing in my Suez Canal memowabilia for Show and Tell." Amanda really did have a collection, Stephen Lombard having once sent her maps and a key chain from Suez when he'd passed through Egypt. "She'll teach us to use a dweidel."

It was a matter of urgency that I leave the manor house immediately, that I get to the library where my mother worked. The Mrs. Kraselnik information could not possibly be true. Amanda and I were nothing to each other in school. In the mornings we waited for the bus together on our driveway but once we climbed the steps, even before we found our own seats, we no longer knew each other. This unknowing was an unspoken and mutually agreed-upon law. We weren't embarrassed by our connection. It was only that we were entirely different persons outside of the orchard. On the way home we were with our friends and could not say hello. The second our feet touched the gravel drive we were again familiar, restored to our Velta-Volta selves, planning our after-school activities. It could not be explained to my mother why Amanda being in my class was a violation; I knew only that it must not happen.

Because my mother was the director of the library, and because there was no place in town except the tavern to gather, the gossips came to the circulation desk to tell all. In that way Nellie Lombard knew everything, the font of knowledge. I made an excuse to Amanda and left my glitter picture. Always in the Dolly kitchen I hurried past the door that led up the stairs to May Hill's part of the house. It was a fact that she lived right overhead, but it was a fact I did my best not to consider. Her house, even though it belonged to the same structure as the downstairs, was in a different plane, a different realm. This truth also could not be explained. In any case, I ran down the back stairs of Amanda's house, only to see Sherwood at the basement sink.

"Hallo, Francie," he said. "You interested in seeing—" He held up a root of some kind but I didn't look, didn't stop, said I had to get home, although Velta was not my precise destination. I ran down the drive, past the barn, down the orchard path, up along the potato garden and the marsh, skirting the near hay field, past Gloria's cottage, up to the baseball diamond, and ragged with running that quarter mile I burst into the library. My mother was at the circulation desk checking out the Bushberger children, Mrs. Bushberger putting no limit on the number of picture books each of her six children was allowed to take home.

"Francie, my goodness," Mrs. Lombard called to me. But she wasn't going to pay real attention until every single Bushberger book had been scanned and neatly stacked in the six baskets, each child talking about the plot of the book she loved best, Mrs. Lombard somehow listening to all of them at the same time.

Here is the reason my mother was a favorite person, children and adults, men and women flocking to speak to her: Mrs. Lombard was on the board of the American Library Association, headquartered in Chicago, the representative of rural libraries, and furthermore she'd won the Outstanding Librarian Award (for Populations Under Five Thousand) in 1991. But even if she hadn't been a nationally famous librarian you wanted to loll around in her company because of her very form, her skinny legs and broad hips, her nice, midsize plush bosom, the gap between her two long front teeth, comic and also glamorous, and in addition to those pleasant encouragements her brown eyes were soft with what seemed like sincerity. You wanted to be with her in the cozy library that was filled with only the good books. She was no beauty by any standards, she once told us, but she said in her la-di-da voice and trailing a moth-eaten scarf that beauty was unimportant as long as a person was captivating. We knew she had something, whatever you wanted to call it, because our father with his tremendous shock of straw-colored hair was famous among his apple-selling haunts, his smile, his beamy, white straight teeth a radiance. Every woman apple customer surely was in love with him, and in fact there wasn't one person we knew of, besides Sherwood, who didn't think the world of him.

When at last the Bushbergers were gone I burst out with it, I cried, "What is this about Mrs. Kraselnik? Teaching us, me and Amanda? I'm not going to be in the same class as Amanda. I'm not."

The librarian of the year usually knew exactly what to say. In this circumstance, however, she was not her usual quick-witted, award-winning personality. I reinforced my position. "Mrs. *KW*aselnik," I spit.

My mother coughed a little. "That will be a tough one," she had to admit.

Mrs. Lombard didn't try to assure me that competing with my genius cousin would be perfectly all right, and she didn't predict that I'd change my mind, nor did she insist on the situation. She said, "I wonder what she's like, the doctor's wife. They're moving in this week sometime. We'll have to go up to greet them."

Another patron came to the desk, cutting me off, and another, my complaint strung out for quite some time.

That very night the new neighbor herself came to our door. My future teacher on the porch, knocking. I was in the middle of telling William that under no circumstances was I going to be in the same class as Amanda when the rapping started. My intuition told me: *Mrs. Kraselnik*. We slunk into the living room, waiting for my mother to be the greeter.

It's hard to say when I first knew I adored her. Certainly in our hall, in that glimpse, I noted her loveliness. She was slender, her features delicate, her hands graceful, her clavicle, her wrists, every part of her a bony elegance. Later, when she leaned on her desk in the classroom, her hip settling on the edge there, you thought *flank*, the horsewoman's firm flank on display. Her silky brown hair was always in a ponytail, bound by a grosgrain ribbon, and she had a little mole near her nose, the first real beauty mark I'd ever seen.

"Where's the doctor?" I whispered to William.

"Doctors are never home." He somehow knew this.

In a very backward welcome Mrs. Kraselnik had brought us cookies and a plant, my mother going berserk about how wrong this was, thrusting the goods back into Barbara's—

that was her name—into Barbara's hands. They were laughing, and before we knew it the equestrian was in the kitchen, and my father was there, too, all of them sitting at the table. Never before had there been a teacher in our house drinking a cup of tea. Jim Lombard offered up every kind of country living help he could think of: machinery, books, advice, his own strength.

When my mother called us in from the living room, as we approached the table Mrs. Kraselnik said, "Mary Frances Lombard. My heavens. It is . . . it is you." She didn't smile. Her voice was surprisingly low, her diction a little severe and in truth somewhat frightening. "A face for a name. This is always a thrilling moment, when the list becomes real. The real girl right here."

I looked at my mother. And back to the woman with the thin, pliant lips in a fresh light-plum shade, the tenderly etched lines by her large blue eyes, her softly glowing skin, the peach tones. There was sweetness itself, but sweetness tempered by the tang of her voice and her erect bearing, Mrs. Kraselnik the horsewoman of summer fruits. "William," my teacher said, "I'm very sorry you're too old for me."

My parents laughed. "I'm sorry, too," William said sincerely.

There was no further discussion at home about the four–five split, my objection forgotten. Both Amanda and I, even before the first day of school, were determined to make Mrs. Kraselnik love us best, both of us full of Mrs. Kraselnik lore. "Her name," I told Amanda, "is Barbara."

"Befowah she mayweed huh name was Bawbawa Baker."

"The doctor is bald and he looks a little black." I added knowledgably, "That's because he's an Ashkenazi Jew."

"He's a wadiologist."

"Her horse is Suzie. Not Chief."

"She's a Thowoughbwed."

Where was she getting her information? "Brianna Kraselnik," I said, "has hair to her waist."

"She's going to babysit me sometime."

This stopped me cold. I had never been babysat in my life, one of my parents always at home, or Gloria came over if necessary. I had only seen Brianna from a distance and maybe she was nearly as regal and lovely as her mother, but still—I said scornfully, "*Baby*sit!"

I had gathered some of the facts myself, on occasion quietly making my way up to the Cortland line, the row that abutted the Kraselnik property. On several afternoons I'd climbed a tree, keeping watch for our teacher. Once I saw her drive into the garage, a heart-stopping moment. Followed by her taking groceries into the house. As children have been for time immemorial I, too, was stricken by the revelation: My teacher cooked food and she ate. On another day I watched her work with her horse, walking the animal around on a lead-line. Any view from the Cortland line was partially obstructed by the cedar trees but I could usually see the bright ribbon on her ponytail, and here and there the swish of Suzie's own tail, and I could hear the firm commands, Suzie naturally being a good girl for her trainer. When I mentioned to Amanda that she might join me in the reconnaissance we both sat on a sturdy limb, waiting. We ate Fig Newtons. Our patience was at last rewarded, the goddess appearing on the driveway, and there she shook out a small blue rug. Amanda froze. She fortunately understood how still a witness should be. Amanda, my companion in Velta, observing the rite, the Mrs. Kraselnik devotion. She couldn't even chew.

Then school started and by order of the law we were required to be in Mrs. Kraselnik's presence for roughly six hours for the next 188 days, not counting holidays and weekends. It was on the very first morning that our teacher told us we were going to be studying Shakespeare and the Greek gods and the planets, and we were going to investigate big cats at risk, and also we would memorize the highest elevations, the longest rivers, the driest deserts, we'd track violent storms, as well as study our school neighborhood and climate. We would do so, she said, in service to learning, each of us creating our own minds. "Do you realize, boys and girls, that you can create your own mind? Creating your own minds," she repeated, a habit she had when the message was crucial. Our learning, she went on, would also be essential preparation for the Geography Bee.

So, Amanda had been right. She smiled at me not in a gloating way but as if to say, *Can't you hardly wait, Fwances?*

What Amanda didn't know was that when Mrs. Kraselnik came to the apple barn on the weekends to buy a bushel, a forty-pound weight that would include all my favorite varieties, I would be on hand to assist her. Amanda never helped at the barn. Instead of giving my teacher one red apple I could bestow upon her a whole orchard's worth. *Mary Frances, how in the world can you tell all these varieties apart? Never have I seen a girl who could do such a thing!*

There wasn't a moment to be lost, Mrs. Kraselnik was saying. Each of us was going to participate in the bee in November in order that the winning student could go on to the county competition, and then state, and possibly to Washington, DC, in March. "You will discover this year, boys and girls, why geography is at the heart of every subject you could ever hope to study. You will discover this secret and at the same time you will become informed citizens of the world."

Informed citizens of the world? Amanda and I, pencils in hand, notebooks open, were prepared. I was already certain that it would be I, Mary Frances Lombard, who would go to Washington, DC, in March, boarding a plane, hand in hand with Mrs. Kraselnik, turning to wave on the steps to Amanda and the rest of the family, and also pausing to respectfully listen to the high school band's selection for our send-off.

6.

The Incident During
the Fifth Cloth

A few weeks later we had a day off from school, a misery,
a punishment. When we left the classroom it was clear that
Mrs. Kraselnik didn't want to be without us on a weekday, either, a mournful tone in her good-bye. The so-called holiday
took place right after she announced an assignment that she
said we could do in pairs. To my dismay, before I could make
my choice Amanda had raced across the room and chosen me
for her partner. There was nothing I could do, no wriggling
out of her hold. It was an important, primary-source research
project—that's how Mrs. Kraselnik had described it. We were
to interview someone in our community, someone who had
valuable information about the history of our region, or who
held a job of interest. Because Amanda had snapped me up
I told her that I would chose the subject of our interview,
that this was only fair. I was thinking of my father, because

he was the chairman of the Farmland Preservation Committee for our town. Or Mrs. Bushberger, who was a member of the Reverend Moon's church. She'd even had a baby for someone in her congregation in Chicago, Reverend Moon having demanded that charity of her. Stephen Lombard then crossed my mind as a subject. Did any other classmate have a relative who was probably a secret agent? He was going to be with us at least for the harvest and maybe longer now that he and Gloria were supposedly in love. But he was not someone who was truly a part of our community, Mrs. Kraselnik probably taking off points for our failure to follow directions.

At dinner the assignment slipped my mind because Mr. Gilbert, a library patron, the man who always came in with his snake, Rosy, wrapped around his neck, had been arrested for possession of drugs. My mother told us all about it. The police had discovered not only marijuana in his house but also his exotic pets, the bearded dragon, the leopard geckos, the poison dart frogs, the veiled chameleons. My mother said that the one time she'd gone to his door to collect a fine the smell was overpowering. So because of the Mr. Gilbert story I had forgotten to ask my father if he would submit to the interview.

The next morning, with no school, William and I wandered over to the apple barn. By eight o'clock my father and Gloria were already hours into their ritual of cider making on the precarious old press that had been in service ever since we could remember. Their fuel, their drug, was the assorted sweet rolls in the bakery box, bismarcks stuffed with crimson jelly and long johns with the jolt of chocolate inside, fritters and crullers, Danishes and elephant ears, and if Dolly happened by she'd want an ordinary dull brown donut, so my mother, the shopper, always included that drab puff in the mix. When the cider makers wished most to sleep they ate another cruller. William and I had a few questions about Gloria, questions a person couldn't ask her directly, which was one of the reasons, besides wanting a sweet roll, that we made the trip over to Volta.

For years, for all of our lives, cider day was the fourteen-hour stretch wherein Gloria always sent my father her love note. So, the immediate questions: Was she going to do it, now that she had run after Stephen? If Stephen himself was in the cider room would she act as if she'd never done the love note, not ever, and would my father understand that the fifth-cloth fun was over?

To make the juice, ten thickly woven cloths held in place by wooden forms were one by one filled with apple pulp and stacked up on a stainless-steel tray, a stack taller than my father. The cloths were submitted to pressure, short planks set in crisscrossing fashion on the stack, stout blocks of wood on top of all of that, and finally the jacks, which would be turned periodically, the whole package compressed, tighter, tighter, every last drop forced from the pulp. Gloria's job was first to put the apples through the washer, giving them one last inspection to make sure there was no habitat for an E. coli–type mold, or mold of any kind, no cuts or deep bruises. From the washer the fruit went into the grinder. My father then poured the pulp from the buckets into the cloths, cloths one to ten, folding them up just exactly so. My father, the master. Together he and Gloria would have decided the recipe to make the best possible blend from the available seconds. A Jonathan–Golden Delicious recipe—we are not talking the green, dimpled atrocities from Washington State, but our yellow, delicate, ripe, blushy feminine Goldens, ours a lovely, shy apple—this blend was a favorite, with whatever odds and ends were on hand and needed to be used up, varieties that wouldn't tip the sweet-tart balance.

Every week, for the fifth cloth, Gloria put a surprise through the grinder for my father. It might be a bushel of pears or a wild variety she'd gone and picked for the occasion, or a box of something special she'd hidden away in the cooler. He'd watch the mystery pulp coming through the grinder into the bucket, white mash speckled with the green or pink skins. With his hands sheathed in the XXX Large rubber gloves he spread what looked like coleslaw evenly into the cloth. He'd smell the mash as he smoothed it, he'd pause to think, he'd take a guess. On that morning of our holiday he said, "The wild tree by the Jonathans? Is that it? Those little apples, the spotty—"

"Afraid not," Gloria said sadly.

"Am I close?"

"You mean geographically?"

"Glooria," he said in a teasing fashion. "I need a hint."

"I don't know, Jim," she lilted. "I may not be willing."

They were talking that way in front of Stephen. He was standing right there on the platform above the press, leaning on the old milk tank where the cider was stored before it was bottled, Stephen reading the newspaper and eating a Danish.

Just then Aunt May Hill came to check on the mechanism she'd engineered for the bottling line, a clever switch that turned off the flow of the cider at the top of the jug. She walked in with her head down, directly to her work. William and I always straightened up and looked at the ground when she appeared, maybe stealing glances at her but otherwise pretending no one unusual was present. She wore a checked shirt tucked into her high-waisted pants, the faded jeans that were neatly patched, and a blue bandanna on her head, knotted in the back, no hair showing. No part of her broad face with the knobby nose, the manly eyebrows, the fleshy mouth was ever obscured by a coiffure. While she fiddled no one said much of anything and to our relief she soon left the room, looking balefully at the box of sweet rolls on her way out. Next news, Sherwood was at the door. "Did you get the order ready for the Greek Ballerina?" He was speaking to my father.

"The pears, and she wanted Paula Reds, too?"

"A bushel." Sherwood didn't like the cider. He didn't think perfectly good apples should be ground up for a drink. He stood at the door staring at the drain, refusing to see the work at hand.

My father said, "I was thinking you had the order in mind."

Sherwood then looked at his brother, at Stephen, a Lombard who had the nerve to read the newspaper during the harvest. Sherwood said, "You want to make yourself useful?"

"What?" Stephen said.

"Do you want," Sherwood repeated slowly, "to make yourself useful."

Gloria turned off the grinder in order to come to Stephen's rescue. She said, "There's a box of pears in the middle room, Sherwood, a box that would be perfect for the Greek Ballerina. The stage of ripeness she likes."

The Ballerina was no starlet but a sixty-year-old who'd been coming to the orchard since she was a young woman. No one had ever thought to call her by any real name.

Sherwood, with his wondrous red curls and his childlike absorption in his projects, was captivating, and yet it was safe to say that the slab of his forehead and his small, deep-set eyes had knocked him out of the running in the family beauty contest. He said to Gloria, with what seemed like sincerity and also amazement, "Oh, you know that, do you? The stage of ripeness she likes?"

My father stopped his tinkering with the stack. He said, "Yes, Gloria does know exactly that."

We quit eating our long johns, wondering, for the first time, if Sherwood minded that Stephen was living at our house. Stephen, the streamlined Lombard, each of his features in gracious proportion to the whole. Plus, what did he think of Stephen getting together with Gloria, the employee who was in the Jim Lombard camp?

One more entrance, Dolly sticking her head into the room, three yellow jackets flying straight to the bottling line. A fun fact about Dolly was that she hated most fruits, and especially apples. She didn't eat them. No one would dream of telling her to shut the door, and while she summoned Sherwood back to the sorting shed four more wasps gleefully sailed through to get a lick of juice coming off the tray. "This order for Mrs. Dolten is driving me up the wall," she said with an exasperation we all could share, Mrs. Dolten famously impossible. Dolly then looked Stephen up and down as if she, too, could not believe he was taking his leisure. She plucked her donut from the box and disappeared.

That's when Sherwood noticed us sitting on two milk crates, sweet rolls in hand. He started to blink, the sign that he was about to have an idea. "Say, Francie," he said pleasantly. "You might want to talk to May Hill."

Talk to May Hill? What for?

"She knows about our ancestors," he went on. "She's the expert around here. She's the one who's organized the files." I must have looked confused. "For your interview," he explained.

Having dispensed that piece of advice he went out the door.

I looked at William, who was alert if not also shocked by the proposal. Always, always and forever, when we saw May Hill or when her name was mentioned, in the back of our minds there was the chime, the word *Scram-bambow*. Maybe the toolshed had not happened—no, but it had, because that word was lodged within us. Neither one of us had ever been in the upstairs of the manor house, Aunt May Hill's domain. It was a place we would hate to have to go.

"The files?" I whispered to him.

"That's a great idea, Mary Frances," Gloria called, she apparently also in the know about our project, even though I hadn't said a word about it to her. "May Hill has wonderful photographs. And letters. And receipts from the old carriage factory. The diaries of your great-grandmother. There are locks of baby hair tied up in ribbon."

"Locks of baby hair?" William said.

"Pressed in books," Gloria replied, as if that were an explanation. "And baptismal gowns, elaborate dresses even for the boys in the olden days."

Stephen broke an elephant ear in half and started in on that confection. One of the strange things about Gloria was the fact that she could recount far more Lombard family lore than most of us. Because she visited May Hill in the upstairs she knew almost as much as my father about who and where and when. And she knew, for sure, our own histories, quoting our remarkable toddler sentences to us, shaking her head in wonderment. For a reason we could not put in plain words, Gloria's mastery of our legends embarrassed us for her; and furthermore, we didn't think Stephen liked her familiarity, either. He was the one to state the obvious. "I doubt May Hill wants to do an interview."

"I wouldn't be so sure," Gloria said. "She loves to talk about history."

All that time my father, while he sloshed around the press in his big galoshes adjusting the wooden forms, was trying to figure out the fifth-cloth mystery. "Liveland Raspberry," he called out. "You saved some Liveland Raspberries!" There really was an antique variety, a punky-striped early apple with that wrong-fruited name.

"Oh, Jim!" Gloria cried. "I made it too easy for you."

"Wow, Gloria."

Stephen was back to reading the paper, no interest, it seemed, in Gloria's skulduggery. He said, "I hope they choose Birch Bayh to speak at the convention. Indiana! Give up your native son so we know you've got more in you than Dan Quayle."

My father was maybe laughing at Stephen's joke but he was also still smiling at Gloria's whimsy and at the care she took to delight him. He said to his cousin, "That would put Bayh on the map, wouldn't it?"

"This is terrific about Bill Foster," Stephen said, moving on to the sports page, to the Baseball Hall of Fame topic.

"About time they put him in there," my father said. The amber liquid was already running down the stack of cloths and into the broad tray at the bottom of the press. He took a paper cup from the sink and stuck it into the flow. "Oh, golly, Gloria, I've got it. The tartness of the Liveland. Right at the back of the tongue. This is powerful. This is just the kick I need."

Then how pleased she was going to be through the rest of the morning, standing in her yellow waterproofs at the bottling line, filling jug after jug and screwing the caps on very tightly, her bare hands raw.

"I'm not," I muttered to William, "interviewing May Hill."

He was staring at the press, the way you do when even if you want to you can't blink, you can't turn away. In that trance he made a slow pronouncement. "I...think...you should."

"I want Mr. Gilbert. I want to see his exotic pets. His poison dart frogs."

The grinder started up again, the noise snapping William back to earth. "You can't," he said. "He's a felon." He said, "Frankie?"

"What."

"You have to. You have to interview May Hill."

When we were downstairs playing with our cousins we sometimes heard her heavy flat footfall, May Hill doing what up there? Gathering locks of hair, apparently. Pressing the hair in books.

"Maybe she'll take you to the attic," William said.

"I'm not going!" I wanted to remind him, in case somehow he'd forgotten: *Scram-bambow.*

"There's a sea captain's trunk up there. The first Lombard's trunk."

"No, there isn't."

"There is. Sherwood told us. Pa said so. And a cage for a circus monkey."

"So what?"

"It's your chance," he said. He was staring again as if in the presence of a mystery. "Your chance," he repeated.

How could William be on Sherwood's side? Because, what if it was a trap? Sherwood sending me into the lair. To be put in that cage. I said then what would surely end the discussion. I said, "I'll go if you come with."

"It's an interview," he considered, ignoring my proposal. "You ask her questions and she, she talks."

We had hardly ever heard May Hill speak and so it was preposterous, the notion of conducting an interview with a subject who was mute.

"Frankie!" he said.

"What."

"I'll be downstairs with Adam. I'll wait for you at the door."

"No."

"I'll be right there."

"But what if?" First of all, there was May Hill herself to consider. As if that danger weren't enough, what about Sherwood and the cage? And yet if Sherwood was sometimes unhappy about being in business with my father, and bossed around by Dolly, and annoyed by the cider making, he was also full of fun. It didn't make sense to dream him up wicked. But again, what about the war between Velta and Volta? Maybe the war had made Sherwood want to take us as prisoners.

"It looks like Joe Klein wrote *Primary Colors* after all," Stephen reported, continuing to bring the news of the country to the workers.

"I don't want to," I said.

"Frankie!" Once more William said, "This is your chance."

I was about to stalk away. I almost got up but I stopped. *Wait,* I said to myself. I could come back from the upstairs— if I came back—like Ernest Shackleton, William's favorite explorer. He'd be at the door, longing to hear every single detail of the ordeal. All at once I pictured the two of us in our room, in our bunks, it's dark, and I'm telling him about May Hill— about being in May Hill's house, and maybe even seeing her bedroom. Her bedroom, seeing her bedroom—supposing she even had one, May Hill with a room, a bed, a hairbrush, a pillow. Maybe lace on the edges of the case.

"Lace?" William might say. "Really?"

"They were still pretty firm," Gloria said to my father about the Livelands. She took a cup from the sink, filled it with cider, and went to the platform, standing below Stephen, holding the drink up to him.

Finally he looked over the top of his newspaper. "What," he said to her. He didn't even realize she was making an offering.

For just a minute we had to stop thinking about the interview. We could see that it was going to take a great deal of effort and endurance for Gloria to incorporate Husband Number Two, Stephen, into her routine of being Wife Number Two to my father, when Jim Lombard, surely, was always Husband Number One in her heart, Jim Lombard the receiver of the fifth-cloth message.

7.

The Mysterious Family Photograph

For some reason or other, perhaps at Sherwood's urging, May Hill agreed to the interview. He arranged for it, as if the assignment were solely Amanda's project. I had never discussed May Hill with my cousin, I suppose because the old aunt was someone we for the most part took for granted. I knew, also without discussion, that even though May Hill lived overhead Amanda did not like the idea of going to her house. And yet we must. Sherwood had said so, had told us the time. He had said we should go up the stairs from the kitchen, that we shouldn't use the formal front entrance. May Hill, he said, would be waiting for us.

At the appointed hour after school Amanda and I opened the door according to our instruction. There before us, the back stairs. "You girls are in for—" Dolly for once was unable to finish a sentence. It was no secret that she hardly talked to May Hill, that neither one had much truck with the other.

"Good-bye," I called to William, who was through the pantry in the living room. "We're going." I didn't want to say in front of Amanda and Dolly that he had promised to stand at the door. "We're going now."

Sherwood was down the hall in the small room reserved for the piano. He'd been working on *Well-Tempered Clavier, Book I* for as long as I could remember, thumping out the "Ave Maria," the metronome holding him steady.

"Good-bye," I called again, over the music.

"Tally-ho," my brother called back. We were not allowed to watch television after school, one of the reasons William liked to play with Adam, the two of them drifting back and forth between computer and TV. It was too late to go get him, to make him stand exactly by the door.

A bare lightbulb hung from the ceiling over the staircase, the film of dust on the stairs thick, because May Hill did not use this way for coming and going, of course not, because she'd then have to walk through Dolly's kitchen. So it was dusty, and up at the top there was not another door, but a wooden gate. Dolly called *Yoo-hoo*, to let May Hill know we were approaching. Our hearts were beating wildly up those stairs, and harder yet when we couldn't undo the latch of the gate. Amanda was scared, too. *Let's just forget it*, we both thought. But then May Hill appeared, sliding the bolt easily and opening up, letting us through, the gate snapping shut.

"Come," she said without looking at us.

Amanda grabbed my hand, which I was of two minds about.

Without my shaking her off we followed Aunt May Hill down the dark hall, past closed doors, one after the next after the next, many small rooms rather than the grand downstairs rooms. May Hill's portion after all had housed Sherwood and his siblings in the olden days, plus the parents, plus the orphan girl, enough sleeping space for eight people.

The base line of a fugue from down below was clean and clear. "Dad's pwacticing," Amanda needlessly pointed out.

The hall ended at the living room, the two long windows looking out over the north orchard. If everything that May Hill owned was shabby, all of her belongings were nonetheless arranged neatly. Underfoot was a thick old braided rug of many dark colors, and there was a blond, scratched-up coffee table, and a television on a rickety cart, and shelves sagging under the weight of books, and a corduroy sofa mostly covered up with a diamond-patterned orange-and-green afghan. It was hard to think that May Hill herself had been the crochet artist. The place smelled of coffee, which seemed funny. And apples, there was the fragrance of applesauce on the stove. It was maybe a home, that is, May Hill's home, where for some reason—neither of us could think it through—we had happened to find ourselves.

There was surprisingly nothing all that unusual in the living room unless you counted the eight card tables along the wall. Who owned that many card tables? They were set end-to-end, and they were covered with stacks of books bound in worn leather, and photographs in plastic sleeves, and a dagger, it looked like, and teaspoons, and a mink, the whole stuffed animal complete with toenails and the raisin nose and bright glass eyes. There were fragile-looking pieces of paper every inch filled up with faint cursive, and yellowed lace, and ivory kid gloves that a lady with slender fingers would have worn, and a pair of boots that buttoned up, to match. Each object was displayed as if the place were a museum.

"Sit down, Mary Frances," she said. Her indoor voice was husky but also soft. She had to clear her throat. "And Amanda," she added. She pointed at the folding chairs that clearly had been put in place for the interview. My heart was still racing but I was able to think two things: She remembered our names, and mine especially because I'd been named for Mary Frances Lombard, a special great-aunt, a semi-famous violinist. A woman who, despite the name, was not a Catholic, as I also was not, something I occasionally had to say to adult acquaintances. At any rate, May Hill had given us enough thought to keep track of us, which was either good or bad. And number two: William was downstairs. We could always leap up and make a dash for it back to safety, if, that is, we could figure out how to open the gate.

"Now then," Aunt May Hill said. She rubbed her hands together, signaling readiness. Her fingers would not have fit into the lady's gloves, but they were surprisingly thin. It seemed, even though it wasn't true, that her lips, dry but fulsome, were for just a second turned up into something nearly like a smile. She appeared to be taller in her house and because she wasn't wearing a hat or bandanna, an article that was always a part of her outside apparel, I could see her gray hair, which— and this was maybe the very strangest thing—was pulled back into a ponytail. May Hill with a little ponytail? I looked at Amanda, who was staring rudely at the beefy eyebrows. There was the broad, bony front, May Hill flat-chested, May Hill thin in some parts but she had a thick middle, her jeans zipping up snugly over the swell of the stomach, those jeans snapping halfway up her rib cage. You didn't want to think about that middle part of her, or her wide, flat bottom. Gloria naturally should find someone to love but you'd never, ever think so about Aunt May Hill. My father always said she wasn't a misfit, that no one should ever have called her by that cruel name. Whatever she was, I might tell him, she had a ponytail.

She walked back and forth, inspecting her showcase items, touching some of the books, wondering, it seemed, where to start. Although we had made a list of questions according to Mrs. Kraselnik's specifications we didn't remember any of them, nor did we recall that the instructions were in my pocket, or that I had a notepad and pen in my hand.

From the far table she picked up a small clothbound book. "The diary," she murmured, "of Elizabeth Morrow Lombard." She smoothed the first page before she looked at us. "Do you know who that is?"

We did not. We knew nothing.

She stood blinking, considering how to explain any of her card tables to people such as us. "Elizabeth was the cousin of your great-great-great-grandmother," she said slowly, "born in 1801 in New Hampshire." May Hill didn't have a lisp exactly, but there was a slushiness when she hit an *s* or a *th*, which no one had ever mentioned. She lifted a pair of glasses that hung around her neck by a shoelace, set them on her nose, and began to read so quietly we had to sit forward.

I cannot recall a more dreary June, the dampness will be the death of us. Father has taken the two ponies off to Mr.

Harding in hopes of a fair trade for a pair of oxen. I am desolate without Mother, and Cudworth is too sick to be of any use.

First of all, Cudworth? And second, was it possible that in real life May Hill was reading to us? Again, I couldn't think how such a thing had happened. As she read on about Elizabeth's day scrubbing the kettle and weeding the turnips and airing the bedding, you might have thought May Hill was in the middle of a murder mystery. She was glued to the page, and her voice, so quiet at first, was getting louder. Her energy made me feel sick once more, as if somehow my stomach had become the eardrum, the words going straight to that sensitive place, and also, it was as if her excitement was something sad. Amanda was slouching in her chair and swinging her legs. It almost seemed—almost—that May Hill was nothing but a regular old lady. Someone pitiful who lived alone, who had nothing to care about but the diary of a pioneer. What if she had brought out the card tables in order to make the displays just for us? That notion was a heavy sinking thing, something I didn't want, something I was trying to forget—but wait! Suddenly there was an Indian in Elizabeth Lombard's house. An old-fashioned redskin in a loincloth. Amanda stopped the swinging. I sat up straight. "*The smell was terrible,*" May Hill was reading. "*He looked weak, his chest frail, but his eyes were blazing at me with hatred.*" There followed three sentences in which Elizabeth Lombard snatched an ax and brained that savage.

We both covered our mouths. May Hill looked up and that time I was sure of it, certain she was smiling at me. It wasn't a large goofy grin or a pretty showing of teeth, but instead a smile of satisfaction, of having expertly accomplished a task. Her blue eyes, which were ordinarily cast down, were wide, those eyes asking the question, *What do you think of that!*

"*The bleeding on Mother's braided rug was something awful,*" she read, "*and I could not help but think, with the swiftness of the death, and what I could see was an easy acquiescence, that he had been ill, that he'd been feverish.*"

I lifted my feet from the rug because if it was the very same rug that had absorbed the Native American's blood, then, as we'd been taught in school, you should not ever touch someone else's bodily fluids, wet or dry, because of AIDS.

It had begun to rain in New Hampshire in 1820, the brother, Cudworth, had woken up with the commotion, and the two of them dragged the corpse to the burning pile and set it on fire. "*When Father came home he commended me for my bravery, but he was sorry that I had had to do the work of a man. I was not sorry to have killed a savage because there is no good savage alive, and I did feel proud even as I prayed to our Lord to forgive me, and to show me mercy at the final judgment.*"

May Hill looked up once more in that new way of hers, May Hill serenely triumphant. Amanda was scratching her knee. "Oh," I managed to say. William was downstairs, I said to myself. I could stomp on the floor if I had to. And scream. We might have moved on to another artifact but the diary reading continued. In Elizabeth's life there was a trip to market, more rain, a visit from a traveling preacher, rain again, the new ox hurt its foot, two rabbits were killed for dinner. No further mention of the ax or the butchery, no mention of removing the stain from the rug. I kept waiting for the subject to resurface but after a while it began to seem as if it, the murder, was a secret that May Hill had told us. Some-thing you'd say only once. Amanda and I continued to forget that we were supposed to ask our subject questions. But even if we'd remembered our assignment May Hill gave us no op-portunity to butt in. Where before in our whole long lives she had rarely spoken a few words in our presence, where we had imagined that she was willfully mute or maybe even a lit-tle brain-damaged, now we suddenly worried that she might never stop reading the diary.

When at last she finally did set it down even so she went on talking. She moved from table to table, every object, every story holding for her equal excitement. The relative who dug up bodies in the cemetery in order to study anatomy just as captivating as the price of corn in 1835. Moses Lombard's death in the Civil War by saber no more astonishing than the number of beavers in the marsh in 1909. The presentation to us of the great etc. grandmother's baby curl, a silky blond loop, made me again feel unwell, Elizabeth Morrow Lombard, I thought, perhaps responsible for that curl, the baby murdered and burned. No, that wasn't right. It couldn't be. But the curl, all by itself, in a ribbon—I wanted to clutch my throat. May Hill went on about the Lombard fanning mill factory, the pur-chase of the business by J. I. Case, the establishment of the dairy farm, the run for the state assembly by Thaddeus Lom-bard.

Amanda by then was as close as you can get to lying down on a chair, her eyelids drooping. I kicked her just the once. It was hard to tell how much time had passed. I myself might have eventually fallen asleep if I hadn't noticed a photograph in a plain black frame on a bookshelf on the other side of the room. May Hill was picking up a small silver-handled pistol, the size of a cap gun, when I cried out, "Who is that?"

It was the only photograph from modern times in the entire place, at least as far as I could see. No solemn ancestor with muttonchops, no girl with a gigantic bow in her ringlets and a lacy white dress, but rather a clean-shaven boy, older than William, a high school student, probably.

May Hill looked startled, as if she'd been intending to take a shot with that little pistol but now she had to answer my question. I'd covered my mouth again, feeling shame because as my mother often reminded me, I was impetuous. She was forever telling me I needed to learn self-control. What had I done but forgotten to exercise it in a place where I should have been supremely careful. Nonetheless, May Hill replied. She said, "That's my nephew."

He had light curly hair and an eager smile, and straight teeth, and a smile in his eyes, too, a twinkle, you might even say. What was his name? Where did he live? And why did May Hill, who didn't like children or people, why in her living room did she have a large framed color photo of someone in whom she should have no interest? She set the pistol down. "Do you have any gwahm cwackhuhs?" Amanda asked.

All at once May Hill and I were on the same exact side, both of us stunned by the question.

"I eat them like I'm a beavuh." Amanda made as if to put a cracker to her lips and gnaw at it. The girl with the monstrous IQ was sometimes the stupidest little baby, and it must have been from nerves, or let's say a wish to elevate the conversation that I blurted out a legitimate interview question—although it was not at all the question I'd wished to ask. I said, "How did your father die in the silo?"

I knew the technical answer, knew that silage produces gases that are colorless and can kill farmers quickly, or a grown man can die in his sleep hours later if he's breathed too much of one gas or another. May Hill's big brow wrinkled. Her mouth was slightly open, no trace of the smile. It was at that moment when William called up the back stairs. "Excuse me? Um, Aunt, Aunt May Hill? Frankie? Excuse me."

We had been in the living room well past the scheduled hour and my brother had come to tell me it was time for our piano lessons. Additionally, he no doubt wanted to see what he could of the long hall with scuffed flooring, the walnut doors, the yellow light from the kitchen. The place I had been brave enough to enter. Without thanking her, without doing more than mumbling good-bye, Amanda and I sprang from the chairs and ran to the gate, which William was holding open for us, we tore past him, flew to the bottom of the stairs, safe at last in Dolly's kitchen. We were out of breath, too dazed to laugh or cry or say anything at all.

"Did you girls get what you needed?" Dolly said.

The interview! No! We'd gotten nothing, not so much as a word on my pad, not even a little tiny period. We were going to Fail, something we had not ever imagined possible. But even worse, Mrs. Kraselnik would suffer disappointment. Her two star pupils, those marvels of scholarship, not living up to her expectations, not fulfilling our promise. She'd be shattered. "I think so?" I said to Dolly.

There was my piano lesson to get through, that weekly tragedy. And then dinner, in which my parents also asked me about the interview. My mother wanted to know if we'd gotten good information, and my father said that May Hill must have been pleased to show us her stash. I nodded. All I could think of was the bloodstained rug and the photograph of the nephew. I might have told them about Elizabeth Morrow Lombard and the Indian but more and more that seemed to me May Hill's secret, something I shouldn't repeat. There'd been the half smile on her face when she'd bestowed her treasure upon us, a piece of history we hadn't asked for, a story we didn't want. For some reason I said that May Hill had given us graham crackers and my mother said, "Wasn't that nice of her!"

It wasn't until later in our room, the door shut, the two of us finally alone, that William was able to ask me about the trip to the upstairs. I admitted it, admitted that we hadn't been able to ask May Hill even one question from our list. He was on the top bunk reading Tintin. "What do you mean?" he said.

I was standing on the first step of the ladder, starting to cry, handing him up the sheet. "Nothing," I whimpered.

He pulled himself to sitting and read the questions out loud:

What year were you born?
Where did you go to high school?
What is your profession?
What historical events have you lived through?
What do you consider the greatest invention of your time?
What is the most interesting thing about your town?

William said, "You didn't ask a single question?"

"I couldn't. She—she talked."

"What do you mean?" he said again.

"She talked and talked. More than Dolly. More than anyone, more than Mrs. Bushberger. She kept talking. She has a sort of lisp. A sort of lisp, a lisp."

He snapped his fingers in my face. "Wake up!"

I cried harder because maybe I had been hypnotized. I had almost thought during the interview that May Hill was something like a normal person but I had to come back, come back, back to my understanding of her true nature.

"Imp! You must have gotten some information. You must know some of the answers." He read again, "*What is your profession?*"

"*What is your profession?*" I echoed.

"Hmmm," he logically said. Even though May Hill was a part of our family the question was unanswerable. We felt like numskulls but justified; indignant, even, about our ignorance. Because our bafflement was all her fault. She was like a hired man but she was also like an English gentleman, owning property and working sometimes. Or you could say she was a mechanic in a garage, but then again the stock market had made her wealthy. At least that's what my mother thought.

I didn't tell William about the photograph of the nephew. He kept rereading the questions, both of us thinking to ourselves about the answers. "You can interview Pa," he said to me. "Or someone else. How about Gloria?"

"Gloria?"

"Why not?"

While I knew those people were possible candidates a curious thing had been happening while he'd been repeating the questions. So that the next day, when Amanda came over after school and while she lay on the floor and made Sculpey animals, I typed up the interview. It wasn't hard to do after all. Because May Hill was old and strange I wrote that she was born at the turn of the century. A twist of a doorknob, the turn of a century, May Hill walking over a threshold and entering a new time. Most of my story—for as it happened it was a story more than an interview—was about May Hill's father being trapped in the silo, in his case the door closing behind him, no way out of that dark round chamber, the smooth walls, the sink of silage, the gasping as he suffocated. His time over and done. May Hill, a girl, knowing already that her face and her big body would never improve, was standing outside, down below, screaming. Which was why in general she talked so little now, having long ago exhausted herself while her father slowly perished.

That's the answer I'd wanted from her when I'd asked the question in the interview about her father's death. I would have liked to have been a real reporter. What were you doing while your father struggled to breathe? Who found him? Did you want to see what he looked like? And then right away, did your mother march to the barn and hang herself? Mrs. Kraselnik always instructed us to write using detail.

She was named May Hill, I wrote, because she was born on a cold winter day, and her parents wished her to know that spring would come. As I was writing, without realizing I began to want May Hill's story to contain some bit of happiness. It probably wasn't possible to bring a suitor into the assignment, Mr. Gilbert who kept exotic reptiles maybe a logical man friend? Or Melvin Pogorzelski, the big reader who was writing his novel in the back room of the library, day after day? No. But there could be someone living whom she felt devoted to. So I wrote another something that was perhaps not exactly nonfiction. I wrote that she had a picture in her parlor of a beautiful boy and that every day she closed her eyes and prayed to him, even though he wasn't a god but a person. For extra credit I thought I might someday write a sequel, a tale about May Hill walking into the manor house for the first time as the orphan. That would be a scene to think about, everyone staring at May Hill, learning that she was going to be the new sister.

Without showing my work to Amanda I penned our names on top of the five-page project, mine in bright purple, hers in standard black, and the next day handed in our assignment to Mrs. Kraselnik.

8.

Meanwhile Stephen Lombard
Halfway Moves in with Gloria

This was how we knew Stephen Lombard was a certifiable spy. A few summers before the Gloria romance he'd been visiting us. He had come upon William and me in the upper barn, and for some time, without our realizing it, he'd watched us. It was a cool rainy afternoon, no dust streaming in through the slatted boards, the stinging, chaffy heat at bay, the nocturnal creatures, the raccoons and mice and bats, burrowed into the bales or tucked up in the beams, far above us.

That day, first, Sherwood had appeared, as he sometimes did when we played in the barn, calling out *Hallo, Francie, hallo, William*, respectfully announcing himself. He'd taken a swing or two on the rope that hung from the ceiling, jumping onto the wooden seat from the high place, the endless long sweep through the air, Sherwood yipping. We couldn't believe it, always we could hardly laugh, the rope or the beam, both, creaking, Sherwood sounding like a Native American. "That's enough for an old man," he'd say before he went off back to work. Or he might stop to tell us the gravity-defying stunts he'd done when he was a teenager. And we'd say, "Really?"

And he'd reply modestly, "Oh, we did all kinds of hijinks up here."

Then he'd go away, and we'd begin. We could do hijinks, too. In our games I was the royalty and William the servant. He liked this arrangement because it was then his task to make my splendid life possible, or he could save me from the cruelty of my captors with a contraption he'd have to build. Where Sherwood's inventions didn't always work, William's creations usually delivered water to me or helped me slide down from a high perch.

That afternoon after Sherwood left, I was in my bower of hay, demanding that the two kittens keep their doll bonnets on properly while William worked on his pulley system. We were both talking to ourselves, William explaining his thread-ing process, and I suppose to the cats I was deploring the king for depriving me of food and water.

How long had Stephen been watching us from just inside the granary door? Practicing his spy craft. I went on chattering about my plight even after William had straightened up, staring at the tall man in the shadows. The man with a telephoto lens. When at last I understood that we were being observed I, too, stood still, a scream lodged in my throat. Did Stephen call out to assure us as an average citizen would have? No. He said nothing. For the first time I felt not just embarrassed to be a child, but ashamed. It didn't seem possible to return to our private world after he went out through the granary door, although we did eventually gather ourselves back into the story. Stephen was nothing like Sherwood coming to have a swing. Stephen was not a yipper, for one, and for another, he had not called out *Hallo*.

Fast-forward a few years, to the summer of Gloria. At dinner one night our mother, having drunk perhaps more than her usual one or two glasses of wine, said so merrily, "We all think you're a spy, Stephen."

William poked me under the table. I nodded, *Yes, yes, Stephen is a spy. Remember the time in the barn?* He was slippery in his loyalties and he was probably a practiced liar, we alone understanding the extent of his capacity to infiltrate.

My father laughed at his ridiculous wife. "Not true," he said to his cousin.

Stephen was in the middle of putting a spoonful of bright green pesto in the center of his glossy noodles. He raised only his eyes, giving my mother a long, keen look, his spoon in midair. He said, "Nellie." The word chilled us, her name. No one would want to be interrogated by him. "I...am...not...a spy."

"Okay, okay!" She laughed nervously, her hands up, as if to say, *Don't shoot.*

To his noodles Stephen said, "If I could find another job that had the same benefits and vacation schedule, a job that offers a sabbatical every ten years, I'd do it." He suddenly sounded tired.

"I wish you would," my father said. "It would be good to have you home, really home again."

We didn't know what he meant by *home*. Was home for Stephen the entire United States or was it our town or the manor house or maybe—was it our house? His most particular home at the moment didn't seem to be on the outskirts of the orchard with Gloria, although he'd taken his big duffel bag over to her cottage. Even after he'd moved he sometimes sat in our kitchen for hours after dinner, the last to leave for bed. He was not domesticatable, so said my mother, a word that had something to do with sleeping, eating, folding laundry nicely, picking wildflowers as a present. I'd come downstairs to find the two of them, my mother and Stephen, in quiet conversation at the table. Gloria and my father were long gone, talked out and sound asleep. My mother had once mentioned that Stephen was the kind of person who opened up to you when you least expected it, no knowing when he might reward you with a confidence. Seeing them there at first always gave me a shock: What if—what if time had wavered, backward, forward—what if everything was now the same except that Stephen, Stephen was our father?

During the day for the most part we were happy he was staying on to pick apples. The harvest was a wild living thing that you were trying to tame while all the while it was dragging you behind, arms out, flailing, in the chase. But here was the miracle: Despite the chaos, the lack of planning, the bad feeling between Sherwood and my father, there was also an overriding unity of purpose, a reverence for the family history, a love for the soil within the property lines. Despite Sherwood's and Jim's temperamental differences the apples grew. They were harvested, thousands of bushels a year. Money, real currency, flowed from the customers' pockets into the sellers' wallets and thereafter to the secret cardboard boxes and elsewhere, and finally, when my mother could get around to it, into the bank. No one else had time to do the deposit. There were weeks in the autumn when there was money everywhere, envelopes hidden in the clean laundry, in the cat food bin, in the sock drawer, the visible reward stashed away. Sherwood, permanently on guard in the manor house, slept with the grandfather's shotgun by his bed, and May Hill always put a chair against the basement door to trip up the robber, the clatter the big alarm.

On the golden-and-blue afternoons the driveway filled with customers, whole families piling out of cars, to taste and decide, to load up their trunks with bushels of apples and pears, with cider and honey and knitting worsted from the sheep and white packages of lamb chops and legs and shoulders. The Ukrainian women from the city liked the kidneys and tongues, and the Yugoslavs had to butcher the animals themselves, in the back barn. There were plenty of people who felt, the minute they started down our long driveway, that they were returning to a bygone time. "Don't ever change a thing," they cried. "Don't fix that shed," they beseeched. "The old surrey is down there, isn't it, and the Model A? We love this orchard, you guys. It's real, it's special, it's—" They sometimes got teary. "Tracie, Lizzy, get in here once and take a whiff of the apple barn, oh Lord, this smell!" Years before those customers had come with their parents or their grandparents, and they were returning with their children. It was nature itself, nature at every level that forced the Lombard operation to work. And if Stephen Lombard, with his great height and long arms, his strength and his stamina, was on the crew, we should not mind that he was in our kitchen far into the night. We shouldn't care at all that he slept into the morning and that he was sometimes still picking apples in the dark. We should try to be happy he was home.

After Mrs. Kraselnik handed back the interview I put it somewhere or other. She had given Amanda and me ninety-three points. One hundred percent for creativity. Eighty, that shame, for not following the rubric. One hundred for grammar and vocabulary. Not long after that assignment I came downstairs, somewhat walking in my sleep, looking for Butterhead, the old cat, and there Stephen was, not with my mother and not with my father, not with Gloria, who was tucked up in her cottage. Stephen was sitting by himself, staring at the darkness outside even though he wasn't technically living with us anymore. The light was on over the stove, one dim light, not enough to see even your own reflection in the glass, Stephen looking, then, at nothing. Because I was not quite awake the dreamscape of our kitchen with Stephen in it didn't seem especially frightening.

I came to the table and began to talk. I told him our farm stories, we, the real children, with our own tales. I mentioned the autumn afternoon when Julia Child, Julia herself, a very old lady, a giant, taller than May Hill, in a tweed skirt and a cardigan, a pooch of a belly, got out of her car along with her friends, the queen of cuisine happening by the Lombard Orchard. Mary Frances Lombard bagged up three pounds of Wealthy apples for her, no charge, a variety from the chef's youth, an apple that made her raise her famous voice in exaltation. I was the only person in my class who knew Julia Child, I boasted. I said again that she was a giant.

Stephen opened his hand, a gray wafer in his palm. "What's that?" I said.

"A travel alarm clock."

"You going somewhere?"

"Never know."

"Because you're a spy?"

"Everyone really thinks that, don't they?"

I must have come fully awake then, because I was surprised to find myself in the semi-darkness looking at Stephen's chiseled handsome face. And more surprising, excitement was blooming in my chest.

"If I was a spy," he said, holding between his thumb and index finger what looked like a dime, "don't you think I'd be able to figure out how to put a battery in my clock?"

"That depends."

"It does?"

"You could maybe truly know how to insert it, but you're pretending to be clumsy. For your cover."

"Ah ha," he said. "You are very clever."

"Are you afraid, sometimes, in your job?"

I think he was looking at me in his hard, keen way, although I couldn't be sure. "Yes, very frightened," he said, "but not for the reasons you imagine."

"Well," I said importantly, "maybe a lot of jobs are like apple picking. You could fall and kill yourself but mostly you don't do that, and instead, you're working hard all day long and sometimes it is very boring." I had heard one of the lady apple pickers speaking about the harvest in exactly those terms.

"But guess what?" Stephen said conspiratorially.

"What?"

"When Sherwood shows up, it's not at all boring because

he's telling you the cell phones of the future will play movies, TV shows, anything you want to see."

Stephen was speaking about his own brother, Stephen clearly on our side in the future war.

"And," I said, "Sherwood's also building a telescope out of aluminum foil, old storm windows, a good pair of binoculars, a rearview mirror, and a cheesecloth."

Stephen rewarded me with laughter. "Don't forget," he said, "it also turns inside out to examine your liver and kidneys."

"Reversible," I said.

"Plus," Stephen said, "it's a cell phone."

We both began to laugh and pretty soon we couldn't stop. What we'd said about Sherwood wasn't even that far-fetched. We covered our mouths, heads to the table, our laughter coming in snorts through our noses. Were we maybe on Sherwood's side as well as my father's? I wasn't sure. For certain I had never been so happy in the middle of the night, in the moment falling in love with Stephen, although I wouldn't have called it that. I said, "You should stay here. You shouldn't ever leave."

That idea made him sober up. "I shouldn't?" he asked, as if I were the one to decide.

Supposing he had children with Gloria: I suddenly could see that they wouldn't necessarily have to be our rivals. Because they'd be so much younger they could stay on as our workers. They wouldn't be owners or partners, but reliable hired girls and boys. It seemed to me that William and I had just made those future children a generous offer. No Lombard should have to leave the farm for any reason.

Of all the surprising things that Stephen said to me that

night, the last question took the prize. He said, "Why do you
think May Hill prays to the photograph of her nephew?"

"What?" I said. My face was at once hot.

"Are you going to be a writer?" he asked.

"No."

"You aren't?"

"I'm going to be a farmer."

"A farmer, eh? You should maybe think about writer."

I shook my head furiously, saying, "William could put that
battery in your clock. It would be so easy, nothing to it, do
you want me to wake him?"

"It's a tempting offer, but, between you and me, the CIA is
testing me with this problem. I'm sure, pretty sure, I'll be able
to solve it."

Another wave, such heat, Stephen trusting me with his secret. Plus, it was dawning on me, past my blazing face and into
my mind, that he'd somehow read my story about May Hill.
Which for one thing was more evidence of his occupation.
The interview was information for his *files*. I felt as if I might
faint and in order not to I stared at him. He definitely looked
like a Lombard, the long nose and the square chin proof, but
he also resembled a Japanese emperor, somewhere along the
line an impurity sealing his beauty. He was the most handsome
spy in the world.

I said, "Isn't Gloria worried about you?" I was still thinking,
He read my story.

He didn't hear my question because he was saying, "Even
though this clock doesn't work it's probably safe to say it's time
for us to go to bed. Don't you turn into something unattrac-
tive and impossible if you fail to get eight hours of sleep?"

"Yes," I said.

"Well then, Francie, good night."

"But I don't really want to go to bed."

"We can have a standing date, every night at—what time is it?" He squinted at the microwave clock. "Two in the morning! Every night at just this minute I'll meet you right here."

He probably didn't mean it. He was living with Gloria and he wasn't. He stayed in our house although it didn't belong to him. He was soon going to float off into the world, a man who himself hadn't been able to be a farmer. He was someone who didn't always know what time it was. Plus the travel alarm clock was too hard for him to understand. I started to wonder, as I got back into my bunk, as I tried to go to sleep—if a place might make you more than you were. Was that possible? The puzzle was like a dread story problem. And then, without that place, say you lost it, or couldn't get back to it, or couldn't stay there for long, it could turn out that you really weren't much of anyone.

9.

Winner and Loser

Those of us who were especially interested in preparing for the Geography Bee stayed after school two afternoons a week for more intense drills, Mrs. Kraselnik having to do little to twist the arms of the smart boys to join in, for they were in love with her, too. Her goal undoubtedly was to try to bring them up to our level, Amanda's and mine, so we would have serious competition. We knew that Mrs. Kraselnik loved us best not because she obviously had pets but because we were the most lovable, that is to say, I was most and best. I heard my mother say that Barbara may have regretted bringing the bee to our school, that the fevered Lombard cousins in their dead heat were probably driving her over the bend. The error of that statement was an embarrassment to the speaker, poor Nellie Lombard out of her element.

Mrs. Kraselnik for certain had rare gifts, her cool beauty and her excellent low voice only two of her many teaching tools. I later understood that in our day-to-day work she somehow made Amanda and me feel that together we were a great force, and separately we were special in a way that required no comparison. When Amanda was excused every day after lunch so she could walk up the street to sixth-grade math, Mrs. Kraselnik allowed me to sit in the quiet corner and read a difficult book or work on my memoirs. If we were both raising our hands with equal urgency she called on someone else. We were both enlisted to be mentors for students who needed extra help, the only class members accorded that honor.

A week or so before our class bee, that long-anticipated night, a fight broke out on the playground, a fourth-grade boy beaten up because he was for Bill Clinton. After lunch, it seemed that Mrs. Kraselnik was looking at me especially when she began to talk about the purpose of life. We were doing a tour of Europe and in particular Spain, our teacher more imposing than usual in a black bolero jacket with red trim, and black gaucho pants, and tall black boots. "Why," she asked, standing before us, "why, boys and girls, are we on this earth? What in the world are we doing here?"

No one had ever asked us that kind of question. Even Amanda didn't know the answer. "What's all this for?" Mrs. Kraselnik sounded almost angry, as if our ignorance, our lack of curiosity on the subject, was unforgivable, as if she couldn't stand to think of our carelessness. Not one of us ventured an opinion, no one in fact saying anything, all of us a blank.

She pierced each of us with her gaze. She said finally, "Boys and girls, we are here to put good in the world."

That was it? She was again looking very hard at me. For

what seemed like a full minute she wasn't just looking at me, no, she was glaring. Had I done something wrong? Or was I going to misbehave in the future, Mrs. Kraselnik an oracle? It was as if she wanted Mary Frances Lombard, more than any other student, to understand the simple instruction. Even though there was nothing to her statement she repeated it. "We are here only—only to put good in the world." She clutched her notebook to her chest, her lips pressed firmly together. "You must," she said, "you must always, always remember this." I gazed back at her with all my heart, hoping she knew I would never forget her message.

At home in those weeks before the bee I'd started to notice something peculiar. My father quizzed me, always discussing the possible answers in depth, both of us poring over the maps that detailed imports/exports, religion, migration, air currents, the landscape beneath the oceans, endangered species, song and dance, painting and theater, oil, gas, coal, diamond deposits, all the spices of life, and the remarkable flux in time and space. Now and then he'd say, "Just think how much you know! That Mrs. Kraselnik! It's amazing how much you've absorbed in such a short time, what a virtual encyclopedia you are."

That pleased me.

But then he'd say, "The reward is right here, Marlene, in your knowledge." For no reason that anyone could remember Marlene had always been my father's pet name for me. "It doesn't matter, you know, if you don't win. That doesn't matter, not a whit. You've already won by knowing all that you know."

Those remarks made no sense. I hadn't won, couldn't possibly have won since the big night had not yet occurred.

My mother, who had always kept track of my studies, was strangely uninterested in my preoccupation. When I asked her if she'd quiz me she'd find an excuse not to, or she'd say I already knew enough to do just fine. William wasn't exactly indifferent, and he did put his time in, firing off the questions and getting involved in the answers, but he, too, seemed not to care about the final result. He lay on his top bunk saying, "I never liked competitions," as if all of his experience was behind him. I pointed out that if I won, Mrs. Kraselnik would spend many sessions a week preparing me and the participating sixth, seventh, and eighth graders for the county competition. If I won up in Madison, I'd then take a written qualifying test to ensure that I was championship material before the event in Washington, DC. If I was even a third-place winner, even if I was not national champion, I would win thousands of dollars in scholarship money.

William said, "If that's what you want to know about, Frankie, about geography, I guess that's okay. I guess that's good."

"Geography," I said, "is at the heart of every subject. For your information."

Every day Mrs. Kraselnik had a different way of explaining the importance of our overarching study. "Everything we know and are, boys and girls, begins with the land in your community. Think. Do you live near a river? In a desert? Do you live in the mountains? Where do you get your food, your water? How far away is your school, your church? Are there people like you where you live or are you a minority? Who"— she paused, moving her tongue along her demure upper lip— "is your tribe?"

Kyle Covell laughed and called out, "I'm not in a tribe!"

That sent us all fluttering around the room, to the dictionaries on the LANGUAGE! shelf, and to the computers in the back to define the word *tribe*, and to think how or if we belonged to one.

One morning Mrs. Kraselnik said what I was already well aware of. Among her other talents, as I intimated, she was a mind reader. She said, "Do you understand that everything about the place where you live determines Who You Are?" Her flank was against her desk as she looked sternly at each of us. "Who You Are," she said again. "You would not be who you are if you did not live right here, in this town, in this county, in this state, and in this time."

"Okay," was all William said, when I tried to replicate her speeches.

It was Gloria who set the actual problem before me. I was at the cottage one afternoon, having offered her the opportunity to quiz me.

What state does not experience frequent tornadoes? Florida or Iowa?

The Maldives are located off the southeast coast of what country on mainland Asia?

Which New England state has more forested land? Maine or Vermont?

"Do you and Amanda quiz each other?" Gloria first asked me. "Do you study together?"

"No!" I said.

"No?" We were sitting cross-legged in her living room, on her hard, bare floor. "Mary Frances?" she said, in an odd warning tone.

"What?"

"I want to ask you something." The beating of my heart, for some reason, sped up. She said, "How will you feel if you win?"

What kind of question was that? The answer was: Elated. Triumphant. Victorious. *I will feel victorious.* She saw she needed to elaborate. "If you win and Amanda doesn't?" Gloria with her long blond braids and her enormous gray eyes behind her glasses said something more. She said, "Do you understand that it can be harder to be the winner, harder to win than to lose?"

That could hardly be true. She was making something simple seem complicated and confused. I said, "I'm older than Amanda." All things being equal that was the reason I should win. However, in our after-school practice sessions lately I often had the slightest edge, Amanda probably spending too much time on pre-algebra.

"Yes, you are older," Gloria said, as if my logic had been wrong, as if I should let Amanda win precisely because of my greater age. Was that what Gloria was asking me to do? Amanda had recently gone to the hairdresser with high expectations, Dolly allowing the stylist to cut her daughter's long hair and give her a perm. Instead of glossy curls, though, the black hair fell straight from a center part before it became a dry frizz. Was that disappointment my responsibility? She'd gotten glasses, too, the frames tinted purple.

I had not envisioned Amanda being the winner until Gloria let a sliver of that darkness into my mind. If anyone else had made the suggestion I would have thought it mean, a jab intended to knock me off balance. I didn't want to think why

Gloria would wish me to lose, and I left the cottage soon after, trying as best I could to dismiss her idea.

I wandered over to the library, where right away there was another disturbing conversation. Traditionally, if Dolly had the need to tell my mother something she'd walk the hedgerow path and no matter the delicacy of her news bulletin she'd stand at the circulation desk and talk. She and my mother rarely spoke on the phone, and I doubt they wrote each other emails. Even if Mrs. Sherwood Lombard went into my mother's office, the rest of us out in the stacks, the patrons and those people who had jobs shelving, could hear at least her side of the conversation. The two wives had the joke of calling each other Mrs. Lombard. "Mrs. Lombard," my mother would say, "how are you?"

"Don't ask, Mrs. Lombard"—Dolly usually laughed—"don't ask."

In any exchange Dolly had to first tell my mother a little something about Adam and Amanda because a day didn't pass without one or another of them excelling, and there was always a catastrophe involving her Muellenbach relatives.

After I'd left Gloria's cottage and had been in the library for about five minutes, in comes Dolly for the usual exchange, *Mrs. Lombard, hello*, and, *Don't ask, Mrs. Lombard.*

Dolly said to my mother after the opening bit, "It's going to be tough, is what I think."

I looked up from my spot in the beanbag chair by the Junior section.

"I know, I know," my mother said, lowering her voice, glancing my way, "but maybe, you know, someone else—"

"Mine is fixated on the money."

"Oh God."

"...already planning how to finance college."

They both laughed.

"You think we could rig it?" my mother said, which made them laugh again.

"Oh well, Mrs. Lombard," Dolly sang out.

"It's in the Lord's hands, I guess," my mother said.

Maybe I had heard most all of their conversation and maybe I hadn't but whatever drift I'd gotten made me understand that my mother, who was not religious, who for some reason had invoked Jesus, was talking about me.

In those weeks before the bee I was only happy in school, when Mrs. Kraselnik said to all of us, but looking at me, that she'd never had a group of students who were so enthusiastic about geography. She'd never seen all of her boys and girls working so hard together to learn such interesting facts and to master map reading. In her book, she said, we were all winners, even though Amanda and I, and maybe Max Peterson and Derek Casper, were clearly in a realm apart from our classmates. Sometimes, though, in the middle of thinking and working, in the middle of eating or brushing my teeth, Gloria's absurd question rang out: *Do you understand that it can be harder to be the winner?*

I'd chew briskly. I'd brush with more vigor. If Gloria ever had a real baby, I felt sorry for it already.

The night of the competition we were lined up on stage in the gym, all twenty-seven of Mrs. Kraselnik's champions. I was wearing a French brushed cotton blue-and-white-striped dress with a yoke, which Gloria had found in a resale shop, white tights, and blue ballet flats. My clean straight hair was without

tangles in the customary pageboy. For the occasion Amanda
had decided on navy pants and a red blazer, a jacket a busi-
nesswoman, a banker, would wear. She had nylon stockings
under her pants, and black pumps with a slight heel. Nowhere
in evidence was the girl who wanted to eat her crackers like a
beaver. She stood next to me with her hands folded behind her
back, and she stared far past the audience, the EXIT sign apparently her portal to knowledge. I remembered right then that I
should put good in the world, a generosity that surely would
ricochet back to me. And so I said to that weirdly dressed girl,
my cousin, I said, "Good luck, Amanda." That moment was
something no one knew about but the two of us, a secret, the
virtue of Mary Frances, a point on the scorecard.

I looked out to the audience, to the way the spectators had
arranged themselves, as if there were the bride's section and
the groom's section. Sherwood and Dolly and Adam were on
one side of the gym, and my mother and father and William
and Gloria were on the other. Everyone in their proper places,
waiting for the action to begin. Even before Derek Casper was
eliminated, before it was just the two of us, Amanda and I,
goodness must have been working its wayward logic in my
mind, winding itself up of its own accord. Goodness waiting to
pop up again, the cheery clown, goodness bobbling helplessly.

Many of our classmates were serious and well prepared and
it therefore took an hour for everyone else to go down. Sherwood always blinked in that thoughtful way of his when Mrs.
Kraselnik asked the question, Sherwood thinking, thinking,
weighing his own answer. You felt he was on the side of each
contestant in the freighted moment. Adam was playing his very
own new Game Boy, a forbidden item for us. Dolly also had

a new haircut, her hair spun into a glossy black bubble. She had taken so much trouble with her hair but nothing she could do would ever make her beautiful. I didn't want anyone in the world to be ugly—what if you were ugly?—and yet ugliness for some reason had to exist. Someone had to do the job of carrying it.

When Derek Casper was finally out we arranged ourselves, Amanda and I, on either side of Mrs. Kraselnik.

"Well, here we are," she said. "Amanda. Mary Frances."

I looked at Amanda, her shoulders pinched back, her hands clasped by her rear, her long gaze past the audience. She didn't seem to be aware that I was on the stage with her. It was as if she were already the ambassador to Egypt, so that I both wanted to laugh and also was slightly unnerved.

"Which state," Mrs. Kraselnik asked Amanda, "has a climate suitable for growing citrus fruits—California or Maine?"

That was so easy it was not in any way funny. "Cali-FONia," Amanda snapped.

"Mary Frances," my lovely teacher said, "which country has the world's largest Muslim population—Indonesia or Mexico?"

Up flipped my mental map of world religions. Symbols across the continents, arrows flashing to show the way. It was additionally helpful to know that Mexico had been settled by the Spanish, who generally are Catholics. I knew that Indonesia was the correct answer, and I knew, also, that I would say so. I noticed Dolly on her side staring at me, her little teeth, her pointy bottom teeth on purpose cutting into her upper lip. My father, about six rows back, on the other aisle, was sitting forward, his head down. My mother was looking at Gloria's lap, and Gloria herself had turned to face the clock. Only William was watching me, his chin up, a slight smile, no blinking. I remembered the once upon a time when he'd told me the story about how our house would come to find me, it loved me that much. *Once there was a girl who lived near the end of the world.* A place no contestant in the Geography Bee could ever know or find.

"Indonesia," I said.

"That's correct," Mrs. Kraselnik pronounced. The audience clapped, although so long into the contest their tributes seemed halfhearted.

For Amanda: "To visit the ruins of Persepolis, an ancient ceremonial capital of Persia, you would have to travel to what present-day country? Iran or Syria?"

Again, a cinch. "Eye-wan," Amanda said.

I was asked a question about physical geography with the answer of isthmus, and Amanda had another improbably easy question about what a barometer measures. "You girls are spectacular," Mrs. Kraselnik said, "aren't they?" The audience clapped in earnest, a few people cheering. "My goodness, you really are both winners."

I noticed Dolly again. She wanted to look like a respectable person with the hairdo, like someone who lived in a subdivision. Like the mother of a winner. How was it that Sherwood had married her, so that forever he had to be in public with the former Miss Muellenbach? Dolly having latched on to him for her single and only dream: Adam and Amanda in cap and gown. Her children were going to go to a great college, she always said to customers at the apple barn, maybe a place hidden with ivy. By hook, she said, or by crook. Her children, she'd explain, scored off the charts. A logical *therefore* kind of question: Therefore, what did I need with a scholarship since I was going to stay on the farm?

Maybe Dolly didn't just want Amanda to win for the sake of it. Maybe she needed her to win. That's why she was biting hard into her lip, about to draw blood. Because of the impossible sum. Fifty thousand dollars for national champion, far more than my father and Sherwood ever made for themselves in a year. I began to sweat. Was this what my parents, what William and Gloria had been trying to tell me? And maybe, yes, Mrs. Kraselnik had, too, her whole sermon about putting good into the world meant only for me.

I had to say to Mrs. Kraselnik, "Could you—could you please repeat the question?"

By allowing Amanda, the girl in the business attire, to win, would I, the cheater, in fact be a force for good?

There were a few more rounds, both of us answering without much effort within the twenty-second time period, and yet I was dizzy and warm, the sweat running down my back. The thought I'd had about cheating was insane; I was maybe going crazy, a foaming in my mind. But remember, remember, Mrs. Kraselnik had been practically teary in class when she'd been imparting her message about goodness. She'd been suffering because of what she was asking, because of the enormity of my sacrifice. I had a fever. That was it, I was suddenly ill. I was going to burn up and fall over, my vision failing, Mary Frances soon to go blind. Poor good blind girl, blind and then dead. I felt that in a minute I might die.

Nonetheless, my turn came again when I was still standing. "Which Canadian province produces more than half the country's manufactured goods?" Mrs. Kraselnik was wearing an orange cashmere dress that came to her knees, made shapely by a giant leather belt with a huge O buckle, clothing to lay your face against even if you yourself were boiling.

I knew, of course, that Ontario borders all the Great Lakes and also has access to the St. Lawrence Seaway. Ontario, therefore, was the reasonable answer. There was a hitch in my throat and sweat in my eyes, that sting. I turned to look at the orange softness of Mrs. Kraselnik. She nodded at me supportively. *Put good into the world, Mary Frances.* I looked at William, at his uplifted, bright face. *Do it, Imp.* Amanda was not going to become the farmer, no, she was going to leave home. She would have to prove herself everywhere she went in her heels and jacket, whereas the farm would be ours, William's and mine. Was that not winning? Was that not the real prize? Everyone had been trying to tell me the answer and maybe even I myself had known it all along: Amanda should have the Geography Bee. If I lost, and because Mrs. Kraselnik knew about my secret vein of goodness, she would gather me to her. She would thank me, whispering in my ear, her wet cheek to mine. And I'd choke, *Oh, Mrs. Kraselnik!*

Thank you, my love. Thank you, Mary Frances.

Come on, Imp, let her have it, William beamed to me.

Do I have to, William?

Yes.

It was something William would do, kind good William. I felt his eyes not only on me but boring into me so steadily they were nearly my eyes, too, his good deep-brown eyes.

And so I said it, I said, "British Columbia."

The startled hush in the crowd. *Is it right, is it wrong?* "I'm sorry," Mrs. Kraselnik said quietly, the audience groaning, the audience sorry for me although glad, too, that the evening was soon going to be over. They could get home for the end of the Packer game.

But not so fast. The winner had to answer another question correctly, the contest not yet done. Our course could be reversed—there was still hope. Instantly after the corrupted answer I knew that I did not want to be the loser; I didn't want to put good in the world after all, no interest, none, in that project.

Mrs. Kraselnik began a narrative question, which by and large she'd avoided. "Hundreds of wooden and stone churches, Amanda," she said, "containing both Christian and Viking symbols were built during the Middle Ages in what country that borders the Barents Sea?"

Russia, didn't Russia border that sea? Amanda didn't answer immediately. She was breathing heavily, her lips tightly pursed. The harsh gym lights, the sound of her breathing, the trick question, the digital clock in front of us—all compounded my illness and fatigue. Mrs. Kraselnik hadn't said a Nordic country, which would have been expected if the answer was Norway. Were there Vikings in Russia in the Middle Ages? Maybe I'd missed that unit. I couldn't think exactly where Norway was, and what of Finland, my mind was suddenly no good, the maps gone dark. It had to be Russia, Russia touched the Barents Sea. With two seconds on the clock Amanda said, "No way."

No way? *No way* was not a country. *No way* most certainly could not stand as the answer. And yet next I knew Mrs. Kraselnik was hugging Amanda on stage, this before our teacher outlined the future. "Right here, in our presence," she then said, "a possible county champion, and who knows, a girl who could get to state and maybe beyond." Never, Mrs. Kraselnik said, had she worked with such dedicated students, but now in our gym she meant that only Amanda was the truly dedicated one.

As an afterthought Mrs. Kraselnik said, "Let's give another hand for the excellent Lombards."

I had slunk down the steps, even though I was supposed to stay on as the loser, as the runner-up, the alternate, in the event that in the weeks to come Amanda had a change of heart or broke a limb. Or damaged her vocal cords trying to learn Standard English. I ignored my mother's outstretched hand and went to sit next to William. He may have spoken to me— I don't know. I wanted to stand up and shout the truth, to explain my reasoning. On the way out many people tried to hug me but Dolly especially made a point to draw me to her ample breasts. She'd never hugged me before but I had to let her. "You girls did so well!" she screamed even though I was pressed into her. "So wonderfully well!"

Gloria hugged me, too. She murmured one of her incomprehensible Gloria sentences. She said, "You have so many advantages, Mary Frances. I'm very proud of you."

When William and I were grown, when Dolly and Gloria were old ladies, maybe we'd put a plate of pie by the door of the manor house. Say the men had gone away, and it was only the history hermit upstairs, the farmer's wife downstairs with her black bob, and Gloria, the three women stuck with each other. They would all be closed up with May Hill, and like May Hill they wouldn't even celebrate Christmas or

Thanksgiving, never a holiday. Maybe we wouldn't feed them at all.

That's what I was thinking all the way home in the car, while my parents and William kept talking about how much I knew, their praise and jubilation no more noise than a door banging in the wind or hail on the roof.

10.

How Hard Must the Pumpkin Visitors Work?

At the County Geography Bee in December, which I was too ill to attend, Amanda stayed in the contest for an admirable length of time. Ultimately the hopefuls were defeated by a seventh-grade whiz kid, a boy predictably from India. It was said that she cried on stage. That was too bad. After the four–five split bee I'd more or less recovered from my loss, our teacher making me the assistant director for the class holiday play, Mary Frances Lombard with clipboard, pen tucked behind her ear, keeper of the details. Even so, I was sick to my stomach for the County Bee in Racine, and stayed home.

For that competition Stephen did his duty as uncle and went along with Gloria, my mother riding with them, which she afterward said made her want to put a bullet to her brain. Even though my mother's exaggerations were not funny, we'd understood after Halloween why she made such dire comments about the couple who were something like newlyweds.

In that fall she was often asking my father accusing questions as if Jim Lombard were responsible for the couple, questions such as, "Why can't Stephen be good to Gloria, Jim? Why can't he just once look at her when she says something? Would it kill him to act as if she exists?"

My father didn't have an answer, my father unable to choose sides.

We did wonder if Gloria put her arms around Stephen the way she did to us, kissing his head longingly although he was right there firmly in her clasp. We thought she might do that, and therefore we were squarely in Stephen's camp. Until, that is, until the night the pumpkin visitors came to the Lombard Orchard for the last time.

We took it for granted that everyone understood the utmost importance, every Halloween, of the pumpkin visitors coming to Velta. If you'd heard about them, of course you understood. For the special guests to appear, it had to grow dark. We sat at the table eating spaghetti and store bread soaked to sponge in garlic butter, and probably we were describing our classmates' costumes when suddenly, suddenly, there, out the kitchen window. A pumpkin, was it a pumpkin in the night? Its lopsided toothless grin all joy, glowing at us?

"Papa! Papa! The pumpkin visitors have come!"

"What?" He'd hurry into the kitchen from somewhere or other. "Where?"

"Look!"

"They came," my mother would say in a hush.

We ran to the front door to see if the sidewalk visitor had

made the trip, and yes, there he was, crooked teeth as usual. Up the stairs we chased to find the two roof visitors outside our window, the ones with question marks for ears and eyebrows thin and curved like seagulls in flight.

"They came!" I had to needlessly point out.

Gloria, wearing her gypsy costume, having followed us, put her arms around me, singing out her *hello, hello,* as if through the double-paned glass they could hear her. The visitors sometimes left us notes, not of course inside their shells with the burning candle but on our pillows, formal, short messages wishing us good cheer and fortune. Once, when William started to wonder how they occupied themselves during the rest of the year, he started to cry. He had made the mistake of thinking outside the bounds of their magic, glimpsing their loneliness, such sad creatures who could only be useful one night of the year. The Easter Rabbit, too, doomed to 364 days of leisure. My father soothed William by involving the pumpkin visitors in Kind Old Badger's life and times, the visitors' rotund fleetness an asset for any number of adventures. But even so it wasn't long after William's upset that my father decided to bring him into his dark enterprise.

When I was seven we were at dinner as usual, the spaghetti, the garlic bread, the discussion of the costumes at school. I happened to look up from my plate just as a tower of flame shot into the sky out in the hay field. "William!" I screamed. "A rocket!"

He ran to the window. "It's—it's . . . the brush pile? The brush pile, ohmygosh! It's on fire!"

"How in the world—?" My mother was too surprised to finish the sentence.

"Could it be—?" I tried. "Do you think—?"

"What could it be?" Gloria sang out, the bells on her gypsy costume tinkling.

"The pumpkin visitors?" I said it, what no one else had yet understood.

"The pumpkin visitors! The pumpkin visitors!"

All of my family was with me, no possible way anyone at the table had made it happen. I was not so stupid as to at least wonder. "A whole bonfire this time," I shouted. As always we flew to the front door. The proper visitor was on the walkway, and we tore upstairs, our old friends there on the roof.

The following year I had to learn—it was necessary to be told—that William had climbed out of my father's office window and lit the perfectly appointed woodpile. He'd lit the pumpkins, too, before he'd slipped back into the house. The fire hadn't roared up until he'd been peaceably eating his dinner. I would have been glad to pretend not to know, everyone forever doing the trick to amuse Mary Frances, but that year I was called into service.

My grandmother was dying up in St. Paul. She had been in a locked ward for a few years, a little lady in her own room with a swivel table over the bed for mealtimes. For the most part we didn't listen to the bulletins of her suffering. Finally, my father got the call and he had to break away from the harvest to drive to Minnesota. Only a catastrophe could get him out of an apple tree. He arrived and an hour later Athena Hubert Lombard died. "Very peacefully," he told my mother on the phone, so that she said, "Oh, Jim, I'm glad." We had seen the ram on its back kicking and kicking right before he died, when the shearer had nicked his artery, so we knew what she meant.

When he returned it was Halloween night. He was almost too tired to eat, my mother sitting close by, pointing out what was most delicious.

She had instructed us to do the work of the evening. The pumpkin visitors, she claimed, would cheer him up. Even though it was Grandmother's time, even though she'd died in her sleep, he still would need the comfort of tradition. We understood the importance of doing it perfectly. While my mother went on speaking quietly to my father William and I stole outside. The barn cats were like minnows in the shallows, moving around our legs as we carried the visitors from the bushes and went pumpkin to pumpkin, lighting the candles. Once the faces were illuminated even the big-headed torn-up toms crouched low, frightened and full of respect.

When my father at last turned to see the toothless beauty in the kitchen window he did something that surprised us. All of him right there at the table seemed to dissolve. My mother didn't shush him or say that soon he'd feel better. Together they huddled in his wide old chair, both of them weeping. There was no comfort—we could see this, none to be had— and so we crept away to our room and into our bunks. We cried not for our grandmother, a woman so ancient she didn't know us. We were crying because the visitors, for the first time in their long history, had failed to bring happiness. We had done the work wrong, or it wasn't for us to do, or their powers were over and done? Somehow, we had made a mistake.

Later, my father came upstairs to tell us how much he loved the magic. He said he couldn't have imagined a better homecoming, and if Grandma were still with us—plus, he meant, still had her mind—she would have enjoyed the story. It was a nice try. We appreciated his effort but we knew that the pumpkin visitors would never come again.

It must have been the next Halloween when Stephen was more or less living with Gloria. Again my mother was the one who made the suggestion about the visitors. Why didn't William and I make them appear at the cottage? We promptly forgot about the disaster of the previous year, all of a sudden excited and serious. With utmost care we picked out several pumpkins from our private patch. There was the carving to do, the four of us working together at the table, the great emptying to make the creatures live, the wet pulp in mounds on the newspaper.

When all was ready we set out. My father had the brute in his arms, my mother with the moderate girlish one, William and I each carrying two small howling faces. In a line we crossed the road and went through the old orchard, the long knobby branches laid out in shadows on the moonlit ground. We trooped past the potato garden and the marsh, considering the muskrats deep inside their thatchy houses. At the cottage we went to our stations, working in complete silence, as a spy must, setting the visitors on the porch and the walkway and in the back window. My father had hidden a ladder near the barn early in the day for the purpose of placing one pumpkin on the roof, outside the bedroom.

We were hiding in the bushes, admiring the display, when the door opened. Gloria came sweeping out in a long, floaty gown, her hair wrapped in a leaning and towering scarf. She wasn't wearing her glasses, but on that night perhaps full vision was hers. Gloria, who never wore jewelry of any kind, was covered in beads and bangles and she had long glittery earrings, each a set of chimes, a percussion section unto herself. In her hand she held a taper, her face ghoulishly lit. We laid ourselves flat, trembling with glee as she drifted among the pumpkins, singing in her high thin voice, greeting them one by one, a shivery vibrato in her *thank you*s. We remembered what was easy to forget, that Gloria every year often became nearly as magical as the visitors. On that night, there the peculiar and graceful spirit was, dancing in the yard. A spirit who had somehow intuited that she should be ready for the spectacular.

The door opened once more. Stephen, in ordinary clothes, stepped out. "Where'd these come from?" he called. He apparently, somehow, was not familiar with our customs.

"The pump-kin visitors," Gloria sang in her fairy voice, the coins around her waist jangling. "The pumpkin vis-it-ors, oh, the pump . . . kin visitors, have come"—up went the note in a wild leap—"have come to us."

Without saying a word Stephen leaned over the big fellow on the porch and blew out the candle.

"What's he doing?" William whispered.

On the walk Stephen pinched the light inside my little screamer. "Make him stop," I said.

"Time's up," my father pronounced, moving low on monkey hands, he and my mother going in their knuckled run. We started to scoot after our parents but in the same instant we turned back. Gloria had stopped singing. She was standing at the bottom of the slope facing her dark cottage. There was only the single pumpkin on the roof still shining into her bedroom, the one visitor who must do all the work, trying to bring generosity and merriment to that place and to that couple.

"Come on, Frankie," William said, but I wanted to look a little longer at the last pumpkin visitor. There would never be another. And so together we stood saying our own private farewells.

11.

My Mother Is Right

As my mother had predicted, there came an end to the Stephen Lombard era. In that next spring his so-called sabbatical was over, Langley no doubt offering him a plum position. I alone knew that he had somehow proved to the CIA that he could successfully insert a battery into his alarm clock. Even if Stephen was merely the writer of spy manuals his work would be plentiful. The first World Trade Center bombing had already occurred, those years a time when agents were brushing up on their Arabic and being redirected. We later considered that maybe he had gone to try to prevent everything that was going to happen, listening in on phone conversations, attempting to avert the tide of history.

It was my mother who announced his departure, coming to the table with the pot filled with butternut squash risotto, cookbooks by a tyrannical Italian woman her new enthusiasm.

In our neighborhood noodles had not yet transitioned to pasta, all of us resisting the change, lobbying for regular old macaroni and cheese rather than bucatini with tomato and pancetta. She had stood obediently stirring the mail-order arborio rice for twenty-three minutes without saying a word. It was when she set the pot in front of us that she said, "Stephen is leaving."

"He's what?" my father said.

"He's leaving Gloria, I guess is more to the point. He already returned his library books. Thirty dollars of overdues."

"You waived his fee," William said, as if it were an order.

"Sadly, yes."

Her nonchalance about the departure, her dwelling on the details was her way of saying, *Told you so.*

"Why would he go now?" My father asked the basic question. "His sabbatical isn't over yet. He was going to be here through June."

"I didn't interrogate him," my mother said.

"What about Gloria?" William asked the other fundamental question.

"He can't go," I said.

"Why, really, would he stay." My mother's remark did not seem to be an actual question. William and I would have liked to know how he could leave the kittens, and anyway hadn't he been wanting to quit his CIA job, get out of that racket? Why wouldn't he stay for another harvest when he knew we needed him? He'd been devoting himself to reading and therefore weren't there still books he wanted to check out?

My father shook his head slowly. "Gloria," he murmured. "Oh, Gloria."

"Yes," my mother said, as if that was an answer.

We thought of Stephen bundling everything he owned into his duffel bag, all of his life in that lump, and going to a city like Cairo, a city so thick with people and cars you had to bribe a policeman to get yourself across the street. Or he'd be locked away in a compound in Saudi Arabia, or stuck in a hovel in Africa. He obviously should not go anywhere. He was a gifted and dedicated apple picker, probably as capable as my father and maybe faster than Sherwood. With his tremendous wing-span and grace he could lean and twist to get into a jungly place where the largest, most perfectly ripe apple hung on its thin stem. While everyone else was knocking apples down accidentally you never heard the *th-whump th-whump* from his tree. And he was swift, running up and down the ladder, a picker who always kept in mind that time was marching on, the cold winds were on the way, the winter snows upon us.

My father, his thick hair in its messy weave, that high hat above his wonderfully lean face, the delicate knobs of his cheekbones, his short dignified nose, and his eyes that were sometimes green and sometimes, no, we thought blue—he finally made the pronouncement: "Stephen should stay. There is no reason for him to leave."

My mother froze in her pop-eyed amazement. "You do understand, Jim," she was able to say, "you do understand he cannot do that."

"Why not?" I said.

"Because."

"Because why?" William asked.

"Because," she said evenly, "it would be difficult for him to work alongside the present management. How exactly would he fit in?"

"There's a place for him," my father insisted. "He knows that."

"I'm sorry." My mother shook her head as if she truly wanted to apologize. "I just don't see Stephen leaping into the operation, taking any kind of charge. For one, this isn't something that Sherwood wants. At least that's my guess. Anointing the little brother who, in his mind, in his exceptional mind, is the goof-off. Which is terribly funny, when you think about it. If he stayed on as a picker—well, being part of the crew is not exactly a career move."

"He could stay," William said meekly, doing what he could for our father.

"He's Adam and Amanda's uncle," I reminded the table, the trump card, Stephen's title surely winning the day.

William said, "He should not go."

Stephen hadn't been a child, not really, not in a way we could believe in despite all his stories. But what if—what if, beyond our poor powers to imagine, he actually had been young? For the discussion's sake, let's just say he had once been four or five or six. How, then, could he leave? We were at once certain that Stephen was the sorriest person in the world. Through dinner and even into dessert we could almost—I say *almost*—understand why he'd blown out the pumpkin visitors. They had come to the cottage but he couldn't have them. They weren't his anymore. He had gone away and lost the ability to recognize them, all of his life now and forever a poverty. We wanted to call him or maybe even run to the cottage to say, *Don't go, Stephen! You don't have to leave us! We forgive you about the pumpkin visitors, we do.* This sudden generosity ran thickly in us.

The night before his departure for Washington, DC, my
mother had a long-planned party for her librarian friends from
Chicago. We did not like her parties with book lovers because
for a few days beforehand she banished us from the kitchen. It
was as if her favorite authors were coming, or real celebrities.
Then, once the librarians sat down to dinner, they'd go into
their ridiculous swoons over the novels they adored, and they'd
end up arguing about who was great and who wasn't, the pro-
fessionals growing increasingly noisy and high-spirited while
the spouses glumly ate their food. That night, my mother was
just about to recite for the assembly what, in her opinion, was
a perfect description of a human being, her performance piece
for special occasions. In college she had committed an entire
page of Edith Wharton to memory, a paragraph devoted to the
physical description of a single character. She was about to begin with, "*Mr. Raycie was a monumental man.*"

Right before she opened her mouth my father made a face
that was a problem for both of them. He didn't just close his
eyes. He shut them hard, he shut them tight, not, however,
as if he were going to have a restful little pause. No, in order,
it seemed, to blot her out. It was hard for him when she was
that animated, when she was that monstrously joyful. Maybe
there was a Lombard gene that made it difficult for the men in
the family to endure too much enthusiasm or energy, so that
even someone as quiet as Gloria was excessive for Stephen.
My mother happened to notice her husband as he was bracing
himself, right before he shut his eyes, just before the wince
sealed his face. That wall against her seemed to have a specific
temperature; for her, it, his very head, that wall, was hot. So
hot it scalded her eyeballs, so hot she had to scrabble for her

empty plate, blindly grabbing at it to save it from the heat. Instead of rescue, though, she raised it, she turned her whole body from the table, from him, the plate in the air, for a moment still whole. And then with all her strength she brought the china down, the blue-and-white pagoda scene smashing into slivers at her feet.

The librarians looked at my mother. They looked at my father, and next not at anyone. "Whoops," Mrs. Lombard cried.

"Whoooa, Nellie!" one of the women brayed, the oldest joke in my mother's book.

Even before one of the husbands said, "Time to go!" my father was leaping up to fetch the coats.

William and I had already gone through the D.A.R.E. program at school and we knew our mother was a real true Alcoholic, and that the glass or two of wine she had at dinner on many evenings, and the three she had at her parties, were going to ruin her life and eventually kill her. My father occasionally joined her but usually he drank cider so he was safe. When there was half a bottle corked on the counter we sometimes poured the rest of it down the drain, to save her from herself. She made the excuses that Alcoholics make, the kind of thing Officer Radewan at school had warned us about. My mother insisted that red wine was good for the heart, that it reduced low-density lipoproteins and was also instrumental in reducing breast cancer—at least some doctors thought so. "Oh, for goodness' sake," she'd say, "wine is food. It's part of a meal. William, do not look so sad. I'm not in danger. Get this out of your heads, you two, that wine is evil, will you please? If you don't, I'll really have to become a drunk."

She said that if we wanted to see what an Alcoholic looked

like we should inspect the postmaster more carefully, or her patron, Mrs. Prinks. But we were not fooled. We usually forgot during the day that she had an addiction, a *disease*, but at dinner we again remembered, her affliction on full display. Officer Radewan had shown the class a photograph of an Alcoholic's liver, the crusty, shriveled black slab, our mother probably already secretly on the list for an organ transplant. When we recalled that she was an Alcoholic we knew that her occasional violence was first and primarily the result of the wine. But even if she was merely drinking water the closing of my father's eyes, the blotting-out, always made her temporarily lose her mind. Sometimes we did think he could have closed his eyes a little less firmly, that he didn't have to look as if he were about to have a knife plunged into his chest just because she was going to recite Edith Wharton. We didn't know that our parents were objecting to the other's self, that enormous hulking thing each possessed, that a self of course is not inconsequential.

The day after the party my mother went off to work, still furious with her husband. Stephen, all set for Washington and beyond, had asked my father for a ride to the airport. Gloria, he said, probably wouldn't be equal to the task. We had to go along to pick up the secret agent because on the way to the city we were hopping off at our friends, the Plumlys.

My father parked on the gravel down the slope from Gloria's cottage. We got out of the car thinking to quickly play with the cats on the porch while the luggage was loaded, while Stephen and Gloria had their smoochy good-byes. When we all got up the little hill Stephen opened the door. He leaned out, saying to my father, "Got a small problem here. A glitch."

"You all right?"

"My passport is not, ah, it's not available."

Gloria appeared next to him, her face a reddish blotch, the puffiness of her eyes magnified by her glasses. She crossed her arms over her chest and stood staring as well as she was able at Stephen, her lids so swollen her irises were hardly visible.

My father talked softly to her. Stephen went back inside but she remained guarding the entrance, now staring at my father's lips, staring in a determined blank way, as if to say that every word coming from his mouth had nothing to do with her. He made simple statements. "You know you can't hold him here." "It's time." "In a few minutes you'll go and get the passport." "Gloria, please, now, get the passport."

His lulling, gentle demands finally prompted her to disappear into the house, the clock ticking away to the airplane's departure. Stephen returned to the door, he and my father standing there not saying anything. When she came back she slapped the document into her lover's hand.

"Thanks," he said.

"No." She shook her head and began to cry. "No!" She tried to get the passport out of his clutches even though she'd just given it to him.

My father grabbed Stephen's arm and pulled him onto the porch. "It's time," he said again.

"No!" This was a crooked noise, jagged, not at all a Gloria kind of sound. She pitched herself at Stephen, as if by sticking hard she might be able to go along with him to Washington. Even though she didn't look or sound or behave like herself, so that it seemed private, these various aspects of her, we set the cats down and gawked.

My father yanked Stephen toward the car. Gloria jerked him

by the other arm toward the house. Stephen had a felt hat
with a ribbon around it, the kind of hat fathers wore to work
in the 1950s, which made him especially look like someone
who should not be at the center of a tug-of-war. In one brilliant motion my father both let go of his cousin and plucked
Gloria from Stephen's coat. He held her, her back to his chest
while she screamed and kicked and flapped her arms, trying to
scratch. "Go," my father cried to Stephen over her commotion, "get in the car right now."

Stephen stumbled down the slope of the yard holding his
hat to his head with one hand, and in the other the long green
sausagey duffel. He threw it in the back of the van, dove in
after it, and locked the doors. To us my father said, "Find
Mama."

The library wasn't far off. This errand was more important
than being the instruments of the pumpkin visitors. We had
rarely been so excited and certainly never felt so essential as
we ran, as we steamed into the library to the circulation desk.
When she saw us she instantly intuited the general circumstances. She called to Hildegard Bushberger to keep an eye on
the place, and somehow, in her clogs, she galloped across the
baseball diamond, through the stand of cedars, and up the in-
cline to the cottage. She took Gloria from my father's arms—
Gloria was beginning to get tired out, bent over and sob-
bing—and led her into the house while my father hurried to
the car to drive Stephen away. In the heat of the moment we
had all forgotten that we were supposed to go to the Plumlys'
house.

My parents had also forgotten their anger about the dinner
party and the broken plate, so that was good. We thought every

time the librarians visited and my mother tried to behave in a sophisticated way, like an intellectual, maybe Gloria could have an emergency that would force them to work together. We sat on the porch and petted the cats, not looking at each other, for a while not speaking while we listened to Gloria wailing inside. She must have realized the truth about Stephen, that he'd once been a Lombard child, and that's why he needed to stay. She'd only been trying to get him to live where he was meant to live, everyone, except my mother, who liked to complicate matters, on the same side. We had to cover our ears, Gloria's sorrow pooling out, as if she thought her distress would reach Stephen even as he drove farther and farther away.

When she quieted somewhat we remembered how she had found us in the woods when we were lost, and so it seemed only fair that we perform a feat to help her. I reminded William that when we'd been curled up in the tree's roots he had told stories to comfort me.

"I didn't tell you stories," he said.

"You did too. You told me about the girl who lived near the end of the world. Our own house picked up its skirts and came to find me."

"You made that up. That's your own stupid fairy tale." He pinched me on my arm. William almost never hurt me, and although I could not have put words to it I understood, I think, that he was pinching me because of Gloria's upset. Still, it was unjust. I was about to screech when a Gloria blast came from the house, a cry out of proportion to my injury. William and I looked at each other and shut up. Maybe I was mistaken about our fright in the woods but it didn't matter because I would always believe that while we were lost William told me stories, and also, with or without stories, we would never be as lost as Gloria seemed to be in her own cottage.

After some time Dolly came along the path from the manor house, the news apparently having traveled. It wasn't that she didn't see us, right there on the porch, but that we didn't concern her. She didn't say hello. Her approach to the door was cautious, her voice at the screen tentative. "Yoo-hoo? Nellie? Are you there?"

My mother came clonking down the stairs from Gloria's bedroom. She let Dolly in, instructing us to go to the library and make sure Hildegard was all right. We again felt important as if, if Hildegard wasn't all right, looking after her own children and the circulation desk, we would manage the library ourselves.

Later we learned that my mother and Dolly were trying to settle Gloria and at the same time figure out how to get her committed; her case seemed that acute. It was my father who ended up staying in the cottage for three days and three nights before Gloria's mother could come to care for her. He had to stay with her because she refused to come to our house, his camping there the last resort. The work of the orchard was suspended for him, no way to get those spring days back, a long falling-behind. Gloria then went away for two months, back to her hometown in Colorado, two entire months when the Lombard Orchard needed her for grafting and planting, mowing and lambing.

When the excitement was over my mother asked my father, "Why did you save Stephen? Why didn't you let him figure out how to get out of his own mess? You betrayed Gloria by doing the rescue, you know."

"It wasn't possible to stand by and do nothing," he said.

"No, I suppose not." She went behind him and chop-chopped his shoulders the way he liked. "They'd probably still be in a standoff on the cottage porch if you hadn't shown up."

Although by then William and I knew well enough that we couldn't marry each other, in those days we were even more determined to live together in our house and sleep in our bunk beds forever. I know this because the night of the incident I said, "I'm always living here." William's soft bristly hair first appeared over the side of the top bunk, his forehead next, his eyes, and his skinny arm, which he extended to me. I reached for his hand. He was not only saying he was sorry about the pinch, he was making his promise.

MIDDLE

12.

The New Hero

The first time I saw Philip Lombard it was spring vacation, Amanda, William, my father, and I in the back shed, the four of us concerned with the lambing. This took place in the time of the four–five split. Philip's father was May Hill's older brother. He'd been in college when his parents died, via the silo accident and then the mother hanging herself. An older boy, therefore no need to be adopted by Sherwood's family. That man and his son were visiting, something that we'd learned from Dolly was going to take place. Philip, ah ha, May Hill's nephew, the boy in the photograph. The pair, father and son, were going to sleep in one or two of the closed-up rooms in May Hill's house, May Hill receiving visitors, an event we couldn't remember ever happening before. Philip himself was now in college, we'd been told, in Portland, Oregon, and had grown up in Seattle. That was the extent of our knowledge about the poster boy, the living person among May Hill's historical pantheon.

Out in the sheep shed, the three of us underaged veterinarians were used to examining the ewes' long pink vulvas, watching for a bloody drip, the first sign of impending birth, without suffering any embarrassment. We also didn't bat an eye at the new mothers lying in the maternity stall leisurely chewing their cuds, their lambs sleeping nearby, the pink balloons of bag and fleshy tit sometimes promiscuously exposed. On that day Old Speckle Face, the problem ewe, as usual had done her yearly prolapsing stunt, the enormous blister, the veiny globe that was her birth canal dangling from her behind. We did not allow my father to ship her even though she was a liability, and anyway we knew he loved her, too, and wouldn't have done such a thing. William straddled her and I held her head. Amanda's job was to hand my father the tools while he tackled the back end. It took him a while to tenderly tuck the gigantic bubble in, and quickly he then inserted a beer bottle up into that delicate place—a technique that often worked and kept the real vet out of the picture. My father was concluding the procedure when a person wearing a red stocking cap, green Wellingtons, and a red-and-white-checked flannel shirt appeared in the doorway. First of all, his clothes seemed like a costume, attire you'd imagine you should wear for The Farm. The gigantic Christmas elf blocked out the sun. "Hey there," he said.

My father was still adjusting the beer bottle. "Philip," he cried, glancing up, "hello!"

"How's it going?" The intruder stepped closer. He squinted at the swollen parts of Old Speckle Face and in a girlish way his hand went to his mouth. "Looks kind of intense in here," he managed. Next he noticed us. "Hey, cousins."

"Hey." William had never said *hey* before in his life.

Amanda and I said nothing. Philip was a second or third cousin, a relation that was so dilute it hardly counted.

"We're hoping to keep this lady from delivering prematurely," my father explained. He took a large darning needle from Amanda, a thin shoestring looped through the eye, and proceeded to stitch a crisscrossing hold for the bottle across the thick walls of the naked pink slit. The poor mother opened her mouth, her square teeth like ours, grade-school-size, and made an otherworldly groan, her eyeballs flipped back into her head. William and I had to keep a firm hold on her.

"Whoa," Philip said.

"There." My father removed his rubber gloves but even so he said, "Consider your hand shaken."

Philip laughed, a sputtery noise. He did not look like May Hill. His nose was without bumps and a modest size. Blond curls peeked from under his hat, and his thick golden lashes plus the particular blue of his eyes were not features he'd inherited from the Lombard side. He was stockier than his aunt, his shoulders were broad, his legs sturdy, his hands meaty, a person clearly graced with strength.

"This is Amanda, Sherwood's daughter, and William here, and Mary Frances," my father said.

"Cousins," Philip reaffirmed. "Great to meet you." Old Speckle Face was released from our hold but didn't know what to do now that she had a bottle up there. She stood looking at the stranger. He said, "She going to be all right?"

"She does this every year," my father replied.

Philip nodded. He started to talk about his hopes and dreams. "I've wanted to come to the farm for basically my whole life. My father's told me stories about you people and this place and I've always been like, Why can't we go visit Wisconsin? What's so important in Seattle that we can't take a trip to the family homestead?"

"It's great you're here," my father said.

William and I looked at each other. In a matter of two minutes we already knew enough to think, *No, it isn't.*

"Thanks!" Philip said to my father. "So, I wanted to let you know I'd love to help out—whatever assistance you need this week. My dad's going off to a meeting in Chicago but I'll be here. May Hill has some projects for me, too, which I'm psyched about, but honestly? If anything needs doing? I'm at your service."

"Wonderful," my father said.

May Hill had projects for him? He was *at our service?* William and I left the shed right away, muttering our good-byes. In the six minutes it took us to trek through the orchard, to get to the road and cross to Velta, my initial impression had undergone an evolution. I didn't just dislike him. I said, "I hate him."

"As much as the Muellenbach boys?" The Muellenbachs were Dolly's barbarian nephews.

"More," I said. "I hate him more."

William nodded, as if I'd given the correct answer.

The spring vacation dragged on. It was the end of March and hardly warm and there was very little to do in the damp outdoors. Adam and William were building a computer from components they'd found somewhere or other. Amanda wanted to do nothing but play chess. The Kraselniks had gone away to the Bahamas, no point in climbing the tree to watch for signs of my teacher. Despite the cool temperatures we were already calling the season spring because my father had sprayed the oil application on the dormant orchard. For us true spring arrived when we first heard the sprayer revving up before dawn, Sherwood or my father on the tractor. It was important to properly aim the sprayer nozzles, the heady brew in the great tank, to shoot the insecticides and fungicides into the trees when the air was as still as possible, thus the early hour.

There was comfort of a kind, waking up to the groaning sprayer engine, even as my father in his orange waterproofs and his gas mask and goggles might have looked menacing to a stranger, driving up and down the aisles of the orchard, at the painstaking, critical task of mass genocide on pests that could destroy the crop.

But also I wasn't comforted when my father sprayed, and I did have the habit now and again of not going to school when it was his turn in the saddle, or if it was vacation I'd stay in bed. It was essential to hold tight to my bunk while he drove through the orchard, important to keep track of him. That is, it was my vigilance that maybe protected him. The especially murderous point was mixing the materials in the sprayer tank, because if even a drop of insecticide in concentrated form made contact with your skin, it would burn a hole through you. From my bed I chanted, *Careful, careful, careful, careful, careful.* If the sprayer was up and running everything was fine, but sometimes it would stop, an abrupt quiet. *Are you hurt? Did you break down? Are you DEAD?* I'd have to wait for the sound of his galoshes, the jangly tread as he came through the orchard, his mask resting on his head. "Screwdriver's not in the tractor toolbox," he'd call up to my window. Implicating either himself or Sherwood for not returning it to its proper place, but probably Sherwood had been the careless one. William and I had not once, not ever, considering going into the locked spray room where the barrels and bags of poison were stored, that shut door a barrier we had no wish to go beyond. No one in his right mind would go in there, which was why the disaster with the Muellenbach boys wasn't exactly a surprise.

The second time we saw Philip just happened to be on that afternoon when Dolly's nephews were hanging around—so many ragtag cousins at large at once. The short history of the Muellenbach boys: Dolly had somehow snagged Sherwood and married him but her sisters had not been so lucky. Melody, for instance, was a mother of four who could not keep a husband for more than a few years at most. She'd had the children, each with a different man, each father gruffer and larger than the last, and also, she chain-smoked, she herself was obese, and there was some problem about her taking prescription painkillers, another hazard we'd learned about in D.A.R.E. Her oldest daughter had had a couple of babies before she was seventeen, again different dads for each. The two mothers and the five boys, ages three through thirteen, lived together in an apartment forty miles away. And some or all of those boys used to come to the orchard now and again for a day with Uncle Sherwood. It was funny that he couldn't convince his own children to perform much farm labor but the Muellenbach boys were always running after Sherwood, dedicating themselves to him, hanging on his arms, climbing him as if he were a pole. William and I worried about the sheer number of those boys—like an entire nation of Chinese males in that two-bedroom apartment. Because of their romantic association with the farm surely they'd want to be part of the operation when they got older.

It was three or four days after Philip had arrived for his visit that my father was in the back barn trying to get the space ready for the shearer. We were aware of Dolly calling the Muellenbach boys in for lunch, for us the promise of quiet while they gobbled up their food. My father was slapping together pens that would be holding areas for the ewes, and clearing a corner to store the fleeces. Sherwood was there, too, working on a contraption that would lift hay bales off their stack in the barn, set them on a roller, and slide them down into the feeder, one of the many rattling things he'd been messing with for years. He had a leather carpenter's apron around his waist, a level in hand, and a pencil above his ear, as if in his heart of hearts he thought he was a builder. It's possible he hadn't realized that the Muellenbach boys had arrived. My father made the mistake of wondering out loud, in passing, if Philip would like to help with the grafting of apple trees, a springtime task.

Sherwood set his socket wrench down. "What business is it of yours?" he said to my father.

"Business?" my father innocently wondered.

"You think Philip is your worker?"

"I—don't think he's anyone's worker. I was only asking if you thought—"

"Always trying to run everyone's lives. That's what you do."

My father wasn't prepared for the biannual argument. It was still early in the spring. For a few seconds he did nothing but stand, holding the wooden gate he'd been about to tie to the makeshift fence. "I run no one's life," he said. "That I'm aware of. It would be convenient if I could. It would be great to run a life or two."

"Philip is none of your concern," Sherwood said, picking up his wrench. And then somehow or other they were deep into the classic dispute, Sherwood saying, "When I went into the army my dad made clear the business would be here for me, that it would be mine when I got back. All of a sudden I learn that you're on the place. I knew then, Jim, I knew how it would turn out, knew Aunt Florence would keep you, that you'd prove to the—"

"You were away," my father said. "Your dad and Aunt Florence—they needed young energy for the harvest."

"I was serving, as a matter of fact."

That was another facet of the argument, the deep cut about the war that had shaped their youth, my father with Conscientious Objector status, working at an old-fashioned state insane asylum in Minnesota, while Sherwood enlisted in the army. Even though he had spent most of his time at Fort Rucker as an informational specialist he had been in some danger when he was in Saigon.

"Yes, you were serving," my father conceded.

"I come back, you're running the operation, you act like you own the—"

"Sherwood! Florence and your dad needed young energy for those years you were away." My father finally set down the wooden gate he'd been holding.

"Young energy," Sherwood echoed in an unpleasant singsong voice.

"Whatever you want to call our strength at the time, our energy," my father said stiffly. "The older generation needed help. Call it what you want."

Even though the Lombard partners had the same argument over and over again their skills hadn't improved much and so far there hadn't been a real breakthrough. Sherwood never punched my father, which might have made him feel momentarily better, in that instant before my father turned the other cheek.

"You think I couldn't run this place by myself?" Sherwood at least was now shouting. He'd remained in his inventor's corner, his shoulders thrust back, his mouth pursed, his nose wrinkled up, an alarming puggish face. That was not the Sherwood we were at all used to seeing. "You're always shooting down every idea I have. Every single idea—you say no—"

"You don't ever communicate!" My father's voice had also become shrill. "How can I say no when you don't tell me what you're going to do? You planted that block of Galas without talking to me. A major decision and you just—"

"There you go, criticizing my work. Criticizing when I'm the one who grew up here. I'm the one who learned from Dad. I'm the one who didn't go out for sports in high school, didn't go to a fancy college, the one who was working—working, Jim, throughout the year, the one who had the long apprenticeship. I'm the one who learned the business."

"It happened, Sherwood!" My father's anger still flaring. "We, you and I, became partners. More than thirty years ago. Time for you to get over it, to get used—"

All at once that wrench was in my father's face. "Shove grass—shove grass, Jim, way, way up your ass."

What? Grass? Grass up— *How would you*—*? Why*—*?* William and I, the two of us nearby in the old cistern with the salamanders, we stared at each other. Did warring men put grass there because then there'd be an explosion, the way wet hay could ignite a barn?

No one, not a single person anywhere had ever said such an ugly, bewildering, violent thing to my father. That was not the way any of the Lombards ever spoke. And yet Sherwood, a Lombard through and through, had shouted the demand, the two of them near the back barn at that point. Those words were far worse than having a wrench rattling near your face. What would have happened next will never be known because at that moment Dolly cried out, pure distress penetrating the war zone. She may beforehand have been calling for her great-nephews, for Jax and Mason, but when we took notice she was screaming, first at them—"What are you two doing in there?"—and then she was screeching "Sherwood! Jim! Sherwood!" The two men sprang from the back barn, running around the long building to the forbidden shed where the spray materials were stored.

Those Muellenbach boys had walked right into the spray room, the door somehow unlocked. Because Dolly was yelling at them they were afraid to come out. She herself seemed too unnerved to go farther in than the doorstep, Dolly shrieking to no one, "Poison control! Poison control!"

Before the men could storm inside Philip Lombard was flying across the driveway from the basement and blasting into the shed; also before we knew it he'd emerged with the three- and the five-year-old in his arms. Dolly snatched Jax's hands from his eyes. "Do you want to be blind? Don't touch anything, you hear me?"

Both of those boys started to howl. One of them was able to say that they'd only been trying to find Uncle Sherwood. Philip set the nephews down and began to examine their fingers and their clothing. My father, who had gone into the shed, said that a bag he thought had been sealed was open, Dolly crying out that they had to go to the emergency room immediately. Sherwood said, "Let's be calm, let's—"

"You explain to Melody why her grandsons are blind," Dolly snapped. "You explain to the judge why you didn't take them to the hospital." She hollered, "Why was the room open? Why was it not locked?"

"Give me your other hand, buddy," Philip said, sniffing Jax's palm.

"Don't you get poisoned," Dolly advised the visitor in more moderate tones. "Wouldn't that just be so wonderful, to send you home at death's door?"

The little boys were whimpering. Sherwood was looking for the key to the spray shed. Philip, who somewhere along the line had mentioned he was an EMT, was spreading Jax's eyelid and studying the pupil. My father was kneeling near the boys, too, doing his own observation. That's when we realized that May Hill was standing on the rise by the pump house, surveying the scene.

"Good job," Philip was saying to the other boy, to Mason. "Stick your tongue out at me, okay, bud? Excellent, excellent, my man, nice slab you got there."

May Hill did not need to announce the obvious, that it was her nephew who had come to the rescue.

We'd hardly recovered from Sherwood saying what he had about the grass, and now there was the blindness of the Muel-

lenbach boys to consider or the burning of their skin through
to the bone, as well as the culprit, the Lombard Orchard partner who had failed to secure the building, not to mention May
Hill standing above us, those big, high-waisted jeans always a
shocker. If she realized that we could see the shape of her, if she
knew, would she cover herself with a poncho? Without discussion William and I went off to dig out our canoe, which we
kept stashed in the brush by the pumpkin field. We'd leave all
of them behind, paddling in the wide deep blue marsh, drifting by the muskrat houses, peering into their hodgepodge of
cattail stalks one on top of the next, great thatched messes.
Good-bye, all of you on land, good-bye!

"Do you think the Muellenbach boys will die?" I asked William. He was always in the stern, so he could steer. I hated
the barbarians but the thought of them dying suddenly seemed
pitiful. Poor little boys with fresh crew cuts laid out in pint-size
coffins.

"Philip thought they were okay."

"Papa wouldn't let them die," I said, more to the point.
"Why did Sherwood—? How do you put grass—?"

William struck the water with his paddle, a thwack.

I couldn't think, couldn't imagine Sherwood being a boy
and believing the orchard was going to be his and only his.
How could he have thought such a thing? How could he have
failed to know that we belonged, too? Although I still loved
Mrs. Kraselnik with all my heart I didn't dream of her adopt-
ing me as frequently as I had at the beginning of the year. And
yet for a minute I allowed myself the worn scene wherein she
scoops me up from our house that's in flames, and takes me to
the mansion on the hill, draws me a warm bath, draping her

fingers through the bubbles while I carefully undress. That romance wasn't as thrilling as it had formerly been in the early days of the four–five split, and I ran my mind over it quickly, obligatorily. Before I could get to the end of the scene in my mind's eye, though, Philip crashed in on it, Philip saving Jax, saving the Muellenbach terror. In real life he was performing the rescue in just the way I'd imagined Mrs. Kraselnik doing, Mary Frances lying on the ground, my teacher bent over me tenderly trying to pry open my eyelid. Wherever I went now, whatever I did, would Philip appear in the frame?

"Stop rocking the boat," William called out.

We had to hold out against Philip Lombard! Right then William and I had to decide for good, for certain, that we would always protect Velta-Volta.

"Stop it, Imp," he said.

"Stop what?"

"The twitching. You're making the boat tip."

"I can't help it."

"You can too."

"I'm never getting married."

"There's no law that says you have to."

"I'm not doing it!"

"Okay."

"Are you?" I said.

"Am I what?"

"Getting married."

"How should I know?"

"You could decide not to."

"That would be stupid."

"Nuns and priests don't get married."

"Stop tipping!"

"Only if you promise not to get married."

"Frankie! I can't—"

I began to not just tip the boat but rock it. I didn't care if we went overboard into the murky depths of the marsh. A normal brother would have gotten furious, would have swiped the oar through the water and drenched his sister. Why was William so nice? That question made me even angrier. Why did he always have to be patient, so patient and kind, too? He made me sick. A sharp awful pain in the head. What was wrong with him? I changed my mind—I didn't want to be an orchard partner with him. You'd have to be an idiot, you'd have to be impaired to be so good. I'd run away to Mrs. Kraselnik's.

He managed to guide the boat to our landing place as I continued to do my best to turn us over. He pulled it from the water, parked it, and waited for me to climb out. I dragged behind, refusing to walk with him. On the way home we had to go out of our way to avoid a great many things we did not wish to see. Sherwood and my father possibly back to their argument. The Muellenbach boys dead on stretchers. We did, against our will, see Philip learning chain saw etiquette from May Hill, the two of them in the orchard about to cut up an old Macintosh that had fallen down in winter. I could maybe like William the slightest little bit because he, too, skirted the path so we didn't have to look.

13.

The Mistake, the Worst Mistake

A few days later in that endless two-week vacation I was wandering around looking for my father when I noticed May Hill and Philip heading into the woods. They were again equipped with chain saws. Philip's father had left us not long after he'd arrived, depositing his son to befriend May Hill, very amusing that suddenly May Hill could have a young person in her life, someone who could be her child, or maybe he was more like a dog, following her everywhere she went. No one said how long he was staying.

Everyone on that afternoon was otherwise engaged, William off at his friend Bert Plumly's, Amanda practicing her French horn, my mother working at the library; Gloria was still in Colorado recovering from her love affair, my new best friend, Coral LeClaire, had gone to Disney World with her family, no one at liberty for Mary Frances. For quite some time in the fall I'd had a plan to steal into Mrs. Kraselnik's house; it was in a dreamscape, that is, my hiding in her bedroom closet and popping out at her. In the sequence she was delighted to see me. Possibly that's why it occurred to me without much premeditation that I could creep up the basement stairs into Dolly's kitchen. Amanda's horn after all was noisy. Adam would probably be in the living room on the computer. As for Dolly, her car was gone, Dolly elsewhere. Sherwood was out by the barn underneath the sprayer, trying to fix a leak. The downstairs was not, however, my final destination. I could get through the kitchen and then run up the back stairs into May Hill's house, open the gate, and find the room Philip was using. I would discover something, surely— evidence. Information about his intentions, information that would discredit him, some no-good incriminating piece. I was not related to Stephen Lombard for nothing, our shared talent a fact he must have recognized that night we'd stayed up in the kitchen nearly until dawn, discussing spy craft. We were both brave. We were both adventurers.

Suddenly the pique I'd felt about my lack of playmates, the dreary vacation, William spending far too much time at Bert Plumly's, even Philip's visit to us, all that misery faded in my fright and exhilaration, tiptoeing up the stairs to the gate. The long hall was dark, my heart at the back of my throat as I began to open doors looking for signs of a college boy. Every room I put my head in was like a jumbled attic, a confusion of artifacts and what looked like trash. The fourth door was the winner, the room by the kitchen, a room that must have belonged to one of Sherwood's many sisters long ago. There was a vanity table with a mirror, the clue. It wasn't much of a guest room but one of the twin beds at least had been cleared of boxes and clothing and books and records, all the stuff that Louise or Margaret or Emma Lombard had once cherished but not enough to haul up to Alaska and the other places they lived. Philip's backpack was on the floor, his notebooks and paperbacks on the desk, underwear, socks, and shirts folded neatly on top of a cardboard box, a little island of Philip things. The notebook: a black-and-white-speckled composition book with unlined pages. I opened it. Lists, he was a list maker. Lists of books to read, items to pack, people to write, music to listen to, recipes to cook, and there were drawings, as well, of mushrooms and flowers, a new lamb, and the bridge-graft he'd done with my father down in the west orchard. No master plan for his life, no mention of love or money or William and me or even May Hill. Only the lists, the drawings, and also he had written out poems, poetry by John Keats and William Shakespeare. I turned every page until there was no more writing. It was the most disappointing document I could have imagined, but maybe he used invisible ink for his true feelings? I spit on a page to see if water brought up a message. No. Nothing. On the desk there was a tube of lipstick in a clutter of markers and pencils, erasers and paper clips, the relics from the time of Louise Lombard. I took the cap off, the dull red tongue of it brand new even though it was something like fifty years old. Without thinking I carelessly applied it to my mouth and then I planted a kiss on that fresh page. "The end," I said. "Ha, ha."

Where, I wondered, did May Hill sleep? I was no longer quite so frightened or alert, an easy thing, really, to steal through someone else's house, especially when they were out chopping down the forest. I went along the hall again and

stopping midway, with exquisitely tuned radar, I opened a
door. Although at first I thought it was only another junk
room, I saw instead that I had chosen correctly. It was clearly
May Hill's room because on the bed there was a pair of neatly
folded sweatpants and a big top, May Hill's pajamas no doubt,
and by the pillow a book of some kind, her nighttime reading.
You had to be attentive to the clues, however, to understand it
was a bedroom because the place was filled, from floor to ceiling, with boxes, a narrow aisle to the adjoining bathroom and
a corridor also to the window. I carefully made my way along
the towers in order to look out to the orchard. Down below
I could see my father hauling brush and all the way across the
road there was our house, May Hill able to keep track of everyone if she took the time to squeeze along through her maze. I
would leave in just a minute, I thought. Wouldn't William be
surprised by my expedition!

Since the interview I had sometimes imagined that May
Hill might be one of those people who made whole miniature
towns out of bottle caps, or she'd have fabricated a family of
paper dolls that were intricately cut with tiny little scissors, the
kind of thing lonesome people do to keep themselves occupied. But there in her room were no astonishing worlds, her
boxes stuffed with what looked like newspaper clippings and
some of them had labels such as CHECK STUBS, 1978–80, and TAX
BILLS, and BANK STATEMENTS. There were several towers of an-
cestral letters, documents I guess she needed to sleep with. A
few items seemed nice, an enormous jar of buttons on a shelf,
for one, and a crock of marbles for another, and a blue padded
book of the sort my father had, filled with coins of silver. I
opened it up to see the half-dollars. So there were those pretty

things to look at, and to be glad about, too, glad that May Hill had a great many unusual and ornate buttons, and maybe the agates and the coins were worth hundreds of dollars, which probably made her happy.

Had I been looking at those precious things for a long time? It didn't seem like it, but when the footsteps sounded on the back stairs I snapped to attention. Where was I? May Hill's bedroom, that's where. I instantly curled up by the radiator, very tightly, behind a box column, listening to the flat quick footfall coming closer, closer. It could be none other than May Hill herself. The person, she, stopped. The door had been left open, how stupid could I have been! She must have been thinking about that unusual fact before she took the simple action of closing it. There, it was shut. She then went farther down the hall to the living room. She was possibly looking for something and maybe she found it or maybe she didn't. I thought I might throw up. After a while she went down the front stairs and from what I could hear she was out the door to her work again.

My inner ears seemed to have taken up my entire head— that's how hard I'd been listening. Time to reverse my steps and get out of the manor house, steam away home. I went to the door. I turned the knob this way and I turned it that way. It didn't, it wouldn't open. I rattled it, I looked through the key-hole, and I pulled at it with all my strength. *No*, I kept telling myself. *I'm not locked in.* I hurried back to the window to see if my father was still driving the tractor along the rows. He was gone, no hope of holding up a flag, or making a sign that said SAVE ME.

Amanda had finished her horn practicing; all was quiet

downstairs. I went into May Hill's private bathroom, the sink with a crusted rust stain from faucet to drain, and the small tub also rusty, where she had to fold up her tall thick self to get clean although a person didn't imagine her removing her clothes. I was trapped in that bathroom and in the bedroom, too, the boxes closing in, the bed probably booby-trapped in some way. The water from the faucet poisoned. I knew I mustn't cry and I mustn't be sick. May Hill had smiled at the story of Elizabeth Morrow Lombard and the scalping of the Indian because she, herself, was a scalper—I had to buckle over. *No, but think, think!* If I could jump up and down to rouse Amanda and Adam below. If the storm windows weren't sealing in the regular windows I could thrust them open and climb out on the roof or at least call and call. Or I could leap to the ground, risking life and limb.

In the end all I could do was stick my fingers under the doorjamb, like a cat when he's playing, his paws blindly fishing for whatever he thinks is on the other side. Then I did start to cry, wishing so hard that Mrs. Kraselnik would come and get me, and being furious all over again that William was spending so much of his vacation with Bert Plumly. My predicament was his fault. It soon would grow dark and May Hill would enter and get into bed. That thought alone was passing strange. Or else she knew I was in the room and she would leave me to my punishment, she'd lock me up, day after day, choosing another chamber for herself, plenty of other beds for rest.

I curled up by the radiator again and I couldn't help it, I whimpered. I lay there drawing circles in the dust. And some squares. Maybe after a long time for just a minute despite my fear I fell asleep because when I woke up my worry had come true and it was getting dark. Down the hall I heard the clatter of dishes. My head hurt. I was stiff and sore and maybe bruised. Someone was preparing supper. I was coming to understand that probably, and finally, there was nothing to do but give myself up. Even if I didn't want to, even if facing that prospect scared me half to death. And so, in order to do that, I went to the door and I began to knock, softly at first but steadily. May Hill was moving pots around and probably chopping vegetables, or sharpening her knife—sharpening her knife. And yet I must knock. I knocked harder. I knocked for what felt like an hour, changing knuckles every so often.

When she opened up I was still knocking, knocking at the air without the door. I stopped the little song I was bravely singing. It's probably a fact that she was stunned by the appearance of Mary Frances Lombard in her bedroom, that she'd been expecting a bat to be flying around or a rodent on the prowl. That's probably why she didn't say anything. She'd been cooking dinner for Philip, a boy about to come in after a long day's work for his good supper. From the heap of ages she'd dug up an apron with rickrack, which under different circumstances would have been humorous on her manly frame. She looked at me. I looked at her and then I ducked. I ran past her down the hall, yanked open the gate, practically tumbled down the back stairs into Dolly's kitchen, and another tumble down the basement stairs, bumping into Philip at the bottom—"Whoa, girl," he said, as if I were a horse. He held me, thinking he was doing yet another rescue.

I slapped at him, slap, slap and ran away out the door, and I didn't stop until I was inside our door in Velta, in our kitchen.

"Where were you?" William said.

My mother was at the sink washing lettuce that she herself had grown in a cold frame, her pride. My father was sitting on a bench taking off his work boots. William had Butterhead, the cat who loved him best, in his arms. I was home. Somehow I had gone far away and somehow I'd returned.

"Marlene," my father said.

"Did you have a nice time?" my mother wondered.

William narrowed his eyes in that expert way of his. "Are you wearing lipstick?"

I slapped at my mouth.

"Marlene?" my father asked. "Are you all right?"

"What happened to you?" my mother said, coming from the sink.

"Nothing," I said. "I wasn't anywhere."

14.

Blossom Day

Philip was at long last gone and the vacation over, our school lives resuming. Somehow, though, I did not feel the same after being May Hill's prisoner. That's how it seemed to me, that she had captured me, that she'd put me in her own bedroom, that she meant to fatten me up or starve me. The story could go either way when it came to how much food, but the outcome for the girl, whether fat or thin, would be the same. Ultimately nothing left of Mary Frances but bones. I would have liked to tell William about the capture but for a reason I didn't understand—even though I lived in my own self, and should understand my own reasons—I didn't want to tell him.

Mrs. Kraselnik could see there was something wrong with me, because every now and then when I was staring out the window, in my mind chained to May Hill's radiator, she would say in her stern low voice, "Mary Frances, are you there?

Where have you gone?" I'd have to shake myself back to the four–five split, wishing I could explain how close I'd been to never returning.

If I loved my teacher it's probably fair to say that William was intrigued by Brianna Kraselnik, who was sixteen in her first spring with us. Her brother, David, had been sent to a military academy after he'd been in rehab, Brianna theoretically the good child. The single community activity that she took part in was the Library Cart Drill Team, her parents no doubt forcing her to do volunteer work for college admission. We were still for the most part full of appreciation for our mother's kitschy enterprise, it never occurring to us that the project might have been an indictment of her character, or at least proof of her Alcoholism.

The art of Cart Drill at the basic level is to push the shelving carts to musical accompaniment. Sometimes you kick a leg out, or do a hip swivel, and as a team you make patterns as a marching band does, or you get a running start and glide with your feet hooked around the base, although that's advanced work. Across the nation at that time there were eighty-four teams and counting, Cart Drill not something my mother herself invented. She was hoping we would one day enter the American Library Association Annual Cart Drill Competition in Chicago, and it was perhaps in order to achieve this goal that she invited Brianna Kraselnik, who was on the high school pom–pom squad, to choreograph a routine for us.

We began to rehearse in mid-April for the Memorial Day parade, our single performance of the year. All of our efforts riding on that forty-five-minute spectacle. We were an unusual team because we were not middle-aged librarians in seasonal appliquéd sweaters and gay men employees but a cross section of the community, which highlighted us, the bibliomaniac children. It's customary for marchers in a parade to throw treats at the spectators but when we performed the crowds rained candy upon us. That's how much our townspeople loved the team. We always kept our focus, every member serious and in sync, ignoring the great reward, the crowd laughing and whooping, Dubble Bubble and Tootsie Rolls filling the top shelves of our carts.

At our first rehearsal in the back room of the library Brianna made her entrance carrying her own enormous boom box, a canvas bag of CDs, and a clipboard. She set her load on the banquet table. Behold: Brianna Kraselnik in an aqua leotard with gathers between her breasts, those cupcakes sharply de-lineated. On the bottom half she wore gray sweatpants that were cut off at the knees and dingy pink leg warmers drib-bling down around her ankles, around her soft leather shoes. We'd never seen any dancer's outfit that was so ragged but also obviously professional. She was nothing like the aristocratic Mrs. Kraselnik, Brianna a girl with bovine eyes, the long lashes bristly with mascara, and she had a luscious red mouth, the puff of her lips something you wanted to try to pop, the way we did to Bubble Wrap, and there was the glossy hair all the way to her rump. When she appeared I was already practicing along the wall: forward, back, run, glide, an accomplished pro myself, a team member who was not showing off but rather re-fining her technique. William, sitting on the floor with a book in his lap was squinting at me and his eyebrows were raised, too, and his forehead furrowed, all of that musculature at work at once. As if to say, *Really, Frankie?*

Brianna didn't hang back. She didn't even wait for my mother to introduce her. "Okay, guys," she said, clapping, approaching the whiteboard. "Listen up."

Listen up? I turned to William, to make our gawking face. He, however, was gazing at our neighbor.

She smoothed her hair only to the base of her neck. "I'm Brianna Kraselnik, your choreographer. I know some of you have worked together before, so, wow, this is awesome, all of you showing up. And we've got some new members, right?" She smiled at Ramona Peterson, a third grader, and her friend Brittany Garner. Somehow, like a teacher with a magical list, Brianna knew our names and situations. Before she could say anything more the Bershek twins in their size seventeen tennis shoes came tromping into the room.

"Hola, ballerinas!" she called to them. "Just in time to show off your talents!"

The Bersheks were impossible to tell apart, both of them with sandy hair and glasses, both wearing the same style from head to toe, as if they had no interest in making it easy for anyone to know which was which. They always helped us with our hay, and it seemed a bizarre coincidence that Brianna knew boys that in summer were so important to us. "You," she said severely, "you bad bad boys, you juvenile delinquents, better behave yourselves." And then she squealed, a high-pitched mocking laugh, although what she was making fun of wasn't clear.

One of the twins saluted, snapping his heels together.

"So, like I was saying," she went on, clearing her throat and stroking her own irresistible hair again, "I'm super jazzed to have the opportunity to create your parade event and to work with you . . . athletes? Or whatever. A special shout-out to you, Mrs. Lombard, for inviting me here. Really, I just love this wacky formation biznass. Um, so, okay, I'll show you what I'm thinking, give you"—she made her gigantic eyes bigger—"the grand design, and then we'll do some warm-ups."

The older Bushberger daughters were on Cart Drill, and so was Amanda and there were several adults, including Melvin Pogorzelski, my mother's star patron, the librarian's pet. Gloria would have been there if she hadn't had her love attack, if she hadn't had to leave us. We all nodded at Brianna, except for William. He seemed to have been struck by the lightning that was Brianna Kraselnik herself. A zap just for him.

She was saying, "Is there anyone who would like to demonstrate what this—thing is, for the newcomers, and maybe for review?"

"Good idea, Brianna," my mother called from the sidelines.

Amanda's hand shot up. I would have volunteered but a small something stopped me. I wasn't sure that our choreographer was in fact trustworthy. My mother had invited our neighbors over for dinner back in the fall, but because of the Kraselniks' school and hospital events, and our harvest, we had so far never gotten together. Cart Drill, then, was our first substantial acquaintance with Brianna. Her squealy voice, her mincing and mugging for the Bershek twins, made me wonder if deep down she didn't think Cart Drill was *retarded*. That would be her word, one we weren't allowed to use. And maybe William was arriving at that same suspicion, too, the reason he looked as if, should he be able to move, he might try to slip away.

I could see suddenly the *retarded* aspects of Cart Drill, the outsider's perspective at once unsettling. There was the embarrassment of Mitchell, for one, the autistic patron, thirty-three years old, whom my mother enlisted to operate the boom box. During rehearsal he cradled the box in his arms as he rocked and groaned, taking the job of operating the PLAY/PAUSE button with the gravity it required. And there was dumpy old Melvin Pogorzelski, who was overly enthusiastic, too, sliding around in his stockinged feet, and clumsy Mrs. Johnson, always banging into us with her cart, and even my mother was mortification, The Director on a stepladder looking down on our formations as if she thought she were the Almighty.

But was Brianna mocking us, the team? When she described how the carts would be decorated with shiny silver strips that hung from the lip of the shelf, like a hula dancer's skirt, she did seem sincerely excited. We girls all said, "Ahhhh!" There were fifteen carts that were strictly designated for the drill team, carts that could not be used for ordinary purposes. *Shelvers, stay back.* When Brianna—and not my mother—asked who would like to be on the decorating committee I couldn't help thrusting my arm into the air, even before Amanda did. And I couldn't help, either, my pride when Brianna said that I would be the girl hoisted on the shoulders of Melvin and Mrs. Bushberger, my cart minded by William when we got to, *Oh, as long as I know how to love, I know I will stay alive.* The key message of the song. Amanda could never have been at the top of any pyramid because she was too chubby to be lifted.

When Brianna first played us the song, played "I Will Survive," Melvin observed, "That is not the most patriotic number I've ever heard."

Before our choreographer could defend her Memorial Day

selection William said, "Yes, it is." He spoke softly, so that everyone had to turn to see if in fact it was he who had made the comment. His face had turned completely red. He was looking at the floor. "It is," he said again. "There's no point to freedom—I mean, you can't, um, have love if you're not free."

What in the world?

"OhmyGhaaaad," Brianna said. "That, my friend, is so deep." She shook her head in wonderment. "I can't believe, Will, how incredibly, amazingly profound that is."

Will? Did she already know him? From the middle school and high school bus stop? An acquaintance he'd never mentioned?

"KA-razy deep," one of the Bersheks said.

"You, boy," she barked, "no more out of you, you hear me?"

I was confused, still very much unsure if I liked Brianna, if I maybe wanted to tell my mother right then that I was retiring, but also I couldn't quit when I was going to be the girl riding on the shoulders of the adults. By the end of the hour the Bersheks had decided Cart Drill was too difficult for them, they were too cloddy, and away they went into the library proper. "Oh, too bad," Brianna said sarcastically. "Whatever will we do without them?" She slapped her hands to her cheeks, her lips in the O of astonishment. Some of the Cart Drillers laughed.

With the irritants gone we were able to get down to work. Although in the end the parade was a sensation, most everyone proud and exhilarated, I was not in that camp because of my private knowledge of Brianna's character. Beyond her flirty behavior and her obscure jokes in our rehearsals, there was criminal conduct that I, and only I, happened to witness after our first practice, when the orchard came into full bloom.

*   *   *

This is what happened. On Blossom Day my mother always let William and me stay home from school. We were sent from the house in the morning with a basket of necessities, and told not to return until three thirty, the hours of the official school day. If the sky was softly blue and the sun's radiance everywhere, no dark hole in which to hide, and the air still, nothing in it but bees working, blossom to blossom to blossom, the orchard lit with a snowy brilliance, and the grass plush and shiny, every green blade brimming with light, and here and there a carpet of violets, and swaths of beaming dandelions—then you yourself, you were dazed. You were bumbly and drunk, too, a once-a-year festivity.

On Blossom Day in that spring right after Philip's visit, William and I as usual set up our camp in the hollow underneath a towering wild tree, a brute that produced a tart pulpy apple that was good for about a week in mid-September. We'd named it Savage Sauce-Burger—hilarious. The south orchard was fifteen acres of mature trees, most of them well over twenty feet tall, planted by our Great-Aunt Florence and Great-Uncle Jim in the era before dwarf and trellis trees were the rage. My father and Sherwood weren't able to prune them all every year and some of them were impossibly overgrown, gothic subjects for a photographer rather than productive fruit trees. We had our books, the chessboard, cheese sandwiches, oranges, a thermos of lemonade, gingersnaps, trail mix, the usual goods for an expedition. William had his current Capsela robot masterpiece, half built, the motors and wires and bolts in his toolbox. But soon into our encampment it—or we—

started to feel strange. We'd already stood close to smell the lacy petals, we'd lifted our faces to the sunshine, we'd talked about maybe playing pioneers, building a fire, roasting our own sandwiches on a stick. We'd discussed constructing a fort, with levels in the tree this time, a few different stories. We'd said maybe we should take a canoe ride.

Somehow, though, those old amusements didn't seem interesting. Had they ever been interesting? I wondered what Mrs. Kraselnik was doing without me, wondered if Amanda was answering questions that should have gone to Mary Frances. William mentioned that Bert Plumly called being outside The Nature. As in, *Don't make me go to The Nature.* That was just dumb, I said.

"It's funny," William said.

I didn't have the energy to argue with him. I felt a tick in the fold of my ear, William removed it, we lit a match and watched it sizzle into a dark strand. Even that old satisfaction wasn't fun. We weren't just bored with the world; we were bored with ourselves, or we were hardly in our selves anymore. It was hard to tell what was going on. Maybe, if we could remember one little trick about how we used to be, we could get there, get back, as if we ourselves were a country we'd left.

We were on our blanket, scratching our arms and legs. William was reading *Swallows and Amazons*, one of his old bibles, with *Calvin and Hobbes* and Gary Larson as backup. We didn't look like twins anymore. His hair remained light where mine had darkened, and his face was a longer version of itself now, his nose still turned up, and his teeth, recently so enormous and separate, had settled into his mouth, all of them somehow a modest size, no more spaces between. He took up the length of the blanket, about a foot more of him than I remembered from the previous year. He shouldn't grow another millimeter, I thought; he'd done enough. His lips as usual were bunched into one pluckable bud, and his eyes, dark brown as the river.

Under our tree I took the time to make a vow. When we ran the orchard we wouldn't work on the blossom holiday the way my father always did. No, we'd declare a feast day for our crew. Hot bubbling rhubarb pies would materialize, a haunch of a goat on a spit, loaves of braided bread, and a bucket of marsh-mallow fluff, all set on planks by the tool house. I thought about how Amanda and Adam were not allowed to stay home on Blossom Day, something we'd never discussed with them, Blossom Day our secret.

I was absorbed in the holiday menu when through the aisle of the orchard I saw a girl, a girl who looked like Brianna Kraselnik. And behind her came a boy—was it one of the Ber-shek twins? The arresting thing about this boy and girl in the orchard, however, wasn't the sandy hair or the big eyes or the small glasses frames. It wasn't that they were probably Brianna Kraselnik and one of the Bersheks. The arresting thing was the fact that each was wearing no clothing. No article of any kind. They both did have tennis shoes on their feet, but no socks.

They were floating along between the trees, coming in and out of my field of vision. The girl's breasts were small, noth-ing much to notice not least because the feature that leapt out at you, that stunned your brain, was the huge patch of hair, a black version of the muskrat's straw houses, in her private spot. That was all there was to see of her. I understood in that moment that underpants must have been the first inven-tion of mankind because without them you would never look into your companion's eyes or face, and therefore it would be impossible to invent other necessary tools or think up ideas. But wait, another horror. The penis of the twin swinging into view. I think I made a noise. It was—how long? I couldn't say, couldn't tell, it defied measurement. He walked as if he wasn't aware of it, as if it required no concentration to have such an organ. He kept scratching his back, trying to get at a place that was no doubt a sting of some kind. I was too startled and certainly too amazed to notify William.

Some time passed. I began to wonder if I'd seen them. If they'd been real. They couldn't be real because it was a very stupid idea and scary, too, to take your clothes off and walk around outside. No one would want to perform that stunt. The Lombard Orchard, a nudist colony, ha ha. But then why would I dream them up? Why give Brianna so much hair, far more than my mother had? Furthermore, I could never have imagined a penis that long. I wondered if Mrs. Kraselnik had told her daughter to take the day off from school, appropriating our holiday, maybe the reason they'd wanted to live next to an orchard in the first place. If the couple was real, where were they going? Did it occur to the exhibitionists that the Lombard men might be doing farmwork, that they might bump into the owners of the property? There was then this question: Do I tell Mrs. Kraselnik?

That was a stunner. *Mary Frances, darling, how can I thank you for coming to me? Brianna has been a handful since the day we adopted her. Yes, it's true, I've never told anyone that she is not my own—and that I've never loved her. My own real child would never do such a terrible thing, nor would she have so much of that . . . hair.*

But again: Wait! Another shocking question was coming to

me. Did Brianna know which Bershek twin was hers or were they interchangeable? I almost—almost right then cried out. Did the Bersheks even know which one of themselves was the real boyfriend?

William calmly went on reading while on my side of the blanket the earth kept quaking. The last shock: What if May Hill was in the orchard and saw them?

I said to William, "What do you want to do?" What I really meant was, *We should get out of here*. We had to leave in case Adam&Eve floated past again. And yet it was our property and so we should build a fort. We had every right to throw stones at the marauders. All my questions and knowledge were like beats within my head, a drumming. I started to pick the grass furiously without even knowing what my hands were doing, trying to outsmart the rhythm.

William muttered, "Reading is okay."

"What what what what time is it?"

He looked at me, his book closing, his place lost. "What is the matter with you?"

I wanted to tell him everything, wanted especially to tell him about being held prisoner by May Hill, and how every time I saw her I became terrified, my heart always racing even if she was in the far distance. I wanted to cry when I thought of being trapped in her room, the event having grown more harrowing, so that I'd started to believe I'd been there for a few days and then a week had passed. But instead of describing my captivity I said, "I just saw Brianna and one of the Bershek twins naked."

He was staring at me, *ARE YOU CRAZY?* I wondered if I was crazy, if I'd have to be carted away to an asylum. Why did the worst, the most unspeakable things happen only to me? William had not ever been the prisoner of May Hill— that was something I could guarantee. William did not "accidentally" lose the Geography Bee. He did not see naked teenagers strolling through the orchard. I rolled up into the blanket and shut my eyes, and not for the first time that spring I wanted to die.

Deep into the misery, unaccountably desiring more, in a terrible leap forward I saw that any number of disasters could destroy the crop that was here and now in its perfect beauty. There might be freeze or drought or hail or wind. The trees smashed and withered, the apples stunted or pocked.

William said, "I think I'm going to see if Pa will drive me to school for the afternoon."

"What?" I said, turning my head so I wasn't facedown in the grass. Neither one of us had ever thought to go to school for any part of Blossom Day. "What," I inquired, "do you mean?" I'd forgotten all about Brianna. He was gathering up our things without saying a word, and then he unrolled my part of the blanket. Even as he worked to clear the campsite I couldn't believe what he was doing. Next he was walking away with the basket and the bundle in his arms. When he was far down the path, when he was almost home I was still sitting there asking *What?*

15.

The Historical Beginning of the Infinite World

So, one minute we were children in the orchard, and the next it was decided by someone, somehow, that William and I were too old to share a room. We were eleven and twelve. I couldn't believe it, the bunk beds ripped apart, the steel web that held his mattress no longer my nighttime ceiling, my sky. He swept up everything he loved in our room, all the Lego embedded in the carpet, every tangled wire, every connector and specialized wrench, all his comics, his books, his long tube socks, his two plastic banks heavy with quarters, and he moved down the hall to my mother's office. I stood by the bed, holding on to the post after the top bunk was removed, feeling as if the injury to the furniture had been done to me, as if something of myself had been lopped off. He wouldn't look in my direction as he packed up his possessions, the Tintin compendium stacked on top of *The Complete HyperCard Handbook*.

"Don't go," I managed on his last load.

He was standing in the door with a laundry basket filled with fat white pipes, a dismantled radio, and a samovar-type thing he'd taught me was a carburetor. "You can spread out," he suggested, nodding his head at my doll junk and dozens of pulpy books about the babysitters.

"Don't—" I tried again.

"Francie, don't be silly." My mother swooping in, offering up her idea of comfort. "He's just down the hall. He's ten steps away."

"Don't go," I said once more.

"He needs more space"—the twentieth time for the explanation. "And you do, too."

"I don't. I have plenty."

William turned the basket lengthwise to get it through the door, and out of the room he went.

That night it was impossible to even close my eyes with so much light, so much air above me. I had curled up by William's bed in his new room but my mother had flapped me away, the arms of her black sweater like wings. "Good night, William, good night!" I called through those wings. "Good night," I cried, "good night."

"Okay, Imp," he had to say, "good night."

There was nothing to be done about the situation but wait until the house was still and take those ten steps back down the hall, pillow and blanket in hand.

His arm was draped over the side of the bed, William now so close to the floor, his knuckles in the pile of the rug. I was still wearing zip-up fuzzy one-piece pajamas all the long way down to the enormous plastic feet, mine in red, William's, before he'd forsaken them, in blue. Already the room smelled of him, of us, I couldn't tell which part of our smell he'd taken with him. It seemed important to let him know that I would never ever leave him, and also that I was fine, I was near, a pull of his toe before I covered his bare leg. He did lift his head, his lids fluttering, his eyes open for an instant. I lay myself down in the corner of the hard floor, the smallest bare place between the shelf and the desk, no crib for my head. But it was all right now because his breathing, his adenoidal inhalations, that syncopated stuffiness, was my breathing, too, and mine his. And so we could safely sleep.

Did I not know, had I not been able to see that the separation, the long slow pull, had begun years before there was fuzz on his upper lip? What a stealth maneuver he had to make, that perhaps he was making deliberately, his quietness and his absorption in his projects a step-by-step, a careful tiptoe, past me. It was our first computer, a Macintosh—funny, the name of an apple—that started the marching of time.

Nineteen ninety: The computer arrived in a white carton, the cardboard itself shiny, polished, and there on the side the logo that should have been ours, the psychedelic apple with the smooth bite out of it, and the single leaf on top. It was my mother's outrageous gift to my father, something he didn't think they could afford. He was trying to refuse it, attempting to carry it back into the hall from the kitchen, but William was obstructing his path, arms flailing, legs doing a jig, crying, "P-p-please Papa. P-please. Maps and charts—charts!" He yanked on my father's hand, wouldn't let go. "You'll see, graphs, you like graphs, and charts and maps. You have to—you can do maps, you can map every tree, you can—" He put his finger in his mouth, bit down, the dream so near. William, five years old, having witnessed the automation of the library card catalog, was the prophet.

My father said, "William! It's all right."

"No, no, maps and charts!"

How to explain that my father could track weather patterns, he could invent weather patterns, he could organize the family archives, he could get rid of the ledger book, he could use email, a recent household invention, he could precisely record the spray program—how to make all of that clear before it was too late?

My father said, "It doesn't seem fair, Nellie, if we have a computer, and Sherwood doesn't."

"He can hallucinate one," my mother replied. "He can build a system from a bushel basket and a piece of copper tubing."

My father said, "This isn't something we really can—"

"Please!" William screeched. Never in his life had he needed anything so urgently.

They carefully unwrapped it together, the decision not yet firmly made, or so my father thought. They plugged it in. William took the chair in front of the small square screen, the 512K whirring like a knife sharpener. In the glow of the soft gray light he clicked on the mouse, and down, down he fell into the infinite world.

He had Adam as his forever friend, just as Amanda was for me, and in addition there was Bert Plumly, who lived in the subdivision beyond the south end of the woods. The Plumly house may have seemed the perfect idea of a house to William, two stories with white siding, blue shutters with cutout hearts, and window boxes, and in the back sliding glass doors out to the deck. And on that deck there was a hot tub, a gas grill as long as our canoe, and an iron table with a white-and-red-striped umbrella, the Plumlys at the ready for relaxation. In the kitchen Ma Plumly served Pac-Man mac and cheese in blue plastic bowls and for a treat Dr Pepper in frosted green glasses with pink bendy straws, and for dessert she put the gluey Rice Krispie squares on holiday napkins. Also there were carrot sticks.

The rooms in that paradise opened up, one to the next, the carpet starting in the family room right where the faux-oak flooring of the kitchen stopped, the fans overhead keeping the cool air moving across the different areas that were empty except for the sofas, the chairs. When the Plumlys got tired of outdoor recreation they could enjoy the offerings of their satellite dish, the screens of their many televisions growing larger by the year, like children, until the one in the living room was nearly the length of the far wall. The poor Lombards had the single old TV that got two channels, Mary Frances and William dependent on the kindness of the neighbors. Despite the Plumly riches aboveground, the boys chose the bunker, everything important, as it turned out, taking place down the basement. That was where they lived, where, hour after hour, they sat at the long counter with the two computers, one for Bert and one for his older brother, Max. When William went to the Plumlys for an overnight he took his own terminal, his hard drives, a bag of cables, boxes of disks, and his office chair.

Ma Plumly, passing through the dark cavity in those early days of the Gaming Epoch, on her way to the laundry room, would occasionally suggest an alternative activity. "A game of basketball?" she'd say with little conviction. "Dad fixed the hoop." As if all that stood between the boys and exercise was a repair of the court. "It's a nice day out there." They'd look up at her with an expression so blank she felt compelled to remind them of her identity. "It's your mother speaking. Melissa R. Plumly. Did you want to have a little lunch?"

"In...a...minute," one of them might say. Hours later, finally registering hunger, the three of them, William, Bert, Max, pounded up the stairs. I was occasionally in the family room amusing Crystal Plumly, a girl three years my junior, she and I playing Pretty Pretty Princess and watching *Oprah*. The boys sat at the island, waiting for Ma Plumly to produce the blue bowls. While she busied herself they tracked the robotic vacuum cleaner spinning through the living area, the disk bumping into the wall, the red light blinking, the boys narrating in Gregorian tones, "I meant to do that, I am not an idiot, who put this frigging table leg here."

At the library Ma Plumly said to my mother, "At least the boys aren't into drugs."

"Or women," my mother said.

Their faces, those boys, were puffy, and they wore heavy canvas pants several sizes too big, the bottoms frayed from dragging along the ground, their black T-shirts with a human-type man on the front but no irises in the eyes.

There was the seminal night when William, twelve or so, went to Bert's house, my father shuttling him over there with all the usual requirements in the back of the van, including his new chair, an ergonomic wonder he'd gotten for his birthday. Max had acquired a game called *Posse* through a quasi-legal file share, a new game that he handed off to Bert and William, the two of them playing until eight in the morning, tipping over to sleep on the nubbly carpet for forty-five minutes and waking to continue. They knew their lives were forever changed, the thing that would mark them arrived.

In order to develop their skills they had to play *Posse* starting in the late afternoon and going through the night, William abruptly nocturnal. They were soon recruited by a kid in Iceland to be on his most excellent team and not long after— so dedicated and talented were they—positions of responsibility were conferred upon them. They were in the lineup to be *Posse* Executives, to someday be the CEOs of their own teams, hiring players, assessing their gifts, firing them if necessary. What, really, Ma Plumly said, could be a better education?

Through July and August she as usual went down the basement, laundry basket in hand, walking slowly past the bank of computers to see if anything had changed. Always the virtual missiles were sighted on metal-plated hulks looming in the bleak distance, each live boy wearing a headset, speaking in a new language to similarly afflicted boys out in the ether.

"It's a nice day," Ma Plumly said in her vain attempt. She'd bring them liquids. She made cupcakes in pastel fluted papers. "You do need fuel," she'd remind them. When she spilled some milk she used one of their *Posse* swear-words, shouting theatrically, "Shazbot!" She sprang on the puddle with a dish-cloth, "Gotta go fast"—another of their memes. When I said *Shazbot* at the dinner table William looked up from his hamburger and told me, "You did not just say that." I was not even allowed to speak his language.

In those months I most often played with Amanda, Gloria

sometimes taking us to swim in a nearby lake, Gloria also making do without William. She had returned to us in June, right away taking up her Gloria things, gardening and knitting and working and talking about apples so that we soon forgot she'd ever had to go to Colorado. At the end of summer, William did without question come with us when we went to The Hills, we called it, the annual outing of the Lombards, the spree that took place in the briefest pause between the early apples and the beginning of the Macintosh harvest. Amanda and Adam, Frankie and William got in the back of the Ford pickup, Sherwood and my father in the dented cab, and over the path through the woods we shrieked when we bounced, and otherwise Amanda and I sang, bursting our lungs, William and Adam shouting at nothing, at the world passing. The loggers from the Forest Management Program had made a road right through to The Hills, which abutted our land and was owned by a gravel company, the mining far off in the future. Each grassy hill had been formed by the glacier in the last Ice Age, during the Pleistocene, Sherwood explained, the scooped-out valley a natural amphitheater.

Dolly and my mother met us at the highest peak, The Top Of The Earth, with the picnic baskets. Before lunch Sherwood produced his best invention: waxed cardboard boxes pulled apart with a little curl on the end, that was it, the sleds so simple. He always went down the hill a few times in order to pave the way, so that by our turn the trip to the bottom, with a great push, was as slick as a luge run, we were sure of it, holding tight to the lip of our cardboards, screaming our joyful fright. Sherwood and my father went down, too, behaving just as they must have when they were cousins together, when

they were the boys of summer. In those hours it was as if the
Lombard partnership had not yet occurred. My mother and
Dolly watched from under the lone burr oak at The Top Of
The Earth, Dolly relaying the antics of her siblings, twelve of
them, never a dull moment in the Muellenbach clan. Nellie lay
on her side with her elbow crooked to support her head and
laughed and laughed.

I was at the bottom of the hill, tumbling off my cardboard,
looking up at the mothers when it struck me that they never
went to war. We all knew that it was fine for the fathers to
blow up, we expected their biannual arguments, but the mothers of course would never speak harshly to one another, never
show their true colors. In our kitchen Nellie Lombard might
say fond, somewhat disparaging things about Dolly, or make
jokes about her endless talking, but Dolly would never know
about my mother's unkindness. I sat down at the bottom of the
hill with those thoughts that seemed pleasant, the idea of the
mothers all of a sudden baring their fangs and shouting. Such
a scene could be enjoyable and not at all frightening because I
knew it would never happen. When I climbed back up the hill
they were naturally still laughing.

That summer we were coming home along the path in the
woods when who should we see but Gloria and a friend she'd
made from her knitting club, two women in wide-brimmed
straw hats, both in long-sleeved shirts and loose trousers. They
looked like old-fashioned ladies, women who might find just
the place to set up their easels to glorify the scene. When we
stopped for them it was Gloria who told us the news. "The
princess," she said, "has been in a terrible, terrible car accident."

"Princess Diana," the friend clarified.

We hung over the side of the truck while Gloria told the story of the princess and her boyfriend tearing around Paris, how the princess had left her children and her country to take her own vacation with the foreigner. We all rode quietly after that, a princess who might die, Gloria so shaken she could not say more after the critical details. When we got back to the farm we learned that May Hill had gotten the tractor stuck in the thick mud by the goat shed, May Hill, who never made mistakes, and not only that, the sheep had found an opening in the fence, the entire flock not ambling but galloping up into the east orchard, lambs and mothers, heading into the great wide open. We couldn't leave the farm for even three hours without the tractor getting stuck, the sheep escaping their yard, and a princess suffering an accident.

It was the next spring when my mother took Bert and William to a hotel outside Washington, DC, for the First Annual *Posse* Convention. The boys were unbearably excited to meet the actual players on their teams, which meant they said less than usual in our company, the two of them scraping along the driveway from the bus in their gangbanger pants, bottled up with their great secret life and times.

My father and I thought about them somewhat at first while they were away in Washington but after no more than an hour had passed we became unexpectedly happy on our own. Over the four days we got the garden planted and we did twenty loads of manure, cleaning the lower barn, the sheep dung compacted into sheaves so that instead of digging at them it was an archaeological matter of peeling away the layers with the fork. We bleached the area to cleanse the place of parasites, and afterward we stood in the doorway admiring our work. We hardly had to speak to understand each other.

In the evenings we leaned against the sink and for dinner had menus such as chocolate malts and saltines with melted cheese. No big production necessary.

Back during the four–five split I sometimes used to imagine my mother not dead exactly but removed, so that Mrs. Kraselnik could adopt me. During the *Posse* Convention I recalled the pleasure of my mother being gone, the idea of it. I wasn't wife of course to my father but I didn't feel like daughter, either. He asked me questions as if he valued my expertise, as if all along on a different track I'd always been his partner, and only now had surfaced in this old but new dimension. "Where should we spread this load, Marlene?" he'd ask me as he was heading off to fertilize a field or part of the orchard. At the sink he'd say, "What varieties do you think we should graft this spring? What should we have more of? What do you like best?"

We did now and again bring up the convention, nine hundred boys in the hotel ballroom, boys and their pizzas, boys electrified by Mountain Dew. My father said, "No more hip bone connected to the hip bone in the electronic age. No more thighbone connected to the thighbone. Homo sapiens, good-bye. A new race is coming." He trolled around in his glass for the last dregs of his malt. "The ennobling future, I guess."

We thought of my mother in the hotel on her king-size bed, lying around reading, maybe ordering room service, the only Lombard who didn't work on the farm. I said to my father, "If Mama was a *Posse* player what would her name be?"

"Savage Librarian," he said without having to think.

We had to hold our stomachs to laugh. Next we sat at the table and talked about all the work we would get done the next day, on Sunday, and we reviewed the good works we'd done that day, too. We talked until the candle burned down. It was as if talking at the table and sleeping were one and the same, and by and by we climbed the stairs trailing words and went to bed.

16.

A Possible Marriage Match

Another spring turning to summer, my seventh-grade year over and done, my friend Coral LeClaire bleeding, I knew, even though she hadn't told me. I'd seen the telltale sign, the supplies in her backpack. Also, she had breasts that appeared to be getting more enormous by the second. My mother seemed to think I was not going to need pads for some time or even a serious brassiere, that I was going to be a slow bloomer.

Already at age thirteen, though, I had plenty of accomplishments, the walls of my room completely covered with ribbons from the fair, blue ribbons for my cat drawings, my grapevine wreaths, my hand-spun, hand-knitted scarves, and my zucchinis. Certainly that summer there would be more prizes. In addition to preparing for the fair I would work as always with my father. And just as he sometimes watched a ball game there would now and again be a small holiday for me, a little rest,

Mary Frances briefly parking in the hammock, the mosquitoes at bay, the butterflies fluttering in their warped flight patterns, the sound of the tractor in the distance, the mower going in the orchard, all the labor happening around me while I read lowbrow historical novels, books my mother said were trash, books she wanted to yank from my hands and incinerate.

Soon after our vacation began I went along with my father to visit the neighboring orchard, ten miles away, the Sykes Orchard our main competition. William no longer came with us on our jaunts, the job of keeping my father now falling solely on my shoulders. "Well, Marlene," he said, "it looks like a nice day for a drive to the great Sykes plantation." He meant it was a good day to point out to each other which fields were wheat, which rye, to admire the growing corn, and at one intersection there was always a tired old Appaloosa standing still in her yard, Our Friend The Horse, we called her. Our Friend The Horse now and again used to show up in my father's stories, in the tales of Kind Old Badger. It was on that drive to the Sykes Orchard that I realized I couldn't remember when the last one had been told, or if we'd known it was the last as it was happening. Or even what the story was, if there'd been a conclusion. I wanted to ask my father about Kind Old but I couldn't; I couldn't think what the real question was, and also I had the feeling whatever the question he wouldn't be able to answer it.

Tommy Sykes's estate was a showcase farm, tulips blooming, lawns tended, the houses and buildings in good repair, every apple tree wide open, kept short and flat-topped by a crew of itinerant Hispanic men. "Those trees are hideous," I said at the entrance, "like poor dogs who've been shaved."

"He gets a good yield," was all my father said.

There was a patch beyond the white barn where Tommy kept a few useless things, but first off, it was a small area, and second, the junk was lined up in a shipshape row. He had retired from being a financier and taken up farming, plowing his fortune into shiny new machinery and planting fashionable varieties and always looking for the next sensation. He looked like an executive on vacation, a man who wore fleece sweatshirts to farm, a chiseled, gray-haired playboy in loafers with no socks. Because he'd been sitting at a desk all his life and keeping fit on a treadmill he now had energy to burn, a horse crashing out of the gate.

There was a house up a tree for the customers' children. Even though I was too old for a playhouse I climbed the rope ladder while Tommy and my father talked their business. The house had a bright-red metal roof and yellow shutters, and inside a blue wooden telephone that had stacking parts, a baby toy. What did we have at our orchard for the children? A flock of sheep. Also we kept four goats plus Roger, the neutered billy with tremendous curly horns. Goats and lambs greeted the shoppers, dutifully eating apples from any outstretched hand.

Maybe, I considered, a visiting child to the Sykes farm on the busiest selling day would fall out the playhouse window, land on her head, and be paralyzed for life. But then for probably about the fiftieth time since the four–five split I remembered what Mrs. Kraselnik had said about putting good in the world. Still, I didn't care, I didn't—and anyway where had following her instructions gotten me besides losing the Geography Bee? And what's more, such a wicked wish could not be helped when it came to Tommy.

After my father had talked to the big Mister for what seemed like a full hour we walked through the bright clean selling area, past the sorting shed where the ladies in season wore clear plastic shower caps and gloves to grade the fruit, as if they were in surgery, past the cider room with the gleaming press from Holland, a press that was so mechanized all Tommy probably had to do to make cider was remotely press a button. We toured the storage shed where he kept every supply imaginable on freshly made pallets. The room smelled of that new wood. There were decorated paper peck bags with smiley faces within the apple logo, and bushel baskets yellow as butterscotch with bloodred rims, and towers of plastic containers for their famous pies, and the great tall bags filled with cider jugs, tightly packed in rows, Tommy Sykes a captain of industry.

He used controlled atmosphere, a regulated room with precise amounts of oxygen, carbon dioxide, and nitrogen, to keep the apples firm, and he was also experimenting with a new technology involving 1-methylcyclopropene, a colorless gas that naturally slowed ripening and aging, Tommy always on the cutting age, Tommy with endless capital to invest in his operation. And no Sherwood to dog his steps and blow up at him. He showed us the chambers for each, my father exclaiming, my father reduced to saying "Ahhh," and "Tommy, this is amazing." Although it was summer, Tommy had saved a certain amount of last year's crop for a lucrative taffy apple account, Tommy supplying a high-end candy store in Milwaukee. And so on the way back to our car he offered me one of those lollipops, straight from the assembly line in their commercial kitchen.

"What kind of apple?" I asked.

"The little connoisseur!" He laughed. "More interested in the apple than in the thick shell of gooey caramel? Thick and soft right now—I'm telling you." He was all melodious-like, taunting. "And studded with peanuts." When I didn't respond he said, "The apples are Honey Crisp."

The Honey Crisp had just come on the scene, a variety my father had brought home from a conference in the last year to try. I knew that a Sykes Honey Crisp would be fracturey hard but have no flavor, knew for a fact that Tommy had no idea when varieties were ripe and should be picked. But even under the best of circumstances the showy Honey Crisp was without character, a fruit only a philistine would grow.

"No, thank you," I said.

"You don't like Honey Crisp?" Tommy said. "That what you're telling me, young lady?"

"I prefer the heirloom varieties."

"I see! I see!" He tried not to laugh some more.

I didn't care that I sounded prissy. Tommy Sykes thought an apple with no real distinction was going to make his fortune— so let him.

The men walked on amiably and shook hands heartily at our car. As if I were a small child my father had to remind me to say good-bye to Tommy. "Bye," I obeyed, and climbed into the car.

After some time on the ride home he said, "You're quiet to-day, Marlene."

It was disturbing, how often May Hill came into my head. Just then I'd been thinking how the one thing Tommy didn't have was a May Hill. Even if I'd always forevermore be scared to death of her, even as I carried the Thing That Had Happened Years Ago as if it were a black stone around my neck, still I knew to be grateful for her machinery expertise. I said to my father, "What do you think would happen if a robber got up into May Hill's house?"

My father never laughed at my questions. He said, "Well, let's see. First, tell me—how would the robber get in?"

"Say he knew everyone was out working, and he slipped in to steal the money. Or—maybe just to look around."

"A robber in daylight?"

"Yes. So May Hill wouldn't have put the chair by the basement door."

"Ah," my father said.

"The robber," I went on, "would start looking at—at everything but then, then, he'd realize that she was climbing up the stairs." My heart was beating hard as I told this fictional although nearly true-life tale.

"May Hill coming upon a thief," my father considered.

"What would she do?"

"I wouldn't want to be the robber. Would you?"

"No," I whispered. My voice was failing me. "Would she—would she knock him out? Would she injure him or—?"

"Hmmm," he said. We were at a stop sign. He turned to look at me. I think it's fair to say that if I had ever been in doubt that he loved me, which I hadn't, but if I had, I would have known then that in fact he loved me maybe better than anyone. He didn't drive on. We were at a standstill. He was smiling at me, a small, lopsided smile, and yet it was with his whole self. All the love in the world—it was in our car. "I imagine," he said, "I bet she'd lock him up. The robber. Some of those doors have locks, as I recall. That would be punishment, don't you guess, to be held just for a while, and to wonder how May Hill would deal with you?"

I nodded. I couldn't look at him.

"Plenty of punishment," he said, before he drove on down the road, saying he thought the Honey Crisp was probably a better apple than we had given it credit for.

I muttered, "Okay."

"Give it a chance, Marlene," he instructed.

Later in the summer I went with my father to a new farmers market that had been launched in a town six miles away. It was in addition to Sherwood's market in Milwaukee and the market my father went to in Madison where, along with a crew of five others, we frantically did commerce from first light until noon. This new market, however, was for my father and it was for me.

I was happy for just about the entire vacation because Amanda went to three different band camps and I didn't have to consider not playing with her, and also Coral was at horse camp and then at her family lake house in Michigan. It seemed that I had grown up enough not to need those girlhood companions, grown up enough to have consuming interests and obligations, even. I wasn't at all the slightest bit lonely. Ten hours a week I worked at the library, a real paying job cleaning DVDs and doing the precision job of shelving. I didn't get money for my orchard work, which was fine because I knew that when Sherwood had been a boy he hadn't gotten paid, either. If you belonged to the work there was no reason to get money from it.

Best of all, every Friday, on our market day, my father and I loaded up the van with apple boxes, a basket of knitting worsted, the honeycomb display, the scale, the bundle of bags, the white tent, the cottage cheese container of change, and my carefully printed signs. Along the barricaded street opposite City Hall we made a line of stalls: the Lombard apple girl and man, the bread lady, the cheese lady, the sweet corn man, the plant people, the garlic and onion couple, the popcorn matron, the duck egg woman, the beef and pork guy, and at the opposite end, another apple vender, the Sykes Orchard representative. Tommy sent an employee to work the market who had the title *Sykes Orchard Manager*. He was twenty-three years old and his name was Gideon.

Like every other facet of the Sykes operation the hiring of Gideon, a dedicated, strong young person, was a genius business move by the gentleman farmer. Gideon, which means "Feller of Trees." He had studied ag science for two years at the university before he'd dropped out to live his dream. In addition to his other gifts he was disciplined about waking at dawn, he was unsentimental about nature, and he knew chemistry. As much as Tommy's grown children may have wanted to keep the farm in the family they had no interest in running it or even in living nearby. The understanding was that Gideon would make a life on the orchard, that he would not own the property but when Tommy eventually retired he would be the person in charge.

In July, at our first market, I wandered down to Gideon's stand. I stood looking at his red blushy apples, varieties that were bigger than ours and shinier. "Did you spray for maggot flies this week?" I asked him.

He looked startled, I suppose because most people didn't begin a conversation or an acquaintance with that question.

"Yep," he said, "and for codling moth."

"We did, too," I said importantly. I said, "We're trying that new disruption technology, the CM Flex."

Maybe he laughed; it's possible he was chuckling. "Good stuff." He nodded. "It's pretty effective."

"I know it."

Gideon was undeniably cute even though he was old, a man hardly taller than William, a pixie with soft-looking brown hair and pale-blue eyes. All at once I was aware of my knobby knees, my skinny legs, my shorts, my plain yellow T-shirt, my drab hair, my ragged fingernails. I had occasionally wondered what it would be like to kiss a boy and even though he was old, as I said, you couldn't ignore Gideon's upper lip, which had a freckle smack in the center, right below the philtrum. The other thing in addition to kissing, the thing I'd learned that was very different from the business of the ram and ewe, the tomcat and pussycat, the thing that President Bill Clinton and his intern had taught us—I had blocked that from my mind. Kissing Gideon's freckle, the idea of it, made me feel sick enough. He was about to say something else to me when a woman butted in on us, blaring her righteous question: "ARE YOU ORGANIC?"

My new acquaintance began to explain the Sykes Orchard spray program, the Integrated Pest Management, a system designed to keep chemical applications to a minimum, the farmer spraying in relation to the pests' life cycles. We used IPM, too, and like Tommy were in close contact with the university entomologists, running trials for research, trying to wean ourselves away from pesticides where possible. I had been at market before when those mothers assaulted us. *The Crones Against Cluster Cancers.* That's what William called them. They were women who never wanted to know the hard science of your practice. They weren't interested in parts per billion or the rate of breakdown or the lab results of residue, statistics that, if they'd just listen, would lower their blood pressure and maybe make them reasonable. Those mothers only wished us to know that we were the individuals poisoning their children and Gaia.

I said two things in front of Gideon just then. I said to the lady, "Do you like biting into a worm when you eat an apple?"

"I beg your pardon," she said to me.

To the pork and beef guy right next door I asked, "How do your animals fare after their surgeries?" Really, that's the kind of inane question those women were likely to ask.

Gideon stopped talking. His pale eyes seemed to spin. He said to the mother, "You should check out the Lombard Orchard. I think you'll like their program and their apples better."

The woman walked away. Gideon burst out laughing. He said, "When you're older do you think you might consider marrying me?" He laughed again. "You are hysterical."

His question made me run as fast as I possibly could back to our own stand. I got in the van that was parked by our stall and locked the doors. My first proposal of marriage, my very first proposal—Gideon, I thought, had maybe, in a certain way, meant it. Which made me feel dizzy and warm and pleased and distressed all at once—that freckle on his lip, for one thing.

What did it take to fall in love? That was a ridiculous question to have to ask when I'd seen Gloria topple over and when I myself had been in love with Mrs. Kraselnik. That is to say, you didn't ask for it, you didn't plan, but the spell was cast upon you anyway. Abracadabra: swoon.

Or maybe Gideon Hup and Mary Frances Lombard would have an arranged marriage, our union on the order of the House of Hanover and the Stewarts commingling. My father thought very highly of Gideon. And if William was too dreamy to farm, if he was going to be a *Posse* player for the rest of his life, then I'd have to make do with Gideon. We at the Lombard Orchard would steal Tommy Sykes's manager, Tommy's hope, steal him away in a blaze of duty to our enterprise, Gideon and me, with our expertise and enthusiasm impressing Sherwood and even May Hill. William would realize too late that what he'd wanted after all wasn't for the having.

And anyway if you were Gideon, would you rather have a perfected operation to rule, one that you would never own? Or would you rather, by marriage, possess the property, a place that, yes, was a little bit of a catastrophe, but a place that was crying out for your organizational skills and your brawn, a place where the institutional knowledge meant the apples were truly delicious? Of course he would choose the Lombard Orchard, saying *I do* to Mary Frances and her entire family.

So in that period I supposed, one way or another, that my future was fairly secure. I always avoided Gideon at the market but I considered him slantwise; in the abstract and from a distance he was my betrothed. In my own room at night all alone I'd think haughtily to William, *Gideon and I will do thus and such*, outlining all the orchard improvements we would make. I did that even though in my mind Gideon was like an Amish doll with no face. Still, I was the only middle schooler that I knew of who had a firm proposal of marriage, no small accomplishment.

LATE

17.

In Which We Play Euchre

Many events, some that were logical, and some that were not, took place in the next few years. In my school career I was in several plays and was for a time in love with Mr. Dronzek, the lord of drama who taught at both the middle and high schools. Mrs. Kraselnik remained the best teacher I was sure I'd ever have but she was not long for our particular world. She and the doctor got divorced when I was in seventh grade and they both moved away from the dream house. Brianna probably was responsible for all their unhappiness, but as with so many things, that was my secret. My father continued serving on the commission to study farmland preservation. Sherwood built an apple sorter that for the most part worked, a machine that incorporated Adam's and Amanda's baby blankets as cushioning for the fruit. At the library Nellie Lombard as always coerced young people to read quality literature and charmed babies to a stupor with lap-sit story time. We outgrew Cart Drill and without us it fizzled. Once William got to high school he scored many awards, including a cash prize for his robot up in Madison. No one told him he shouldn't win.

It was after the four–five split that Amanda and I had stopped spending so much time together, depending on each other only when no one else was available. After the Geography Bee I had briefly assumed that our association was over but when she lost at the county level we were equal in our way again. There was no feud that divided us, no concrete before and after. It was funnily enough geography that changed our habits. Once I was in sixth grade we were in different buildings, the universe of the middle school a block away from the elementary school. Also, she had become interested in chess and Russia, her goal to be a diplomat and grandmaster stationed in Moscow. Whereas Coral and I, and our friend Jay, were busy writing plays together and learning lines for Mr. Dronzek's productions, and going to vintage clothing shops in the city with Mrs. LeClaire, Coral's mother. Because Coral had a tremendous singing voice and often spoke in a British accent, because of her general theatricality, my father referred to her as Sarah Bernhardt. To her face he'd say "How are you, Say-rah?" and "Have a good show, Say-rah," which she pretended to be outraged by, calling my father Slim. "'Ey, Slim," she'd say in her Cockney accent. It was extremely hard to stomach, their cornball. My mother sometimes called him Slim, too, which also was not terribly funny.

Although I was interested in the theater, at the end of eighth grade, in that summer, it was against my will that I went to drama camp. My mother forced me to do so, my mother start-ing The Four Rivers Camp Warfare.

The battle started in the spring, a few months before camp, on the day the yearlings went to slaughter. I was fourteen, William fifteen. The lambs had just been shorn, their sturdy musculature plain to see, and without the wool on their faces their watchful brown eyes were nakedly soulful, philosophers, you might think, all of them. Or anyway they were filled with life even though we knew they were terrifically brainless. Wil-liam and I got up early on that April morning to help with the loading. When my father appeared in the lower yard with the grain bucket some of them did their twisting and popping jumps, joy—you could not call their feeling anything less than joy. It was still dark, which made the whole scene even worse. For as many times as we'd been through this exercise, as hard-ened as our hearts should have been, we were downcast. In the upper yard The Old Sheep came to the fence to pay her re-spects, her wool ragged over her sharp hips, her knees bald, her baaing guttural, a useless warning. There was always one in her position, a ewe in her last spring.

My father carefully spread some grain in the feeder, making sure to leave spaces between the portions so the lambs wouldn't crowd as much as usual, so they could be peaceful during their final meal. When they were finished he walked backward, tapping the bucket, toward the pen we'd made for them, a hemmed-in space that went right up to the back of the truck. We hoped we could get them up the ramp, get them loaded without any of them spooking, the whole mob then stam-peding over each other, trampling the weaker stock to death. That's how dim-witted they were.

Because they trusted my father and because William and I were at their heels they followed him, thinking, *More of our favorite and most delicious Sheep Formula? And so early in the morning? Honestly? You're going to give us more?* When the last was inside the vault of the truck I brought down the door. The clang, and another bell tolling with the latch. No childish plea for mercy, no spider weaving words into a web, no last-minute stay of execution. "I'm sorry," I whispered. "So long, Dandelion," I said, the runt I'd bottle-fed. At the slaughterhouse no one would care anything for them, already pieces of meat while still living. They would wait jammed together in a low tight room and be yanked one by one to the death slab.

My father crawled from the back through a small opening into the cab. It was cold but even so he unrolled the window. He raised one hand, the farewell. We waited by the gate while he adjusted the mirror. When he was ready he turned the key in the ignition and with the beeping that signaled "reverse," those solemn notes, the truck moved slowly out of the yard.

We were still thinking of the lambs, still downcast after dinner. It was my mother who suggested we play Euchre, the ideal game for us, four persons, a game that requires some concentration and strategy but allows for sociability. This would cheer us up, she'd decided.

At the table William and I as usual insisted on being partners. There was no other way to match ourselves up even though we, as a team, made the game laughably uneven. The truth was my father became spacey over cards. We played

Euchre several times a year and he couldn't ever remember the rules. Each time we had to explain all the details again, what trump meant, what the left bower was, the right bower, who started when, how you kept track of points. My mother, however, in her own way was worse. She more or less remembered the basics but she was like an idiot savant, not knowing what was going on at a fundamental level, and yet sometimes not only managing to do the correct thing, but blowing us out of the water. William and I, therefore, could not have either one of them as partners, neither the oldster nor the wild card.

We sat diagonally from our partners at the kitchen table, William dealing in his suave high school style, a flicking of the wrist, throwing out the cards two and three at a time.

"Wait," my father said, "how many should I have?"

"You have five," William explained.

"Is that the right number?"

"Yes. Yes it is."

"Five? It doesn't seem like enough."

"Papa!" I cried. "We each get five cards."

"Five," he repeated.

"Good Christ," William muttered.

My mother didn't even scold him. It went to me to make the pronouncement, to order up the suit. I said, "Trump is diamonds." William reiterated, "So, diamonds is trump."

Exactly half a second later my father said, "What's trump again?"

"Diamonds," my mother said. She laid down the first card, an audacious play.

"Whoa, tiger," William said. "Good move."

"Thank you."

"What'd you just do?" my father said.

"Papa!" I cried again. William blazed at me. I telegraphed to him, *He's deranged! And Mama is, too. She is even more. You wait.*

When she put her card down two tricks later William said, "You know that's trump, right?"

"Oh!" she giggled. "I forgot."

I snorted and did the glance at William, *See?* To forget that the left bower is still trump after playing for decades really is mental retardation.

"I always forget that," my father said.

"You should not admit it," I instructed.

"What is wrong with you people?" William couldn't help asking.

My mother glared at her cards. "We're just old," my father explained. "That's all."

"Well, snap out of it." Softening, William added, "Do you want me to review the rules again?"

"I think we've got it."

We paused between rounds for the making of cocoa, the milk simmering, the woman of the house busying herself at the stove. She said, with her back to me, "I was talking to Coral at the library today about the drama camp Mr. Dronzek has been recommending. Up in Hayward."

What was she doing talking to Coral? "I'm not going to camp," I said.

She came to the table with a tray. "Why not?"

"Because."

"May I inquire because why?"

"Because I love summer at home. Because I want to do the

market with Papa. Because I don't want to miss hay making and apple picking. And because, for your information, I'm helpful and useful and maybe, just maybe I'm indispensable."

"No one is indispensable," she said, on her high horse. She set out our mugs and sat herself down. "Except May Hill. I'll give her that."

William was dealing.

"I like this," my father said, looking at his hand.

"It's four weeks," my mother continuing her campaign.

"Good for it," I said. I tried to appeal to my father. "You need me, Papa."

"I always miss you when you're not here," he said somewhat absently. "But you should have your adventures."

"I don't need adventures."

"You're a teenager," my mother observed. "What teenager wants to stay home with her parents? Honestly, Francie, sometimes I wonder if you are a freak of nature."

"Freak of nature?" I repeated.

"Nellie," my father said in his warning voice.

"Are you serious, Mother?"

"Forget it," she said, as if that was an apology or explanation. When she played her second card William said, "Hmmm. Why—why on earth would you do that?"

She hissed in his face. "Do you want to see my cards?"

"Easy, old girl, easy now." He'd been talking that way to her, when necessary, for about a year.

She slapped her hand down, destroying the round. "This is what I've been dealt. See? Do you see? Or are you just going to pronounce me a stupid idiot?"

"Or freak," I said. "Let's say you're a freak."

"Simmer down there, Old Betsy," William said to her. "Simmer down. It's all right."

"You did the only thing you could." My father supporting his wife.

It was as if my mother hadn't spoken to me in that way, as if her question, her wonderment about my freakishness, now existed only in my ear, everyone else excusing her.

When the dealer was again William, when he was shuffling the cards something untoward occurred. Possibly my mother had been hypnotized without our knowledge. Or she was having a stroke. Whatever the cause, she began to declaim on the most peculiar subject possible. "I remember," she said slowly, "when we lived with Aunt Florence in the manor house. And we were trying to have a baby."

"Oh, please," I said. We all knew that when my mother was very young and first married she'd lived with the ancient aunt and my father, who at that point was also old, sixteen years Nellie's senior; none of that was news.

"Florence," she went on, "used to come into the bathroom to wash her teeth, her dentures. Do you remember, Jim?"

"Let's play the game," he said.

She went on, "We were in the bedroom that connects to that bathroom, downstairs, you know, the room that's Sherwood and Dolly's now." She was studying her cards as she spoke. "It was so generous of such an old lady to allow me to live in her house with her nephew. Especially when she'd been living with you already for years, Jimmy, the two of you in your way like a married couple. So generous. I don't know what I can do here, with this hand. Anyway, I used to have the feeling—it's crazy, I admit it—but I used to think that the noise of her teeth in the glass, the clinking of those dentures as she brushed them next door, right by our headboard? Was the sound that sperm and egg make as they collide, as they become one."

William was squinting at her, as if she were difficult to see and hear. I had literally just about thrown up in my mouth. If my father was going to say one thing that made them laugh I was going to ax murder the both of them. Fortunately he looked nearly as disgusted as we felt. He'd even closed his eyes against her for a second. "It's getting late," he noted.

Nonetheless, we arranged our cards, trump was called, we began to take the tricks. It occurred to me, it hit me that Nellie Lombard, as grotesque as her little story was, had been speaking in a riddle, and that the riddle was for me. When it came my turn to deal I couldn't help it. I said, "Why did you bring that up?"

"Bring what up?" my father said.

"I'm talking to Nellie."

"What?" she said.

"Are you trying to say that our birth was the result of the immaculate conception? Teeth plus egg, the clinking becomes William? Is that it? The big reveal? *You were not adopted, kids, but there's something we need to tell you?*"

"Oh, I don't know," she said breezily. "I just remember feeling like I was having a baby by all the Lombards and for all the Lombards."

"Hearts," William called out, staring at me—*this isn't happening!* "Hearts is trump."

"I ... don't know ... what! You are doing," I said elocutionarily to my mother. I was going to remain at home all summer long to be the good, kind, strong daughter to my father, to be indispensable to him. I was going to do so even if I had been conceived to be a worker bee, a Lombard slave. I said, "I'm not going to Camp Four Rivers, in case you did not understand my earlier comment. I have no interest in the rustic cabins, the bonding, the stupid girls, the stupider boys, the competition for parts, and whatever else. I don't care if Coral is signed up. Get it through your head that I am not going to Hayward."

"It's not like Frankie needs drama camp," my brother pointed out.

My mother's jaw was wonderfully clenched, the muscles twitching near her ears. I had perhaps never been so satisfied by anyone else's suppressed rage, but then we Lombards, we freaks, were a tribe renowned for our decorum.

For the rest of the spring I did my best to maintain silence when in my mother's company. Furthermore, when she signed me up for camp without my approval or knowledge, when I found out, I also said nothing. I went through the house and slammed all the doors, making the tour four times. The violence to the structure was, I hoped, permanent. Coral was very excited about going, and maybe secretly I was a little bit interested, but I did nothing to pack, that chore left for Madame Librarian. On the seven-hour drive north I said absolutely nothing to my mother. I did not say good-bye to her or even look at her when the time came to part. During the course of the one-month session, I did not write as much as a line on a postcard, even though we were supposed to correspond with our parents. I lied about my output to the beautiful, amazing counselor Nona Nelson, whom I loved even more than I'd loved Mrs. Kraselnik, something I had not known was possible. When my mother came to pick us up I didn't say hello to her. I got in the car with Coral, and both of us cried all the way home, writing letters to our new friends and gazing at our jars of water that we'd collected from the lake.

When I got back I was further enraged to find that in my absence Philip had returned to the orchard, and that he was once again living upstairs with May Hill.

18.

Mail-Order Bride

Oh, by the way, Philip is spending the summer with us," my mother said as we were pulling in our driveway. That's how she told me. Before I could recover from the shock she said in a haughty way, "And in case you're interested, Gloria is moving on."

"Moving on?" I was able to say.

"Our Gloria, Francie, has found love." Her tone was softer and sad. "We need to be happy for her."

I got out of the car and slammed the door. I shouted, "Why didn't you tell me?"

My mother smiled without showing her teeth. "We were checking the obituaries daily from up north," she said. "Finally we called the camp to see if you were alive." What could I say to that? "When we found out you were doing very well it hardly seemed right to bother you with Gloria's news." She added, "It was a surprise to us, too."

In her spare time Gloria had taken the plunge, using the library computers, and signed herself up for a dating service. She didn't tell anyone about it until she'd snagged a mate. After sixteen years in the stone cottage she was moving to Cortez Island in Canada, to live with a man named Corey, a man she'd gone down to Chicago to meet, also unbeknownst to us. Gloria, who had been our fake mother and my father's stand-in wife, now was going to be like a mail-order bride before she became an old maid. Through the years, aside from her wipeout with Stephen Lombard, we were sure she'd loved my father better than anyone else and that she'd stay indefinitely to help him live and work. It turned out, however, that her loyalty wasn't as permanent as we'd imagined. She packed up the relics of our childhood, the miniature bread pans, the heart-shaped muffin tins, the spindle, her knitting mushrooms, the boxes of fabric scraps—our craft supplies—for her unborn children, as well as the bedding and toys for the two cats she'd kept from the time of Stephen.

It made me furious that not a single person had written about Gloria's departure, and that Gloria herself had not mentioned it in any of her postcards to me.

Two weeks after I'd returned from camp the cottage was empty and she was going, she was leaving. We stood by the car before she pulled away. "Thank you," my father said, holding her with both hands at her slender waist. "Gloria—oh, Gloria." His voice was gloggy because—were there? Yes, tears were running down his cheeks. Suddenly we wanted to cry, too. "Be well," he said to her. "Be well, dear, dear Gloria. Take care. Please take care." No one, we realized right then, would ever again send him a fifth-cloth note, never again the fifth-cloth surprise. "We love you," Nellie said, "so much," the two of them clasped tight. "How can we ever thank you? How can you know what you mean to us?"

Gloria covered her face and shook her head, which didn't exactly answer the questions. "William," she quavered, moving on to him. "You're amazing. You're practically grown up. You're practically on your way to college. Thank you," she said. "Thank you for being my friend." He submitted to her embrace, placing his own hands on her back. At my turn she held my cheeks and one last time bore down into whatever there was to see of my personality. "Mary Frances, my Mary Frances. You'll use your fierceness well, I know you will. Oh, my fierce Mary Frances."

I looked at William through the hug. Was I fierce? Was he her friend? Was he crying? I wasn't going to cry, I wasn't.

Gloria had been a pair of hands, a sturdy back, a loving presence, in exchange for ten dollars an hour and a house, the highest-paid Lombard employee in the history of the orchard. Just like that she could leave us. We stood on the cottage porch waving her off, sobs in our throats, our arms wild flags. "Good-bye! Good-bye!"

When she turned onto the road my mother wiped her eyes, there were great purging exhales, and she blew her nose. "Do you suppose," she managed, "do you think Stephen will feel free to come and visit now?"

My father was still waving even though Gloria was out of sight. He said, "Is there much to do to get the cottage ready for Philip?"

"What are you talking about?" I said.

"Philip's going to move in," he said, continuing to wave at nothing.

I turned to my mother because it was surely she who was responsible for that plan.

"He can't live with May Hill forever," she said.

That night I happened into William's room, the farewell comment of Gloria's pricking my mind, and also the word *forever* applied to Philip's living situation. William, Gloria had said, was practically in college. Assuming he got through the rest of high school, that is. I lay on his bed. He was at his desk, scrolling through the *Posse* Message Board. I said, "Do you really want to go?"

"Go where?"

"College."

"Uh-huh."

"But why?"

"Why?" When I didn't elaborate on the question he said, "Imp, we're going to college. You know that."

"What for?"

He broke away from his work, turning in his chair to look at me. "Frankie—"

I sat up. I asked him, "What do we need to know that we can't learn from Pa and Sherwood?"

His eyes, still dark brown as the river, widened.

"Who will pick the apples?" I said.

"Ah...the crew? It's not like we're out working night and day. There are, you know, Lombard Orchard employees."

"I always pick after school." This statement was somewhat although not completely true. William, though, hadn't worked much for a few years because of his cushy tech job at the bike factory. When he was in seventh grade they'd started him at

$12.50 an hour. They were lost, they said, without him. "I'm a fast picker," I told him. "Papa even says so."

"Uh-huh," he said again. "That's great." He started to spin slowly in his chair. "Think of it this way." He was taking tiny steps, a tap-dance circle on his plastic rug guard. "College is our *rumspringa*. Seeing the world so we can decide if we want to run the orchard. Or to get some education in case—"

"In case what?"

He swung around and stopped in front of me. "Sherwood and Pa can't—"

"Can't what?"

"You know how hard it is for them to make a decision, how they never talk to each other. How they don't plan."

"They can plan."

"I don't know. Ma says—"

He was talking to our mother about orchard affairs? "She says what?"

"I don't know," he said again. "She says the whole thing, the whole organization is maybe too complicated for—"

"Everyone," I said scornfully, "knows it's complicated."

He started to turn in his chair once more, propelled by those little tappy steps. "We should see what it's like to live in a place where people have gotten rid of their rotary phones. Join the twenty-first century."

I said, "We can get a new phone." He was in the nighttime of his slow spin, his back to me. "William?" I said his name as I used to, when I'd reverently asked any question of the boy who knew everything.

Instead of waiting for me to say more he started to spin very quickly, his feet sweeping the floor. Around and around he went. When I grabbed hold of his legs he and the chair jerked to a halt. "Stop spinning," I cried.

His face, which I knew better than my own, all at once seemed swollen and ugly, his eyes flaring, his mouth wide open. "I'm not stopping!" he yelled. "You hear me?" But he had stopped. He was at a complete standstill. "I'm not," he said more distinctly, "stopping." I might have pointed out to him that he was mistaken in both speech and action because in fact he was no longer spinning. But who would I have been talking to? I ran out of the room and slammed my own door shut and turned out the lights and got into bed, covering my head with the pillow.

19.

My Father Holds Back the Waters

No one, however, made me angrier than Philip. As if he had always been part of the farm, as if Gloria had never walked the earth, as if the universe existed to favor him, he took up the role of best right-hand man, the new star orchard worker. May Hill wasn't squiring him around anymore, Philip no longer strictly in the role of her houseboy. Sherwood talked to him and enlisted him in projects and so did my father, Philip on everyone's side. Which, admittedly, was not an easy position, being both a Velta and a Volta man. What else was supposedly good about him? He was strong. There was no doubt about that. He could throw bales and tackle a running sheep, and stack apple boxes, each one fifty pounds, eight-high in the cooler, one after the next, the top one over his head, unloading the whole wagon single-handedly. That was something my father could no longer accomplish—or anyway that's what he said to my mother. But I knew if Jim Lombard had to he could still lift whatever he wished in order to get a job done.

Generally speaking Philip was gung-ho. He acquired a pair of denim coveralls so he could look the part, Philip coming along the path wearing a red baseball cap that said on the front, in black letters, WICKED. Farming had been his dream from his earliest memory, he'd done the whole WWOOF experience in his Gap Year, the work exchange on a farm, his in Italy, and to further his scheme he'd studied global environmental policy in college. Very likely now that he'd graduated he was going for world domination. At college it was he who had started the organic garden, growing produce for the cafeteria, Philip a Slow Food, locavoring, hipper-than–Alice-Waters pioneer. It was in Portland, Oregon, where he'd performed this awesome tilling of the earth. As if any effort was required to foment the revolution in that city.

So technically there was nothing to dislike about him, our cousin. He made friends with Gideon Hup, *my* fiancé, and they sometimes had beers together at the bar in town, sharing knowledge. My mother issued him a library card and although she was breaking the privacy law she freely told us what he was reading. *Middlemarch*, for one, Philip no slouch. He planted not just a standard vegetable garden in Gloria's yard, but perennials such as asparagus, and he made a strawberry bed. That behavior, that long-term putting down roots, was unbelievable. The cheek of it. His furniture was from local yard sales, great finds, apparently, rugs on the floors, art on his walls, too, tasteful block prints, my mother said. Somehow or other I was never available when he invited us to dinner, off to rehearsal or busy with Coral. As if assisting May Hill wasn't enough for him he was helpful to the ladies who had plots in the community garden. Everything about him, clearly, was intolerable.

Furthermore: Old Seattle friends occasionally turned up to marvel at his new life, which he was proud to show off, the extensive tour for childhood friends with names like Billy and Shaver. He called our place, our land, his *home*. I actually heard him say that.

What was going on? When I asked how long he was staying my parents would say extremely vague nothings such as "We'll see," or "He's trying it out," or "He's very young." Of course someone so smart and energetic would naturally have a girlfriend. He felt himself at liberty to visit her on weekends in Chicago, the two of them flitting around the Art Institute and eating artisanal cheeses and going to microbreweries. But that was one of the most critical identifying factors—the letting loose of the mouse to see who in the lineup of so-called princesses would actually faint. He didn't even know that real farmers do not have weekends off!

I did my best not to speak to him when he was at our house for dinner or be in the same room with him alone not only because of my inborn dislike of him, but because of the kiss I had planted in his composition notebook. He may have come to understand that those were my lips, something I hated more than almost anything to remember, that kiss I would've so liked to have been able to erase.

He was always trying to draw me out at the supper table, which was unnecessary since there were plenty of conversational topics. My mother was ridiculously enthusiastic in his presence, and he and my father had a great deal of shop talk, and for William he often had specific questions about hardware and software, updates and crashes. For me, though, the ruby-lipped kisser, it seemed worth his while, for some reason, to struggle.

"You're in *Our Town*, I heard," he said.

I nodded, buttering my bread.

"The stage manager? It's great they gave that part to a girl."

There was no law that said the stage manager had to be a male.

"A lot of lines to learn."

So what. Learning lines was not difficult.

"It's one of my favorite plays."

What do you want, a medal? And also, what really are you doing here?

My mother at that point would bust in with a smattering of questions about Philip's experience with high school drama, Mrs. Lombard coming to the rescue. I'd eat and excuse myself because after all I had a lot of lines to learn.

Nonetheless, against my will I was learning a few details about him, facts a person couldn't help hearing and thinking about. For instance, his mother had been in the grip of breast cancer for years. She'd died when he was sixteen. Which was why he and his father hadn't visited the farm in all the time he was growing up; because that mother had been sick for nearly Philip's entire life, the father and son tending to her, and if they traveled it was to exotic places to try out a treatment that was not available in America. But there was something else I learned, something I could hardly stand to consider. When Philip was in fifth grade he'd had to do a family history project. An assignment for a teacher who was perhaps close to his heart, his own Mrs. Kraselnik. And so what did he do?

What must all children do who have a resource such as we Lombards had at our disposal? He wrote a letter to May Hill requesting information, May Hill after all his true aunt. He was her only younger kin, the only nephew and there were no nieces. Apparently she'd written him back a very long letter that included a hand-drawn family tree. Also precious photographs. And then what happened? They began to correspond. They had what my mother called an epistolary relationship, a courtship, you might even say. They became pen pals, not just temporarily, not only for the first flush of interesting stamps and news from foreign lands, but for years.

He was a very special, unusual person, my mother often said.

So that of an evening when I sometimes saw the young man and the hermit walking together, or if they were down in front of the manor house, digging around in May Hill's garden plot, it was clear that they were behaving like old friends. He'd kneel in a mulchy aisle nodding as she talked, as they picked beans, and they'd put their heads together to examine a bug of some kind, and then she might hand him a sweet little tomato, which he'd pop into his mouth. It was a tableau I'd spy on if I happened to be at a distance and yet it was a miserable sight that always made me feel as if somehow all along I had understood nothing.

In our house, when Philip wasn't around, there were conversations taking place that William and I were not a part of, our parents often talking long after we'd left the table. We'd come upon their discussions and they'd abruptly scoot their chairs back and again make bright little remarks that signified something but gave nothing away. *Okay! So, ah, well, that's that!* My father was nearing sixty but everyone said he looked like a hale and hearty forty-nine. Sherwood had broken his arm the year before and it hung in a slightly crooked way from his shoulder, which didn't mean that he had lost his strength or that he still wasn't a superb apple picker. They were fine, the men, they were lean and magnificent.

One Saturday morning in the first fall Philip was with us I came late to pick in the Jonathan row, late because I was playing Penelope Sycamore in *You Can't Take It with You*. Philip was in charge of the weekend crew, two older women from town and a retired science teacher. I'd slipped on my picking bag and was up a ladder before he saw me. "Mary Frances!" he called out. "Welcome! Glad you're here."

I had never flipped anyone the bird but right then I could completely understand the impulse. He then had the gall to say, "Great performance last night."

Philip had come to my play? As if he was an uncle or teacher or friend? My parents and William had seen it the previous weekend, no one saying the Seattle visitor would be in the audience.

He said, "You played her with just the right edge of daffiness. Not crazy, not over the top, but sweetly daffy." He apparently was an authority on everything. "Congrats."

How could I not say *Thank you*? I had to thank him. He'd forced me to.

Even though I had a natural dislike for him, as I said, it was sometimes, however, hard to maintain an unequivocal feeling about him. It seemed that you could assume one thing about his character but two seconds later consider the exact opposite, and adding to the puzzlement, you might be correct on both counts. One time, for example, my father was trying to corral the lambs in order to castrate them. He went dashing toward a big fellow but missed his mark and was falling, falling, possibly going to smash his head on the shed wall if Philip wasn't by his side, the annoying presence, who before my father cracked his brow somehow righted him and also at the same time scooped up the lamb.

"Philip!" my father exclaimed. "Whew! Thanks!"

The superhero said, "No problem, man!"

And another instance. We were well into high school the night William and I attended a crucial town board meeting, where, to our surprise, the cousin turned up, too. At that point he'd been living in the stone cottage for about a year. We were along with my father because we had some idea what was at stake not only for him but for us, too. My mother had ironed his shirt and demanded he wash his hair. We were proud of Jim Lombard for being the chairman of the Farmland Preservation Committee, the chairman, which, when we'd been small, we'd thought of as a kind of king. For seven years he and the committee had been working on a draft of a land-use document that would restrict developers in order to preserve farmland in the township, a township that through the decades was becoming more and more suburbanized. My father, with a handful of faithfuls, wanted to prevent future piano key subdivisions, no more quarter-acre lots, the farm fields jammed with house after house, driveway aprons, basketball hoops, lawn mower sheds made to look like little barns. The plan was also to prevent the development of the highway corridor, presently corn and beans and woodland, into the usual one long stretch of Walmart/ Home Depot/Walgreens/Taco Bell/Menards/Dollar Depot/ Aldi/Ford Dealership/Mattress World/US Cellular/Wendy's/ Best Buy/Staples/Burger King/Dollar World/CVS/Long John Silver's/Verizon.

The meeting that night was the last in a series of informational sessions and was supposed to conclude in a vote. The board would decide to adopt the Plan or they'd reject the committee's work and permanently shelve the idea of preservation. We'd long known that if my father didn't get his way then by the time we were ready for the farm it might be an island, houses like the Plumlys' surrounding us. The taxes through the roof. But even if we could pay up it would be difficult to spray and raise noisy, smelly livestock, the new neighbors thick upon us, no room for the foxes, the cranes, the field mice, no space, it sometimes seemed, for the stars. My father didn't say that it was so, but we knew that without a Plan, without his vision, there might not be a place for us.

The meeting room was a low dark hall with no windows, the hanging panel of fluorescent lights doing us no favors, the fifty metal chairs set up on the linoleum a respectable distance from the dais, chairs for fifty persons, the clerk's generous estimation of attendance. Four of the town board members were men, their stubby fingers stained with oil, men who worked in machine shops or owned farms, men, my mother said, who would not have been orators in ancient Rome or in any other civilization. The fifth member, Pam Getchkey, was a woman with prickly short hair who bred Dobermans. My father didn't usually imitate people but when he performed Pam snapping her gum we always suddenly realized that he was the funny one.

We took our seats in the meeting room, our blood hot, our hearts pounding. Many of us already hated everyone on the wrong side. We put our heads down and studied the agenda. Sherwood and Dolly sat in front of us and, with five minutes to go before curtain, in comes Philip, washed and brushed, clattering into a seat next to Mr. and Mrs. Sherwood Lombard. *What's he doing here?* I radiated to William, a beam he chose not to receive. There was a scattering of hobby farmers and the old-timers who had the habit of civic involvement, and the local developers were there, too, Marv and Susan Peterson. My father had praise and damnation for them, saying it was better to have residents doing the developing rather than gold diggers swooping in, men who didn't have to live among the atrocities they'd built.

First, again, as he'd done at many other meetings on the subject, Jim Lombard, who'd been given a place on the dais, rose to explain the Plan. His pants would have fallen to his knees without his suspenders, a man with no hips, no rear end, a man who was one thick knot across his shoulders, so muscle-bound he couldn't fully extend his arms over his head. His tufty hair had been tamped down, tidy and strange, but probably land-usey and respectable. In the hall our notable specimen outlined for us the history of the committee. He had his hand-drawn charts and graphs, and he talked about the surveys taken—the proof that informed consideration had gone into the comprehensive Plan. Yes, there had been opposition, and the committee had responded. The goal, he reminded the assembly, was to provide a framework for responsible growth, growth that the township could afford and support, and growth that suited the character of the area and its people. He sounded a little bit like a social studies teacher but we were sure he wasn't dull.

In the middle of the presentation Mr. Reed, an old grouse, called out, "Sounds like socialism, Lombard. We can't subdivide our farm how we want, is what you're saying. By order of the law we got to have open space? A green corridor? Like the Chinks and the Russians do to their peoples? Commie-stuff, just like all your other presentations. How many times we have to hear this?"

"It's not your turn to speak," Mrs. Bushberger cried.

"How many times?" Mr. Reed asked again.

William had brought along a book to read but he hadn't cracked it yet.

Mrs. Tillet, the tax accountant's wife, was the first person in the citizens' portion of the meeting to say her piece. She had to remind us how much she loved living in the country, and how, on their two hundred acres, they were fortunate enough to have orchids and trillium, gray foxes and great horned owls, the pileated woodpecker and other animals that should be respected.

Philip was nodding, in firm agreement.

No one, Mrs. Tillet said, wanted to live in suburbia—that's why, after all, everyone in the room had moved out to our town, to get away from the subdivisions.

"You move out here, lady, you become the subdivisions." A truth-speaking grumbler.

"You want the gates to close but only after you've moved in," Susan Peterson heckled.

Don Tribby, the chairman of the board, pounded the table with his gavel, his big fun in any meeting.

Mrs. Tillet with her silky layered blond hair that she drove to Chicago to have styled, and her toned arms, and her diamond rings up to her knuckles, was not good for the cause. My father, we knew, in a perfect world, would have had her muzzled.

Mr. Carter stood next, the old farmer with a fat lower lip and squinty eyes, and he had maybe three hairs right at his crown, and everywhere else moles, large, medium, small, an array, an assortment. Connect the dots. He was big enough to bellow. "I've given my life to my farm, see," he said, with surprising quietness. "Don't tell me I don't love it the way I'm supposed to. Don't tell me I can't give my wife her dream. She's been a good wife, my Betty. She don't want to be cold in the winter anymore. Don't tell me I got to put half my land in some kind of plan. I need to take her to Florida. She's a good wife."

My father pulled out statistics about how farmers should be able to sell at market value with the proposed Plan but everyone probably suspected this was not absolute. We were suddenly not sure about the Plan, either, curiously sad for Betty and old Mr. Carter.

There followed a stretch of talkers on both sides, people either praising the rural character of the town and supporting thoughtful growth, or protesting that the Plan was government yet again limiting the freedoms of its citizens. We weren't paying close attention until Philip himself stood up, stating his name and the address of the stone cottage.

"You don't know me," he said, "but I'd like to introduce myself. I'm a Lombard relation. I've been here for a year or so and my hope is to be involved with the orchard, the Lombard operation, long-term—" He smiled at my father, and turned to Dolly and Sherwood to acknowledge their potential goodwill.

Long-term? I turned to William. *Is that what he wants?*

Philip had shaved, no sign of any farmhand scruffiness, and his clean hair was loose and golden. He'd even tucked in his chambray shirt, a shirt that brought out the notable blueness of his eyes. "So, I don't know," he said. "I get that it's difficult to try to legislate morality, that one person's moral views shouldn't be imposed on the community. I mean, I agree with that, and yet I think we need to recognize that laws most always have moral aims? Moral aims, and that in many circumstances those aims concern justice."

It's possible I had never felt so embarrassed. I wanted to scream, *He's not from here!*

He scratched his cheek, his lips screwed to one side of his face, a gesture an actor would make on stage, a further mortification. "I guess," he said, "I think that in this situation tonight the committee has tried to be both moral, you know? In terms of stewardship of the land and future generations, and also practical, serving the needs of the citizens in the here and now. I mean, it goes back as far as Plato, right? Philosophers making a close connection between true justice and human well-being. When companies pollute the air and the river, this is unjust because it disturbs every person's well-being. It prevents individuals from flourishing. So then the Environmental Protection Agency is born."

"My achin' back," someone behind us said.

My father was nodding, as if he was not at all ashamed of our relative. My mother was smiling encouragingly. William was paying close attention. Dolly, however, had been rummaging around in a bag and was pulling out her knitting.

"It seems like, from what I've heard and read, that the committee through the years has grappled with issues of justice at every governmental level—"

"Is there any Lombard that isn't full of it?" Marv Johnson called out. Marv was a monumental man, his power in his brisket, that barrel in a red shirt, and there was no ignoring his drooping face with the pitted nose, his skin tending to purple.

Philip turned to him. "Excuse me, sir? I—"

My father said, "You don't have the floor, Marv."

Tribby banged his gavel—"Since when are you the chairman, Lombard? You don't have the authority! That's your whole problem, you people, as far as I'm concerned. You come in here with your college degrees, your whatever elite documents, and you think you can tell us, the real working farmers, the real citizens, how to run the government. You think if you just explain it for us one more time, we'll let you snow us. No one wants this Plan. Hardly anyone at all. I'm in touch with the community. I'm telling you, the people, the real farmers, hate this Plan."

"Actually, my father is a real farmer!" That cry was a hot streak through my mind but also it seemed to have come from my mouth. William grabbed my arm and Tribby banged his gavel; he banged his gavel at me, Mary Frances Lombard. My own words in the air were burning my ears, the clue, besides William's grip, that I had spoken out loud.

I put my head down. What had just happened? Philip had maybe said something important; I wasn't sure. My father had thought so but bringing up Plato? You did not bring up Plato at a town meeting. That was a rule anyone should instantly apprehend, crossing the threshold of the room. And yet Philip must have been right if people like the chairman and Marv Johnson were lambasting him. Think, think: I couldn't very well be on Tribby's side. He had practically beaten me with that mallet. I had shouted without even realizing it, which might mean I was out of my mind. Or very ill. I was hot and shivering, both. Trying to keep my body still, afraid the chair would start rattling. I could feel William not paying the slightest attention to me.

After some time I became aware that Sherwood was standing. Then I had to look up and take note; I had to abandon my own suffering. We held our breath since you could never quite know what Sherwood was going to say. His craggy face, that block of a forehead, was imposing, his curls were still red and made a fanciful halo, his best feature, and even though he wasn't on the dais he had a pressed shirt and his good shoes. There was no need for him to be shy but he was hesitating. For what seemed like a few minutes he looked up at the ceiling, trying to collect his ideas, everyone, even the Lombard–haters, pulling for him. You just had to, no matter what, that man with visible effort intending to speak thoughtfully.

Finally he began. "Consider how much arable land was here twenty years ago, ten years ago, and now." He spoke softly, dreamily.

Philip was nodding at Sherwood, nodding without pause, as if he were saying, *That's right, man*, again and again.

"There are four or five farmers who among them work about twenty-three hundred acres," Sherwood went on. There was a small cry, an *uhhhh* from Mrs. Tillet. All the good land gone, a fresh sorrow to her. "We can say that the shrinkage is due to an individual's right, and his choice to sell, but what if we had a land-use plan that rewards steward-ship, rather than cashing in, a land-use plan that has built into it conservation easements and tax policy, so that we are not only assisting the individual but working for the communal good?" There was spittle on his lips, his hands making larger circles, Sherwood revving up. Philip was still nodding, as if he alone understood the points being made. He had no right to think he knew anything and yet he continued his outrageous agreement while Sherwood gently educated us about the Dust Bowl, about the possibility of hunger, about the richness of our land resource, about our obligation to preserve it. Sher-wood was spirited and tender, quiet in his knowledge, proving Tribby wrong, proving to the assembly that the Lombards' in-telligence was mannerly, that it was not unseemly or puffed up in any way.

"Those of you," Sherwood was saying, "who want out can sell your property for a good price. There's no reason to fear you wouldn't get a good price. Those of us who want to con-tinue farming will feel secure that we're still in a community that values us, that supports us. We are together in this, more than we realize. If we understand that we're together so much of this Plan makes sense."

We almost clapped. Being together was after all what the Lombard Orchard was about, too, and he knew it, he believed in it; he no longer thought he alone should run the farm. This was how we'd always loved Sherwood, suddenly, the joyousness knocking us over the head. It would fade away, the feeling, we'd forget about it, we wouldn't see him for a time, we'd be in earshot of our parents' complaints but then, then he'd appear before us again, unusual and pure.

When he was done he sat down. Even so Philip continued nodding. "Why is he nodding?" I whispered to William.

"Shush," he said.

At last the citizens' portion was concluded. Tribby informed the audience that the board would vote on the Plan at their next meeting.

It was Mrs. Tillet who yelled, "You can't do that! TONIGHT. It said in the paper you'd vote tonight."

A rumble rose from the crowd. "You've made up your minds so just do the vote." Someone on the other side shouted, "Vote when you feel like it, fellas!" Another call, "You vote now, when we're here to watch you."

Tribby turned to his board. He said, "You boys ready?"

"That's what this meeting is for! You're supposed to vote—"

Tribby banged his gavel. "What do you say, boys—and Pam?"

One by one each member indicated that he was prepared.

"I'm going to say what I've said before." Tribby raised his papers in a stack, tapping them together on the table, doing his tidying. "You all know I don't believe in this Plan. Why would we want to approve even more government, bigger government? We've got government oversight in every arena of our life. Uncle Sam telling us when to turn around—"

"The government supports you!" Mrs. Tillet was again irrepressible. "You, personally, Chairman, get subsidies. Look it up, people, on the Internet. Learn how many hundreds of thousands—"

"You want a vote tonight?" Tribby's throat and jaw were a

blotchy red, no way to obscure his rage. "We need any dis-cussion, boys, or have we discussed this thing into the dirt? It's your call."

There was all at once a motion, Pam Getchkey, the breeder of Dobermans, moving that the Land-Use Plan not be adopted. She moved also that my father's committee be dis-solved.

The committee over and done? Forever? A cry went up from the crowd. The faction that was incensed by Pam, by Tribby, got to their feet, the chairs banging against each other, the clangs ringing through the room. The Lombards stayed put because of course by and large we weren't public jumper-up-pers and yet I did find myself standing. Dolly was so amazed she started to laugh, calling out, "What are you doing, folks!" The townspeople, both sides, were gibbering, a few of them shaking fists, some of them advancing toward the dais. My mother actually looked alarmed. "Jesus Christ," she muttered, "sit down, Francie."

"No," I said, although I somewhat wished I wasn't on my feet.

The board members held to their positions. My father said afterward that nothing of the sort had happened in that cham-ber before, a mob of twenty-five or so advancing. Tribby pounded his gavel like a baby at a peg-and-hole toy, leaving it to my father to rise and greet us. He stretched out his long arms, my father. He towered over squat Tribby with the boil-ing face, my father looming and sallow under the awful light. "Sit down," he called. "Please. Everyone. Go and sit down." With his arms out it was as if he could hold us all, as if he could easily contain us.

Tribby continued to strike his gavel. No one looked at

anyone else, everyone receding. We had sprung up without thinking in just the way I had shouted out—but now we were ashamed. Because, in truth, no one knew what was going on at the revolution. No one had a plan. Were we going to topple the table? Punch the board members in the nose? The furious cohort went back to their chairs and those of us who had stood without thinking sat back down. William was fiercely reading his book.

"We have to let this process unfold," my father was saying. "In the next election, you'll be able to vote for change, if that's the will of the township. If there's energy to—"

"Tell us something we don't know," Tribby sniped, still banging away.

Dolly turned around to us and said in her normal loud speaking voice, "You kids should understand that where we are right now? It's the nuthouse. I like to think that everyone will leave this loony bin, that the only people left in the township will be these board members, the cuckoo clocks. I have to say, that makes me happy."

My mother smiled a little, but she couldn't agree outwardly because the town board members were the people who funded the library and in public she must always try to be on her best behavior.

When the motion carried Marv slowly clapped his enormous fleshy palms together, one loud clap after the next. My father's work of seven years, for naught. He got up and we could see all at once that the meeting had drained him of his powers.

"Jim," my mother murmured, even though he was not anywhere near her.

His chest was sunk in on itself, his back bent, the hump of an old person. That's what I thought, an old person, my father. He looked like a man who through his life had not slept enough or eaten enough, a man who had no business being in a struggle with our community, or maybe with any community, with people who were coarse and mean, with people who could give up their farms for Florida.

"That was epic," Philip said on the way out.

"That's how it is around here," Dolly said drily.

My father, I didn't explain to them, would eventually win; he would win. He had to. He would win because he was right in principle. The whole world could not be built upon, the whole earth cement. It might take time but he would prevail. In fact, it wasn't until the recession of 2008 that no new subdivisions were proposed. In that spring the building of prospective homes on those plats that had been approved was suspended. Every single plan on hold for lack of money. Even though my father had done nothing to cause the recession except privately hold to his convictions about farmland, nonetheless, Jim Lombard's deepest dream, his dream for zero growth, of course had come true.

20.

The Fears of MF Lombard,
Part One

I was outwardly more or less perfectly well adjusted, as far as I could tell, although sullen when it was necessary, but MF Lombard—the name I now used—MF in her inner sanctum was generally, more or less, terrified. The towers had come down, for one, when we'd been in school, the entire day devoted to CNN, the planes piercing the buildings, the office workers, those specks, falling through the sky, the buildings collapsing, over and over again. But more frightening than the footage itself was the shock of our teachers, some of them weeping as they watched, and also how silent, at first, the bad students were, the troublemakers, some of them with their heads down on their desks, as if even they couldn't find a prank like that useful to look at.

At lunch I found William, I needed to be with William. He now wore good-boy clothing, Oxford shirts tucked in, his oversize pants with pockets for guns a fashion statement of the past. I didn't usually see him much during the school hours but I had the feeling he was waiting for me, sitting on a bench by himself outside the library. I sat next to him, the two of us not saying anything. We were embarrassed. We didn't know where to start. Everyone would understand our sitting together and yet we ourselves, between the two of us, didn't know what to say. After a minute, however, I began to think that I did have something to tell him. I couldn't explain it even though the feeling was hard in me, the tough little ball gathering speed out in the distance, within the space of my mind, the light of reason: which was, I was right, MF Lombard had been correct that William should not go far away to college. Because, this is what happened, strangers evidently from the land of Stephen Lombard on the bluest, softest autumn day perpetrating evil. Best to stay put, stay close to what was near and dear.

Amanda was already preparing to go to Germany with AFS in the next year, Dolly so excited for that adventure. And Adam was applying to colleges in California, an agricultural state with no water.

"Do you think we could go home?" I finally said to William.

"I have a calc test."

"We're just going to be watching the news for the rest of the day."

"We've been attacked," he said, needlessly.

William's saying so, though, made the event real.

"What if our school is next?" I had to wonder.

"They only hit symbols of power," he muttered.

The bell rang and we were required to move.

In the next few days there was talk of war, of trying to fight the group, the country, whatever it was, that had caught the world's attention, and it was that idea that frightened me most. At the end of the week, on Friday, I was in the back room of the sheep shed, a place I often went for the purpose of crying. The floor was thick with hay, the room warm and close with dung and rumination. The spring lambs came to see MF with her head down, arms hugging knees, Spinky and Sue bravely approaching, nibbling at human hair. So then I could hold them close, clasping their heads to my cheek, my tears wetting their soft white noses. Sometimes I didn't even know quite why I was crying but on that day I was scared about retribution, about William having to march off to the Middle East, and I even cried for Stephen Lombard, because maybe he'd be blown up somewhere along the line.

I'd never known May Hill to come around the sheep shed, and afterward I did remember that she had a pail in her hand, and that she was probably going to give her compost to the ewes. She was all at once looking in through the open windows. "What's the matter with you?" She spoke sternly and yet with curiosity. It was, it seemed, a real question.

I had been distantly in her company in the summers, across the field making hay, and sometimes she walked by the barn when I was working, but I hadn't been face-to-face with her in years, not since my capture. It was possible in the compound, if you were careful about your route, not to bump into someone like May Hill. And since we never celebrated any holiday with the Volta family there was no danger of seeing her around a Christmas tree. But now she'd come upon me at the peak of my frenzy. What was the matter with me? A good question. Certainly I was crying about how the world in the space of one Tuesday morning had completely changed. Maybe, however, there were also other lurking sorrows that had piggybacked on the big one. For instance, Philip with his springy walk and his blond curls and his good cheer working so ably alongside my father, his infiltration going on year after year. I could hardly remember when he hadn't been with us. It was if my father had adopted him, as if he were now the first son. Philip, the second coming. And, additionally, there were the college materials, the sheer mass of the mailings in our PO box for William, every day appeals from institutions that wanted him.

"What's the matter?" May Hill said again.

I sputtered something about war.

"There's always been war," she said sharply. "War is nothing new."

I sniffled and tried to dry my eyes.

"Crying is not going to help."

"I know that," I said.

She next made a somewhat funny remark. She said, "I wish I could sit around and cry when there are apples to be picked."

"Oh," I said. Although May Hill worked hard and was strong by any standards, but especially for a seventy- or eighty-year-old lady, however old she was, and although she was indispensable, she was also upstairs in her own house for great chunks of time probably sitting around reading. Not that I would point out such a fact to her. There that large face was in the window, once again proof that May Hill had none of the typical Lombard grace. Did an elderly person have the need to cry, or was crying something you probably outgrew? I wished something in words that I'd always wished with a feeling, that old situation, a knot, an ache trying to gather itself into meaning and possible action. That is, I wished May Hill wasn't a Lombard, and more than that, I wished she'd disappear. I stared back at her, my tears over and done. *Go away*, I willed. *Fall over dead.*

Her face persisted in the window, that ogre head swelling because—because she was having the same thought about me, that wish engorging her mind. May Hill hoping to erase me as fervently as I wanted her to vanish, our wishes pitted one against the other. That clear fact frightened me so much I scrambled up in order to make sure she hadn't paralyzed me, that her wish hadn't frozen my limbs. I wasn't too old to be that alarmed by her; a person, no matter how grown up, would always be alert to her powers.

I then remembered something my mother always practiced on her unpleasant patrons at the library. A tack that might possibly work, at least a little, on our fake aunt. Mrs. Lombard said that she killed the wretches with kindness, she became simpering with niceness, that being almost unbearably sweet to people who were itching for a fight caught them off guard and defanged them. Therefore, I mustered my strength and I said to May Hill, "I like your shirt." Admittedly that was not the most believable compliment for a ratty piece of flannel, but it didn't deserve a scowl.

She muttered a word that started with an *m*. Maybe it was *mercy*. But possibly *murder*. Or *mongrel*. Yes, *mongrel*, that's what she'd said. She made her pronouncement about me before she turned and went up the sheep path and out the gate.

*   *   *

To mutter like that. The horrid word. And when I was trying to be nice! So the stone of May Hill was again heavy around my neck, all the bad juju of my encounters concentrated in that stone: the interview, the capture in her room, the pronouncement that I, and perhaps each of us, Amanda and Adam and William, too, were people beneath her contempt. Individuals with no breeding. But if there was a leader of the pack it was MF Lombard. I was certain that in her ordered mind I, above all others, was the vermin.

I might not have minded her condemnation so very much if there hadn't been the matter of her plan. My parents now were often talking about it, a conversation I wanted to understand and also couldn't bear to hear. We'd been at dinner a few weeks after the World Trade Center attacks when the topic first came up for our benefit. William and I were startled at the way my parents were speaking, as if the plan was common knowledge.

"What are you talking about?" I said.

May Hill was drawing up a document with a lawyer, my father explained, that would allow Philip to buy her out, to purchase the acres she owned on a land contract.

"A land contract?" I said.

He repeated the fact. May Hill was preparing to transfer her assets to Philip.

"Transferring her assets," William echoed. "Why doesn't she just will it to him? Why does he have to buy her out?"

"That's not information I'm privy to," my father said.

"May Hill is remarkably savvy," my mother added.

"She can't do that," I cried. For starters, we all knew that her property included the right-of-way to the apple barn. She owned that stretch and the half acre the house sat on, but not the house itself. We had always understood that the owner of that strip held power, our great-uncle Jim for his own reasons conferring a certain influence upon May Hill.

"She can do whatever she wants with it," my mother argued in her cross way.

"Of course she can," my father replied.

"She considers Philip her heir."

"That's obvious, Mother," William said.

"Someone has to think of the future," she insisted. "Someone has to take steps to ensure this place isn't going down the tubes."

"That is such an insulting thing to say to Papa," I shouted.

"Oh, he knows what I mean," she said lightly. "Why Sherwood and Dolly aren't in favor of Philip's having ownership is beyond human comprehension."

"It's always a slow process, coming around to change," my father said. He rubbed his eyes. "They'll get there."

"It would be ideal if they got there before you men are wheelchair-bound," my mother said. She then chattered on about how Adam would soon be in college, how the guidance counselor at school had never heard of any of the institutions Adam was considering.

"The farm's not going down the tubes," I repeated, interrupting her monologue.

"Repairs are in order, Marlene," my father said. "Don't say it, Nellie—don't."

My mother started to laugh in that terribly annoying fashion of hers. "Let's see," she said. "Two of the barn roofs have gaping holes. How many sheds are on their last legs? Sherwood spent all spring on that contraption to wash boxes and all summer picking garlic mustard? I mean, really?"

"Sherwood works plenty hard," my father said.

"*I mean, really?*" I mocked my mother.

"Where's May Hill going to live?" William thought to ask.

"She has the right to live in the house until her death," my father replied.

Philip actually owning a piece of Volta? I kept asking that question to myself. He had been learning how to spray, studying for the Pesticide Applicator's Test, something Gloria had never done. But even if he had skills, even so we would always own more of the land than he did and if necessary we could put in a different driveway. We could get to the apple barn without his precious holding. I wondered then about William's question, why May Hill didn't just give her nephew her land, why she needed him to buy it. But wait, I thought, would we have to buy our portion from my father?—No, of course not, he would give it to us. But maybe we'd have to buy Sherwood's shares, something I'd never considered before. How could we possibly find the money to purchase Volta? I very much wanted to ask how William and I would take over, how the mechanics of it would happen. Instead I said, not looking at William, I said, in the spirit of helpfulness and charity and also fear, "Philip is a good worker. And strong." Ah, I was having an epiphany! "He'll be like our Gloria, William." In a snap I'd figured out at least part of the puzzle, Philip always willing to do any task at our bidding.

"Oh, for God's sake, Francie," my mother said. "He will not be like Gloria. He'll have ownership."

"It's a dramatic change, Marlene," my father said soothingly, "but it's important for him to have a stake—"

"It's not something you have to think about right now," my

mother butted into my father's comforting words. "You don't have to decide your future right this minute."

"You just said someone has to think about the future," I cried. "You just said that. But what you meant is, You, MF Lombard, don't have to think about the future you yourself want. You meant that I only have to think about the future you want for me."

My father said, "Let's talk about this tomorrow. *The morning*," he quoted, "*is always wiser than the evening*."

"Just sign me up for camp, Nellie," I said. "Pay an enormous deposit you won't get back, money that could be used for the farm, just send it off without telling me."

With that point made, MF Lombard, the winner of the round, went upstairs. I had a momentary satisfaction before I remembered the more significant point, that Philip was going to own a portion of our property.

My mother's assumption that we would go to college was so stubbornly imbued in her—and probably, to be fair, in my father, too—that there had been little need for her to speak much about it until we were teenagers. Unlike Dolly, who herself only held a high school diploma, Dolly whispering *collegecollegecollege* into her newborns' ears.

By the time we got to high school my mother had become generally cranky, bent on making her pitch both overtly and subliminally for the colleges of her choice. She served us cocoa in her college mugs. She often related her adventures in higher education, stories that she'd suddenly recall.

There seemed also to be more visits than usual from her best college pals, one of whom was the dean of admissions at one of Nellie's top ten picks. The dean, over breakfast at our kitchen table, had intimated that when we applied to Swarthmore, as of course we must, we could very likely expect not only the fat envelope but substantial aid. "You've got everything going for you," she said to me. "Brains, naturally, grades, extracurriculars, and let's not forget, you've got the farm card."

The farm card?

My mother glared, *Do not be rude.*

It seemed to me that the exact minute I'd gone to high school she'd become disapproving of me full-time, a shocked look on her face when I told her I'd joined Future Farmers of America, as if FFA was beneath the station of a girl with a pedigree like MF Lombard's. And when I'd wanted to sign up for auto mechanics instead of honors biology you might have thought I was throwing my life away by shooting heroin or having unprotected sex. She even discouraged me from continuing on in 4-H. "Oh please, Francie," she'd sighed, "not another year showing your zucchinis."

Whereas Dolly's aspiration for Amanda and Adam was a brag-worthy university that would provide them with a marketable skill, Mrs. Lombard wanted William and Francie to become fully rounded, truly educated, cultivated people. She seemed to think that without Oberlin or Bates or Carleton or Williams we'd not know who Hesiod was, we'd forget to vote, we'd vote Hitler into power, we'd confuse *good* and *well*, we'd not appreciate a symphony orchestra, we'd track mud into museums, and most frightening, we'd admire terribly written thrillers and bosom heavers. College was four short beautiful years, she'd go on, when we could open out, all blossomy, when we could experience new ideas, when we could have the privilege of freedom, a time when we could study whatever interested us, although presumably she did not mean auto mechanics. If she hadn't met Stephen Lombard, she reminded us, never would she have visited the farm, never married my father, and therefore we would never have been born. In the beginning was Oberlin College, the light, the way, world without end.

Nellie's friend, the dean of admissions, said to me over breakfast in my own kitchen, "Here's what I want to ask you, Francie. Do you want to farm anywhere—do you love farming? Or is your love for farming about your love for home?"

The question stank of Mrs. Lombard.

I did my best to remain calm. I did not mention that the Lombard property was historical, mysterious, and productive, that the woods were deep, the soil well tended. I didn't point out that Amanda and Adam had no interest in the orchard life, and that someone was obliged to honor tradition. I said, "Most farm families would kill for their children to take over the operation. What, after all, is the point of having children if the parents just want them to go away?"

"Oh, honey!" the dean cried. "A parent wants her child to have a rich, full life. We want you to use your talents, to have the tools to be happy. It's not that we want you to go, not at all! It's that we have to let you go. This, believe me, is the most painful part of being a mother." She went on to explain that college would equip me to make an informed choice about my future. I could study chemistry, biology, business, all courses that would help me if I decided to return to the orchard. I could network with other students who were interested in farming, make lifetime friends with people who would be helpful to my venture.

"I already have people in my life who will be helpful to my venture," I reminded the dean. "I have"—I counted on my fingers, so she could see and understand—"my father and my brother, Sherwood, and also Dolly. And, additionally, Philip."

The dean said what she had no business saying. "Your father wants you to have an education, too."

Nellie, perhaps because she'd been omitted from my list, had to have the last word. She said, "You just want to keep your options open, that's all, Francie. You want to have options."

I remembered my proposal of marriage from Gideon Hup, which naturally I had long since stopped considering, and yet I would have liked to add that offer to my talking points. Nellie Lombard, I didn't say to the dean, had little idea how many options for her venture a girl such as MF had at her disposal.

21.

MF Lombard's Fears, Part Two

Another slow blink and time passed. I went to drama camp for a second summer when I was sixteen. It was my decision. I wanted to go. The jar of lake water from my previous year, the jar sitting on my desk, spoke to me. To my surprise I was cast as Rosalind in *As You Like It*, even though I was not your typical ingénue type. But I'd gotten tall and gamine-like, I guess. I was complimented on the quality of my skin, the typical adjectives, *poreless*, *porcelain*, and a greeting, *Oh Milkmaid!* Fine, I had lovely skin, which was not an accomplishment. Some people in the show were not in favor of my being the lead, including the boy who played Orlando, a person with pillowy lips that he believed were irresistible. It required all of my skills to pretend I was in love with him, and he made it clear that he, too, had to muster his forces. Coral was not in my cabin and was involved in *Annie Get Your Gun*. And so I very much felt on my own, trapped in the Forest of Arden, no one but a character for my friend, Rosalind the person I spoke to and drew comfort from.

When my parents and William drove up for the performance I couldn't let them know how miserable I was. It made me unbearably sad, their driving seven hours one way in order to see me. They probably thought I was having the most wonderful experience, that I'd gathered a few campers to my heart for lifetime friends. That's what my mother wanted more than anything, and as we walked the wooded paths she kept asking in a hushed way, "Who was that girl? What's that boy's name?" I was almost too sad to be angry with her. She supposed that because I had the lead I was popular, but no, my only real friend in the cast was an imaginary person.

My father said, "It's amazing you learned all those lines, Marlene. It's something to think of, having that heroine in your bloodstream."

William said, "You were prettier up there than I remembered, Imp."

My mother laughed.

Each Lombard made other nice comments about my talents and then Mother, Father, and William got in the car and drove away, leaving me for one more week, one last show, *The Miracle Worker*, MF Lombard a blind girl with one short scene. When I got home I was more than happy to have that Four Rivers Camp session dissolve as soon as possible into nearly nothing.

Most of the time thereafter, when I was leading my school life, writing another play with my friend Jay and acting in Mr. Dronzek's masterpieces, all that time doing my extracurriculars and studying, enjoying the company of Coral and a few other theater enthusiasts, *keeping my options open*; even so there was the other real life beneath all of that surface activity, the real life rife with terror—an apt word although if I'd said it out loud I would have been chastised. But *terror* for anyone's information was not reserved for religious zealots blowing up themselves and others in marketplaces. Terror also existed in a black night and an early morning. It could exist at lunchtime in a crowded cafeteria stinking of fish sticks. No escape from that crush. With no warning it beat in you when you opened your locker to the jumble of notebooks, torn assignments, gym clothes, petticoats not yet returned to the costume closet. It could come upon you walking up the hill in the back field, out of the blue feeling as if you were standing on the lip of the world, alone. Also, it, the terror, could occur right before a school dance.

In the fall of my junior year I saw May Hill for the first time in months when Coral and I were posing for homecoming pictures by the apple barn, the two of us in our steampunk finery, our garters and relatively tasteful purple bustiers, bodysuits underneath, little flouncy skirts, our lace-up boots, our thick black eyeliner and long curly black wigs. Jay, Gayjay he'd dubbed himself, was taking the pictures. Coral and I were going together for the sole purpose of wearing our costumes in public, as if the dance were a Halloween party. I was still flat-chested so that my wearing a bustier was Kleenex-filled hilarity. We laughed until we fell over, Coral and I, at her bust size and my bust size, the Mutt and Jeff of bosoms. My mother said periodically that any day now I would require the pads that had been in my closet for at least two years. She said so as if she were a cheerleader, as if she were rah-rahing for my eggs.

In her mind I was apparently not just a slow bloomer but a stunted, stalled girl—which did sometimes worry me, the possibility of a medical condition. For the most part, though, I was perfectly happy without that particular monthly nuisance.

As far as the egg situation went, a week before the dance Mrs. Lombard had come into the exam room with me for my checkup. In my presence she'd asked Dr. O'Connor if I should be put on birth control pills or if I should have a battery of tests to see what was happening with my ovaries. The state of my reproductive equipment was something I had no interest in discussing in a nearly public forum. And even if Dr. O'Connor had thought I had cancer or had injured myself or—truly hideous—didn't have a large enough opening, I would not have the tests, and most certainly I was not going to take birth control pills. It was to my great satisfaction that he told my mother I was not abnormal, and that in the fullness of time I would menstruate.

"You're saying I am not a freak," I said to him.

He laughed. "I assure you, Mary Frances, you are not a freak."

"Okay then," I said, looking at my mother. "Thank you."

At any rate, I saw May Hill before the homecoming dance when I was dressed as a Victorian call girl, bust size 32A. I'm not sure she as much as glanced my way, walking quickly past Coral and me, her head down. Amanda, who had become willowy and beautiful, her dark hair in a French twist, had already left with her date. William was going to the dance, too, with Charlotte Meuweesen, a sweetly bland girl he couldn't possibly like in any significant way.

While we were doing the photographing William had

driven into Volta, to the apple barn, in order to get a gallon of cider for Charlotte to take home after the event. He was wearing a sport coat and, to distinguish himself, a bow tie. May Hill walked past him, too, but she may, in spite of herself, have noticed Charlotte sticking her long leg from the car, noticed the black gown that to May Hill would have looked like a slip rather than a formal garment. May Hill stopped walking. She appeared to be thinking. She glanced at the leg once more, she looked at the gravel, she then walked on. All my pleasure in my getup and hair and stockings just like that was gone, the Shadow of May Hill not simply casting a pall over the evening, but destroying it. She disappeared into the basement. That was the extent of the May Hill episode. And yet a great buzz suddenly was in my ears. I couldn't hear. It was difficult to breathe.

To complete the feeling Philip happened by, Philip coming up the path from the sheep shed. I believed he shouted, "You look fantastic, you guys! You are so meta! Homecoming with an attitude. Homecoming from beyond the past and beyond the future." He may also have said, "Have an awesome time."

"That's enough pictures," I was able to say to Jay.

Coral giggled, instantly becoming idiotic, thanking Philip and simpering. I got in the car and slammed the door.

In theory, and in theory only, it had by then occurred to me to consider marrying my cousin. If I had to. I was not serious on the one hand, but also on the other, it was a real idea. All the way to the school, to the gym for the dance, I couldn't stop shivering. May Hill walking across the driveway was the Queen of Darkness. Philip was her minion. The notion of my marrying him made me ill, the old man and the maiden, plus the crone keeping watch, and additionally we were related and

would have the moronic children. Working alongside my husband would be like playing Rosalind to that dope of an actor at
camp, not for a mere four performances, but for literally eter-
nity. We'd be buried next to each other in the family plot.

"What's the matter?" Coral said to me.

"I think I might be sick," I replied.

There was, however, the matter of Philip's girlfriend, a
woman named Natasha. My father referred to her as the
Countess Rostova. My mother called her The Gorgeous One.
Natasha was the reason the awful idea stayed in my mind.
Once there'd been the talk of succession, of the land transfer,
I'd realized that Natasha through marriage might someday own
May Hill's dirty little right-of-way to the apple barn. It was
then that I'd felt remiss, that I tried to turn over the idea of the
union with Philip in my mind. But it, the extreme altruism of
my act, and he, the flesh-and-blood man, always repelled me,
so that it wasn't possible to concentrate on the concept of our
business relationship.

The morning after homecoming my mother asked me how
the dance was and if we'd had fun. I didn't know. I couldn't
remember anything that had happened except for the moment
on the driveway with May Hill and Philip.

For quite some time there had been no talk of the transfer of
assets and I had come to believe that May Hill had changed
her mind. Or anyway, surely the decision was far off. Certainly
she would never make any legal alterations in apple season, not
when we were all caught up in the harvest. It was something so
futuristic and far-fetched there didn't seem any need to try to
bring up the subject with William. When you thought about

it in a realistic way it made no sense that Philip "Plato" Lombard, the Renaissance man, was going to commit to a lifetime in our burg and our home.

I therefore wasn't prepared down at the library one afternoon when Dolly came through the door. She didn't so much approach the checkout desk as march up to it, the color in her cheeks unusually high. No doubt there was going to be a news flash about Adam, our cousin now at Pomona College in California. He'd gotten a full ride including a travel stipend. Surfing had become an interest. And whales. I was sitting at a nook nearby cleaning DVDs with a shammy cloth. Never had I seen Dolly look so well and so pretty. There was the girlish flush and the tinsel effect of the shiny threads of silver in her dark hair. I smiled eagerly at her but she paid no attention to me, standing firm at the counter.

"How are you, Mrs. Lombard?" my mother as always said so cheerfully to the relation.

"I'm not going to say my opinion." That's what Dolly said. No Amanda or Adam reports, no Muellenbach intelligence, nothing about the sisters' diets or one of the husbands shooting his foot accidently.

My mother understood the topic. She spoke quietly. "I'm not sure anybody realizes how much of his strength Jim has lost in the last few years, Dolly. We need this change. We need it to be legally binding."

Dolly began to hum. She had perhaps come into the library to complain and maybe hadn't expected my mother to have a point of view.

"I'm saying something," my mother said. Never before, as far as I knew, had she spoken to Dolly in that warning tone. "I'm telling you an important piece of information, Mrs. Lombard."

"May Hill has no right to give up her property to that boy," Dolly cried. "That boy could go off tomorrow, for all we know. He could sell it to someone else. He could lose interest. For all we know he could ruin us."

Yes, yes, it was so.

And yet my mother said, "May Hill has every right to transfer her acres to Philip. She has every legal right."

"No one cares about my opinion." Dolly looked as if she might burst into tears. "No one. I'm nothing. All these years and no one listens to me."

"That's not true—"

"You sit up here in the library. What," Dolly asked, "do you know?"

My mother was startled.

"You sit up here," Dolly repeated.

"Excuse me?" my mother said, a foolish question, a nothing question.

Dolly muttered, "You don't work in the business."

That was a fact—what could my mother say?

"I know I don't, Dolly," she nonetheless said. "But that doesn't mean I don't understand the dynamics."

"I've killed myself on that cold floor in the sorting shed. Standing for ten hours, day after day, season after season. Pretnear killed myself."

"Everyone appreciates your work—"

"You," Dolly said fiercely, "have no right to an opinion."

My mother pressed her hand to her lips. Dolly wiped her eye.

"I do have rights," my mother said then in a very calm voice.

"We all do. We have rights, you and I, for some of the same reasons. Because of marital property, for one. Because of family feeling, and there are different reasons, too." Her voice was lulling, smooth, so quiet. "For instance, for my part, the chunk of money that came to me at my parents' death, most of it has gone into the farm. You might not know that. I'm guessing you don't." My mother pulled her thin graying hair into a ponytail with one hand and held it there. "I didn't mind the contribution, but don't tell me I know nothing, or have no rights, or that I've just been sitting around. Please don't do that."

Money was involved? My heart was doing its pricking, my hands cold. The buzz in the ears. Dolly was the stunned one now, staring at my mother. She looked as if a poison dart had pierced her breast; she looked that stricken. My mother, though, seemed not to notice the wild hurt expression shaping up, the little gimlet shine of Dolly's narrowed eyes and the bit-by-bit collapse of the doughy face.

"I never wanted," my mother went on—

Stop! I wanted to scream.

"—it to cause bad feeling, our putting cash into the operation, Jim and I."

SHUT UP!

"I only say so now because it's my *sitting around* over here that has made some of the capital improvements possible."

My mother let go of the ponytail. Time, it seemed, skipped a beat or two, a stillness in the room, no tick of the heart. Did Nellie Lombard have any idea what she'd done? What you'd know instantly if you'd been in the audience? The hands on the clock then moved, the filter in the aquarium remembered to purr. A child shouted on the playground. Did she have a clue that Mrs. Lombard and Mrs. Lombard could never be jolly or even cordial again? The friendship over now that my mother had laid out what had been a fine secret charitable thing, now that she had declared herself the martyr. Dolly was reduced, her pride smashed. For once in Mrs. Sherwood Lombard's life she was unable to say even one word.

But my mother wasn't done yet. She felt the need to say more. Of course she did, because in her blackhearted way she'd been dying to speak about the money, to rub it in, ever since she'd given up her treasured chunk. "I know that May Hill has completed the transfer," she said, "that the land contract is legal, and that we have to accept it. I know she didn't consult us, which is too bad, but it's over. I so wish, Dolly, that you'd understand that May Hill has saved us. For the time being. Saved the farm for now. We need Philip. Surely you do know that."

Then Dolly did something I couldn't believe even though it was happening before my eyes. She picked up a book on the counter and threw it as far as she could across the room toward the stacks. That's how she made her exit, back to the hedgerow path.

My disks were forgotten, the cloth having fallen to my feet.

"My God," my mother said, staring at the door.

I got up from my chair in the nook, walked out onto the floor, across the carpet, past the magazine rack, a short distance to the book, a thick Elizabeth George mystery. It was a heavy book to have thrown so far. I didn't want to touch it, to pick it up. The book Dolly had thrown.

Nellie was pressing her fingers into her eye sockets. "Oh God," she moaned, "I'm such an idiot."

As much as it was true I almost for just a second felt sorry for her, that she herself had to know it and say it. It would have been better on my end if I'd been able to point out that fact to her. I kept looking at the book and thinking of Dolly's soft drooping face, the openmouthed frown. How pretty she'd looked at her entrance. My mother started to talk in her hokey, preternaturally calm tone. Whatever she was stumbling around saying, though, she wasn't anywhere near the root of the matter. Because, the thing is, I knew precisely what she'd done. *Be still, Mrs. Lombard, so I can tell you.* The following, in case she didn't realize, had occurred: My mother in the showdown had won. She had pulled up the prizewinning fact. She'd obliterated her opponent. Good for her in the moment. Score for the librarian. Congratulations.

But now in the aftermath? Now and forever? She maybe was coming to see it, the error slowly revealing itself. Oh no. She should have let Dolly think Dolly herself was the winner. A trick so simple. Let Dolly, who did not have the advantages, who had not gone to college, who did not have any spare family money, let her at least have the satisfaction of prevailing at the library.

I no longer wanted to be in the nook. My feet were moving toward the door. It was cold outside and I'd left my coat behind but I didn't care.

At dinner no one said much of anything. It was as if somehow William and my father understood that Dolly had thrown a book across the library. My father did say obligatorily, "How was your day, Marlene?"

Sherwood had once told Jim Lombard to shove grass up there. And Dolly had thrown a book. Those adults from across the road in Volta were the people who had to be violent in the face of my nice, even-tempered parents, so nice and po- lite and generous, so selfless, giving up their money, the couple of Velta, the upstart Lombards who had come to the farm from the outside world. On my walk home from the library I'd switched over to their side, to Dolly and Sherwood's side. I could clearly see their position, could see why you'd have to shout unpleasant things and throw heavy books. Those hateful nice people, Jim and Nellie. The small acts of rebellion against them. It was all you could do, the book, the grass.

22.

The Fruit Sale

The next morning when I woke up the sunshine was too bright to bear. The sun had hardly risen and already in my window it was terrible. "Francie!" my mother screeched from the kitchen. "It's late!" The Elizabeth George novel was presumably still on the floor at the library, no one daring to move the object that spelled our doom. "Francie! The bus in twenty minutes!" In my room the daylight at once glowed red. It was difficult to open my eyes to such luridness. To keep them open. In the night I'd started to understand a few other unspeakable facts, most especially that everything was ruined because of me.

The story was back to MF Lombard. It was I who had unraveled the place I loved more than anything else in the world, I, who had steadily been at work not only at my own wreckage but at Dolly's and everyone else's, too. It was I who, from the day of the interview in fifth grade, so long before, had started May Hill plotting, May Hill determined to keep the farm from me. The interview during the four–five split was her first hint about my character, and then there was the capture in her room, followed by any number of indications that MF Lombard was the silliest of persons, MF crying in the shed, MF dressed in an outlandish costume going to a school dance, a girl of no substance. A...mongrel. And now it was done, Philip a part of us, Philip the foreigner on our very soil.

With great effort I pulled myself to sit up in bed. MF, a pie dog, destined to roam, bloodied ear, hungry. A cur. It was almost impossible to assemble my Future Farmers of America uniform. To pick up my books. *The Norton Anthology* for AP English, the heaviest. Everything supposedly important in one volume. Putting it in the backpack. Scowling at my mother about breakfast. I could hardly manage the rudimentary motions. Going out, step after step, as the bus made the bend in the road, rattling toward me. No William, because he had departed early for one of his clubs. I would have stayed home if the FFA annual fruit sale, of which I was in charge, hadn't been taking place at school. I did know—I was aware—that William was waiting to find out if he'd been accepted Early Decision at the college of his and my mother's choice in Minnesota. It was one of any number of schools that claim to be the Harvard of the Midwest, a school that had aggressively courted him.

After the weary day going from class to class I found myself standing at the banquet table in the cafeteria, surrounded by boxes of Florida oranges and grapefruits. The Sunshine State. Invaded by pythons. I was looking at the list to see who had yet to show up when my brother appeared with a large white envelope in hand. The collar of his Oxford shirt was carefully folded down over the neck of his respectably drab sweater. He was a boy who was going to go out of state, a place very few students at our school dared to venture.

"What are you doing here?" I said to him. He was not ordinarily in my FFA world.

"I got the letter." He put it on the table in front of me. "The fat envelope."

Although there had been little doubt that William would be admitted I hadn't expected to learn about it at the fruit sale. He had gone home to check the mail, and he'd returned to tell me, as if for some reason he needed to do so in public.

"Are you going to go?" I knew even as I was asking that it was a terribly stupid thing to say. You don't apply Early Decision to the college you most want to attend because you're thinking you might not matriculate. In fact you are honor-bound to show up.

"I think I will," he said.

"Oh," I said. I said next, "When does it start?"

He laughed a little, a small hiccup escaping his mouth. Currently it was November, ten months before college would begin. But the thing is he knew; he knew the exact date without even looking. "September ninth," he announced.

"September?"

"If I was going to be on a team or something, I'd probably go earlier."

"What kind of team? You're not on teams."

"I don't know. Cross-country, maybe?"

"How can you be on cross-country? You're not a runner.

You have to already be that in high school to compete on a college team."

He wiped his upper lip, as if he'd been working hard, as if he was sweating. "I mean, I probably won't, but it's not out of the question. The team there is pretty lame, which means I might be able to join." He looked down at the envelope. "You can come and visit sometime, Frankie."

And I said, "I most certainly would not visit during apple season."

At that point, who should come to the table with her check to pick up her fruit but Brianna Kraselnik, a girl who was supporting her alma mater. We knew she'd returned to our town after dropping out of college, returned to shack up with not a Bershek twin but another local boy, and she was about to have a baby. Mrs. Kraselnik had gone to Connecticut with her horse and was remarried, and Dr. Kraselnik also had a new wife and was living in Milwaukee. Surely the daughter was a tremendous disappointment to her mother, Brianna an uneducated, small-town, unwed, pregnant twenty-three-year-old.

"Mary Frances and William," she cried, "ohmyGawd, you're in high school!" She, with her sleek hair now only midway down her back, and with no makeup, her eyelashes no longer tarred over with mascara, spoke with the astonishment of a gaga adult. "So, how's it going!"

"Great," William said, his greatness having just been confirmed by the fat envelope.

I thought to add a fee to her fruits, compensation for all the apples she'd surely stolen through the years.

"Your uniform is so cool," she said to me, as if she meant it, as if she really did like my dark-blue FFA jacket with the emblem, and the blue tie, the white shirt. She turned to Ashley Klemko, who was also at the table. She said, "Hey! I love your hair." She said this about starchy bangs teased to look like a fistful of curling ribbon. "So, wow!" she went on. "I ordered some fruit for my little guy." She actually squealed, patting her grotesque bulge.

William, I noted, was wincing, as if he were three seconds into the future. He had assumed it would be safest to tell me about college in public but he was realizing he'd miscalculated, that wherever he made the announcement there might be surprises. Nothing for me to do then but fulfill his expectations. I heard the questions, posed firmly and yet pleasantly, issuing from my mouth. I said, "You know all those times, Brianna, those times you used to roll around in the grass in our orchard? On our property? Those clothing-optional sessions?"

She made one little startled birdlike cock of her head.

"I just hope," I said, "that the residue from the spray isn't still in you, that the toxins won't affect your—little guy." I lifted the box onto the table. "Here's your fruit."

"Oh, my God, Mary Frances!" She burst out laughing. "OhmyGod, ohmyGod! I'm so sorry. I am so incredibly sorry you ever had to see me like that—you poor thing! We were so crazy, me and that bad old Nick Bershek!" She squealed once more, a piercing awful noise. "OHMYGOD!"

William was looking at her with both gratitude and curiosity.

"I'm more worried about the drugs I did than pesticides, believe me. But you—! We probably scarred you for life, am I right? We were very naughty, really very very deranged." She turned to William, shaking her steepled hands at him. "Please, please tell me you never saw us." Mrs. Kraselnik's daughter, the only token of my beloved teacher, felt compelled to again say, "Oh, my God."

My urbane brother, so suave, said, "I'm afraid I never had that pleasure."

Brianna whacked his arm. "Oh, my God, you are a laugh riot!"

William was going to college on September 9, and in college he'd say many witty things to many girls, all of whom would incessantly say *OhmyGod*, and he would be gone. He would be gone.

23.

Future Farmers of America

When was the last time I'd felt even a little glimmer of happiness? I couldn't remember. It seemed certain that never again would joy be accorded to me, my mother going as far as to wonder, to my face, if I would consider going to the doctor. She meant a shrink. It was right after the fruit sale when she said to me, "Francie, I want to talk to you."

I was in my room reading *Heart of Darkness*, lying on my bed. She wanted to talk to me? Fine, talk away. She pulled up a chair as if I was in a ward and she was a nun paying the patient a visit. In a conversational tone she said, "I'm worried about you."

Rivets were in short supply in the jungle. I kept reading.

"You seem so unhappy."

I shut my eyes.

"I just wonder," she went on, as if she was having a fun idea, "why you're so hard on us. You walk around glaring at everyone. I wonder if you realize how combative you always seem. And negative. I wonder if you're aware of it."

I rolled to my side in order to look at her, not in a glaring sort of way but because of my astonishment at how little she understood me. If she had known me even somewhat she would have appreciated how full of love I was. She would have understood that in fact I was overtaken by love. Love, at a basic level, was all I had inside of myself. "I don't walk around glaring," I said.

"But you do. I'm trying to help you, Francie. I'm wondering why you're so unhappy, first. And second, I'm telling you that in company you look somewhat murderous. When you're talking to us."

I'm full of love, I wanted to yell. *Most of the time I love you. More than you deserve. I love everyone! I love our life!*

But I didn't shout. I didn't even speak. Because to reveal that information would have been to invite a diagnosis that would sound like a line from a Lifetime movie. *That's the trouble, Francie*, she would no doubt say. *You just can't love the world as much as you do.*

She next said, "I think you should consider going back to Dr. O'Connor."

"I just had my appointment."

"He might be able to give you something to feel better. An anti-depressant. And he could recommend someone for you to talk to, a therapist." When I didn't answer she said, "Francie?"

"No," I said dully. "No, thank you."

"Please don't rule out—"

"I don't need therapy. I don't need birth control pills. I don't need Prozac."

There was no help for my condition. No help for the situation. Nothing to be done.

And still no help for it a week later when William was invited, along with a few other accepted bright stars, to meet with the Math and Computer Science Department professors at the College of His Choice. It was apparently a very special select weekend party, probably all-you-can-eat macaroni and cheese and garlic bread, fluffy French toast, starch and song, obeisance to Alan Turing, prayers and candle lighting, thanks be to Steve Jobs. My father, who so rarely had an outing, was going to drive him to Minnesota, the trip commencing on Friday at 2 p.m., the soonest William felt he could get away from his obligations at school. I was unwell that day, taking the opportunity to reread some of my old favorite books, impossible to get enough of Anne Boleyn's capers with the king.

At about one o'clock, having been in bed long enough, I thought I might take some air. My father was over at the unheated apple barn, standing ready in his thick blue coveralls to wait on any customer who might happen by. My mother was as always at the library. I got the old picnic hamper and stocked it with apples, cheese, bread, water, cookies, and my books, along with a bag of other necessities. Off I headed into the woods in my parka with the fur-trimmed hood. It was a sunny December afternoon, mild for the season. Also, I had, in my pocket, the keys to the car. I went straight to our place of refuge, William's and mine, that old gouge where the tree roots had been upended. In all the years since we'd first used it as our safe haven, that night when we'd been lost, no one had gotten around to cutting up the limbs for firewood.

I climbed into the cold damp chamber. It was considerably smaller than I remembered. A blanket and a duvet just fit, the blanket for the floor of the tomb, the duvet for wrapping up. Cozy, actually. A branch ledge for my basket, enough food to stave off starvation for a day or two. The headlamp in my pocket with the car key, so when it got dark I might read and not strain my eyes. The books beside me, my very old favorites, going way back to *The Baby-Sitter's Little Sister* series and *The Boxcar Children*.

As I read about children who triumph I began to get angry, angrier than I had been in general. Why were children always heroic in literature? Why the brutish lies to us? How patronizing! No, evil, it was evil to deceive young life. Even—yes, it was true—even Kind Old Badger was statistically improbably successful, like a drug those happy endings, the parents feeding the tykes narcotics, so many zombies set out into the world. It was cold in the hole, it was loveless. I should have brought matches. Why hadn't I brought matches to build a fire? It was everyone's fault! And especially William's, that I was freezing out in this hole. Why did he need to go and visit a place he already knew he liked? Why would professors invite high school students to campus when they had plenty of college boys to instruct? I was opening one of the *Baby-Sitter* books when a strange thing happened. The photographs that Stephen Lombard had taken years before, of William and me in the barn playing, those five black-and-white pictures that the spy had snapped, slipped from the pages.

They stared up at me, one after the next. There I am sitting way up high on a bale with the basket of kittens, splintered light coming through the cracks of the barn. The rope is hanging from a beam, the thick braid we used to swing from, that delirious long back-and-forth. Someone had removed it a few years before, May Hill, we'd thought. William is down below, making a pulley device to get water up to my perch, to save me. He's wearing a junior tool belt, bent over his work. Even though in my hiding place darkness had not yet fallen I shone my light on the photographs. They seemed to have appeared out of creation or maybe years before I had stashed them in the book. However they'd materialized, I'd fallen straight down into the barn scene, MF Lombard no longer in her dugout. In one of the pictures William is looking up at me, the girl with the cats, as if he's worried, as if it's almost too late for the rescue, he knows he must hurry.

Stephen then occurred to me, Stephen himself standing in the door of the granary, watching us. Studying us no doubt for quite some time. Had he taken the photographs as a way to insert himself, just for a minute, into our childhood? Wanting to be us, to have us, trying somehow to—what? Could a grown man have such a hopeless wish, trying to get back *there*? Once I had that thought I scrambled to get out of the hole. I didn't want to grow up. I didn't want to someday have the hopeless wish, trying to get back, taking pictures—and longing. Longing, I couldn't bear all the longing that was already in me. And to come, all of it to come. I was running at first and stumbling. As much as I knew our woods it was still possible to go astray in the thickets and so I went in circles.

As I walked and walked other questions came to mind, one prompting the next and the next. What if soon we were unable to pay the taxes on the four hundred acres? What if a multimillionaire bought the woods, the houses, razing the apples trees for piano key subdivisions? That little tin cup we'd once found long ago, the cup we'd discovered and reburied, cemented over for a garage, never again found by a boy and girl? I wouldn't think of it, would not imagine the classic and lugubrious farm auction scene turning into our real and saddest of memories, the closing of the door for the last time, getting into the car, turning back to look. One more look. I had to bend over, couldn't walk—one last look and going down the road. Nothing left but the Stephen Lombard photographs.

I don't know how many minutes or if it was for hours I wandered like that. When I got back to my camp the light was fading. Was Philip our savior? Was it true, what my mother had said, that May Hill was providing for our future? I felt as if my mind might rupture—how long, how long was it going to take William to figure out where I was? I could already hear the scratchings of nighttime, voles scurrying, deer delicately making their way along their narrow routes, the plaintive cry of a little lost bird who had foolishly stayed behind in winter. And always, in the woods, there must be the call of the owl, the demanding *Who who?*

Really, how long would it take William? It should not have been so difficult for him. If he wanted to go to Minnesota that badly he should think carefully about where MF Lombard was with the car keys. It made me so angry, again, that I'd had to resort to this kind of tactic. It should not have been necessary! And why had Gloria left us years before? She should start calling for me now, coming to find me, rather than living on Cortez Island with her own baby, a girl named Sophia.

Four o'clock had passed and five o'clock and six o'clock. Where was he? How dare he not find me. How dare he keep me waiting in the cold, doing the taxing job of holding my ire at the boiling point. It should have been a cinch to find me—how stupid could he be?

At six thirty I crawled out to do my business—*look what you've reduced me to*. Once again I tried to get comfortable, tried to get back the warmth I'd lost, and when I was sick, too, when I'd been so sick. But I would stay, I would stay the night, I'd stay for two nights if I had to, if William was so brainless he couldn't find the car keys right in the hole in the woods. I was making my resolve when finally I heard the bushwhackers. Ten minutes past seven o'clock. It was my father who was calling. "Mar-lee-een. Mar-leeeeeeen! Are you out here?"

Maybe I was and maybe I wasn't.

"Marlene!" A big sharp shout.

They were drawing closer. I burrowed deeper into the duvet. What was going to happen?—that secretly delightful question. Before I could entertain it further they were on the lip of the chasm, their headlamps blinding me.

"Jesus Christ." William spit the name.

"It's okay," my father said to him. "Come on out, Marlene."

Ho-hum, I acted as if I didn't see them, as if they were not present. I opened my book since their headlamps were now providing me with perfectly adequate light.

"Frankie—!" William was too angry to say more.

"Oh, hallo," I said.

"It would be considerate—" He was so worked up he was starting to cry, my brother. "It would be—" Not only had it taken him *forever* to find me, he also couldn't manage to speak in complete sentences. How in the world did he think he was going to conduct himself at college? "Nice," he hissed. "If you could give us the car keys."

"Marlene," my father said, "we're all pretty tired."

That was their problem, not mine. They wanted to be rested and happy, they had only to get a basket and come into the woods.

"Ma's out of her head with worry," my father added.

William just then began to pound, with his bare hands, on the gigantic upturned platter of roots and earth. Very melodramatic for anyone but for William especially surprising. Was he crying or choking? I couldn't tell.

"So go away," I remarked. To tell the truth, it was frightening, his display. I said, "Would you please just leave." I meant it in a local way.

At that he sprang into the hole. "Ow!" I yelled. "Get off me! Stop it!" As I said, the hole was considerably smaller than it had been when we were five and six.

"GODDAMN IT, Imp!" He seemed to hover before he came down upon me. I suppose it happened quickly. The press of him, a darkness in my mind, my brother smothering me. Such weight, the boy himself in his padded canvas jacket. Before you knew it you could be snuffed out, you might surrender, one bright bloom in your head, the last flowering firework, almost a happiness to have everything over and done. I heard him cry out, "YOU ARE SUCH A—BABY."

BABY like an ugly word, like the worst curse. It was close to me, that word in the hole, and yet it didn't matter, the canvas like an old chapped hand, William's jacket covering my face and in my mouth. Before I could try to struggle, even as I was thinking to, my father was yanking William, my father with all his strength pulling his nearly grown son up out of the hiding place. All at once the light was back in my eyes, I was gasping for breath. There was noise, my father I think talking to William, maybe he was saying something, a confusion even though the main action had already taken place. I thought, *Okay, I am now going to climb out.* I could see that there was no reason to stay put. They had found me, I wasn't dead from suffocation, perhaps my point had been made, time to go home. I couldn't exactly think in the moment what the point was. But before I could get out, before I realized what was happening my father had also dragged me up and next I knew he somehow had hauled me over his shoulders. Wait! The duvet had fallen away, my father, as old and as tall as I was, my father adjusting me as if I were a sack of grain, as if he thought I wouldn't come home with them, as if he thought I'd try to fight. I could still feel the weight of William, the jacket, that stuffing, in my mouth. I should tell my father that he could let me down but I couldn't think of the words. *Baby.* That's what I kept hearing.

We set off down the path. William was running ahead probably. I couldn't hear him, didn't think he was with us. I was not easy to carry, my father faltering. I imagined I was going to say *Let me down* and so I must have because he stopped. I was then walking beside him. He smelled of apples, the fragrance thick and sweet, the smell bonded deeply into his jacket and his coveralls, his hair, his skin. Even though I was no longer slumped over his back I felt as if I were being carried along in a dream, the night, my father, the two of us maybe walking forever. Where was William?—Oh yes, in the dream, remember he is gone? On we went until we came out of the woods. We walked down the dark drive of Volta and crossed the road to Velta.

Just inside the door at home my father was good enough not to turn on the hall light but nonetheless I at once remembered my part. I tossed the keys on the floor in the hall, *Fine, there they are, what you wanted*. And then I ran up to my room and I locked myself inside.

It wasn't until I was in my bed that I began not merely to tremble but to shiver in an uncontrollable way. I wasn't even all that cold. As usual I wondered if I was losing my mind. The shivering was not, I thought, prompted by William's unnerving, unique histrionics or my inability to speak to my father on the path. No, my teeth were rattling because of the resemblance that was occurring to me: Gloria. Long ago Gloria had stood in the door frame of the stone cottage, forced by my father to produce Stephen's passport. Had I become Gloria? Had I become a person going insane? There were moments, I could now see, when it was understandable to completely go off your rocker. The easiest and most reasonable and maybe proper thing to do in the world, to lose hold of yourself. What were my parents doing downstairs but probably trying to figure out how to commit me. They were discussing the fact that I was certifiable. So the question before me: Was I indeed crazy?

Yes or no.

MF Lombard driven mad by a departure?

I wasn't sure. I didn't know. Before I could make a determination the Stephen photographs leapt to mind. I hoped they were going to be all right out in the hole for the night. I loved those pictures. I loved them so much I could hardly

stand it, but not, it seemed, in an insane way. Loving the
pictures simply did not feel like lunacy. Loving the pictures,
there was nothing to be done but lie quietly at the mercy of
the suffering.

After some time I got out of bed and went into William's
room. My heart sped up, the thin hum in my ears as I approached the threshold. Had the woods been a dream for him,
too? Would the correct approach be to laugh, to cry, to do
nothing but sit down and lean against his shelf? He was at his
desk playing *Posse*. His fine wispy hair was long enough in the
back so that a wind might make it tickle his neck. I loved his
neck, which he may or may not wish to know.

"Um," I said.

"What," he said.

"Are you going?"

"Early tomorrow morning." He kept playing his game.

I managed a great summoning of my courage and I said
right out, "What are you thinking you will do when you get
out of college?"

He turned in his office chair to face me. His eyes were
bloodshot, I guess from the crying. He looked older than
usual, circles etched under his eyes, the brown of them faded.
His face was somewhat drawn. "I don't know, Frankie."

"You don't?"

"No."

I stared at the floor. How could he have no idea?

"I want," he began.

"What?"

He moistened his lips. He shut his eyes tightly, he opened
them and looked hard at me. "I want to make hay."

"Hay," I repeated stupidly.

"I want to make hay," he said again. "And the rain is coming."

"The cloud is hanging over our heads?"

"But," he said, nodding, "the rain doesn't fall. It doesn't fall yet."

"Because we don't have all the bales in."

"Because—" He suddenly did a lightning spin in his chair. "It's going to wait until we're done."

"Because Papa is there."

"Yes," William said. "Because Papa is there."

We both looked at the floor. "Oh," I said.

"Now would you please get out of here?" He abruptly turned back to his game.

"Okay," I said. I went out into the hall. I was satisfied with his answer.

Maybe it was the best possible answer for the time being. I stood at the top of the stairs, very still, holding as still as I could. William, I knew, was capable of playing *Posse* until morning. It was well past the dinner hour but I could hear my parents at the table in the kitchen. I could see the light downstairs. By the smell of it they were having my mother's famous pork-and-turnip stew and probably she'd whipped up mashed potatoes with buttermilk. Librarian by day, chef by night. I heard her laugh. "Jim, Jimmy, my God." My father had been working all day out in the cold and afterward he'd had to go into the woods to find me. Probably he was holding a cup of tea in his enormous knuckly hands, telling her the story of the search. It occurred to me that I, too, could stay right where I was, holding on to the newel post, until morning. "How did it get so late?" I heard my father say. My mother replied as if it was a real question. "In the usual way," she said. I thought I might stay on the top step, in the darkness, holding to the post, stay awhile longer, but I also knew that in just a minute I'd go downstairs.

Reading Group Guide
for

THE
EXCELLENT
LOMBARDS

by

JANE
HAMILTON

Discussion Questions

1. The Lombards comprise a sprawling, complicated family, and the relationships among them are even more complex. How is the concept of family portrayed throughout the book?

2. What effect does making Frankie the narrator have on your perception of the plot?

3. One might describe Frankie as being both surprisingly mature and immature for her age. Why do you think this is? How else would you describe Frankie's character? Use examples from the text to support your claims.

4. How does a rural setting lend itself to this sort of familial, community-based story? What role does the landscape, which Jane Hamilton describes vividly, play in the Lombards' tale?

5. In many ways, this novel can be viewed as a coming-of-age story. What are some key moments in which Frankie "comes of age"?

6. The question of who will inherit the farm is one of the main conflicts in this book. Do you think that the matter of inheritance is emblematic of some other issue?

7. The relationship between Gloria and the Lombards is very complicated. What do you think prevents genuine feelings between the children and Gloria? Between Nellie and Gloria?

8. "We weren't just bored with the world; we were bored with ourselves, or we were hardly in our selves anymore. It was hard to tell what was going on. Maybe, if we could remember one little trick about how we used to be, we could get there, get back, as if we ourselves were a country we'd left." How does this quote relate to some of the book's main themes?

9. Frankie often has incredibly strong feelings and opinions toward those around her. Analyze Frankie's relationships with other key characters, such as William, her father, Amanda, and May Hill.

10. How does the bond between Frankie and her brother, William, evolve throughout this book?

11. How does Frankie view love? Does it change throughout the course of the book? If so, how?

12. What do you think makes the Lombards "excellent"?

A Conversation with Jane Hamilton

What was your initial conception of *The Excellent Lombards*? Has it changed much?

I wrote many versions of this novel. I have a friend who writes crime fiction. She is often understandably shocked at the inefficiency of my process. "You had *another* failure?" she once lovingly said to me, when I was explaining that yet another version of the novel hadn't worked out. At the start I knew the situation of the orchard family but I kept superimposing ridiculous plots onto the basic structure. For instance, there were several versions involving a nun and the lesbians in the neighborhood. The nun drowns in the marsh. I read *Catholicism for Dummies* and went to Mass. That version was six hundred pages.

How did your own experience of living and working in a Wisconsin orchard farmhouse inform the content of this book?

I certainly couldn't have written this novel if I hadn't lived the life I live. I suppose that could be said for any novel in relation to the novelist, but for this book and my life that statement is especially true. My business associates have for some time been suggesting that I write a memoir about my farm life, but I can't seem to muster enthusiasm for nonfiction. The pleasure and requirement of writing a novel is living in an invented world. There is the basic material that is the novelist's life, the marble, clay, the canvas, and as the work progresses the invention becomes entirely separate from whatever real-life events or situation inspired it. So this book lives in an altogether different plane from my own life and times.

What was your greatest challenge in writing *The Excellent Lombards*?

I had the voice of the girl at the beginning. I knew the situation of the family. But situation is not the same as plot. How was I going to organize all the material? How was I going to make a contained narrative with material that is close to me, and ongoing? What should the time frame be? In several of the many different versions Frankie—whose name was once upon a time Nina—is in college. In one version she is well out of college. In one version her father and Sherwood die, a double accident in snow. Chain saws are involved. At a certain point I realized it was better to limit the passage of time. Also, there are specific challenges in an episodic novel. There needs to be connective tissue from chapter to chapter. The whole thing has to flow and cohere through the episodes. I didn't want to write an eight-hundred-page, intergenerational book with a family tree but rather a book that was relatively short, the girl's narrative a story that is a distillation of her family history, that history contained, you could say, in her body.

In her essay "On the Art of Fiction," Willa Cather said, *Art,
it seems to me, should simplify. That, indeed, is very nearly the whole
of the higher artistic process; finding what conventions of form and
what detail one can do without and yet preserve the spirit of the whole,
so that all that one has suppressed and cut away is there to the reader's
consciousness as much as if it were in type on the page.* I'm not a poet
but that goal of condensing and being precise—that trick!—
was my impossible goal. All that to say, I wanted to write a
short novel about time passing.

Which characters did you enjoy creating the most?

Oh Frankie! I love the clear sight and confusion in the child,
and the fury of the teenager. Frankie cannot bear to grow up.
She cannot stand the idea that her family's ties will have to
change as she and her brother grow older. She is in love with
her family as it is. Her rage as she tries to hold on to time
and place was compelling to me. I loved looking at the world
from her point of view. Inhabiting her mind and spirit was a
privilege.

**Frankie clearly loves her family deeply, but this love
sometimes manifests itself through seemingly bratty
behavior. What do you think love really means to her?
Do you believe that people often struggle to express
love?**

Frankie is trying to figure out how and if she can cement her
future, trying to foresee who will get to stay on the farm, who
will have to leave, who belongs, and what a person is if they

don't have a place that roots them. For her, all of those problems, those conundrums, are bound up in the word *love*. She is at times nothing but raw feeling. She is powerless even as she exerts her powerful self in her household. Back to Willa Cather: In an essay on Katherine Mansfield she wrote, *As in most families, the mere struggle to have anything of one's own, to be one's self at all, creates an element of strain that keeps everybody almost at the breaking point.* Love threads in and out of that "mere struggle." Certainly in Frankie's family each member is at different times almost at the breaking point. It's hard to express love when you are at that point.

Frankie's family structure is unusually complex, especially the dynamic between Gloria and Jim. Is this tangled web of people—and the heightened emotions that accompany it—reminiscent of your own family? If not, what inspired you to create such a complicated group?

A family business is always a good place to observe tribalism, and the subtribes within the overarching tribe. Mrs. Kraselnik asks her class to think about Who Your Tribe Is? (The word *tribe* seems strange to the fourth and fifth graders. *Tribe? We're not in a tribe!*) I first started to think of tribal society not long after I stopped going to ballet school, in the 1970s. The pecking order at ballet school was brutal! And I've continued to think about how we all operate inside and outside of our particular tribes. All tribes, I'm quite sure, are tangled and complex, and my own family is no exception.

Did the character of Frankie evolve much as you were writing? Is the experience of writing a young woman's coming-of-age story ever like going back in time to your own childhood?

That is the pleasure of writing about childhood and teenagehood! Although Frankie was born around 1987, so her childhood takes place in a very different time than mine. She was born just as Steve Jobs was hitting his stride in his first stint at Apple. It's tricky, although not impossible, to imagine being a baby now, swiping through the parents' photos on an iPhone. The challenge and pleasure of writing a child: trying to access how a child lives at a sensory level that is far more intense than the average adult's: heat, cold, taste, smell—the world new, a heady brew to absorb. One must try as best one can to remember how it all felt, and how bewildering the adult world seemed, and how essential it was to create a private world, a place to which to retreat. When I was a girl I lived in and retreated to the worlds I found in books. Frankie has that escape hatch, too.

Jim encounters many obstacles in running and maintaining the integrity of his orchard, a number of which are raised in the town meeting Frankie attends. Are these issues indicative of difficulties faced by your own orchard?

Yes. Land-use issues are issues for farmers the world over. How can we preserve what we've built? How can we live in the world with people who have different values when it comes to land? Should landowners be granted privileges for their holdings, or should they be supported? Are large tracts of woods, owned by a single person, good for the community and the ecosystem as a whole? How much regulation should the government impose when it comes to property and farmland? Time-honored problems.

The section where Frankie interviews May Hill, rather than being a dry, lackluster conversation with an old woman, is interesting in its emotional intensity and horrific elements. Can you discuss what sparked the decision to include this?

May Hill is crucial to the solution of the farm crisis, to the matter of succession. I knew that Frankie had to have a major event with her. Frankie considers marriage to various bachelors who could affect the solution (after she understands that she can't marry her brother—or her father, for that matter). She comes to believe that May Hill regards her as a frivolous person, as a girl who couldn't possibly be a serious contender. That first scene allows Frankie to have her initial display as an unfit future farmer.

What was your thought process behind *The Excellent Lombards* title?

Finding the right title is often a trial-and-error process. The title has to somehow hold the book. At first the novel was called *The Boy Who Could Do Anything*. Then it was called *During the*

Reign of the Lombards. I very much liked the idea of monarchy in the title. But it didn't have the right music, that title. And it was a mouthful. When Mrs. Kraselnik says, "Let's give another hand for the excellent Lombards"—I thought, *The excellent Lombards—that's what this book is about.*

About the Author

Jane Hamilton's novels have won literary prizes, have been made into films, and have been international best sellers, and two of them, *The Book of Ruth* and *A Map of the World*, were selections of Oprah's Book Club. Her nonfiction has appeared in the *New York Times*; the *Washington Post*; *Allure*; *O, the Oprah Magazine*; *Elle*; and various anthologies. She's married to an apple farmer and lives in Wisconsin.